PRAISE FOR BLOOD AND GASOLINE

"*Blood and Gasoline* is a head-spinning mix of stories by some of the genre's dark masters."
   –**Reed Farrel Coleman**, *New York Times* bestselling author of *What You Break*

"Strap yourself in for a wild ride in these testoster-one-driven stories that get your heart pounding. Be grateful you're reading these tales of desperate men and women on the edge, not living them."
   –**Charles Salzberg**, author of *Devil in the Hole*, one of the best crime novels of the year by *Suspense* magazine

"Stories so fierce and ferocious they blister off the page. And edged with a surprising tenderness that elevates the very edginess to the very best art."
   –**Ken Bruen**, author of *The Guards*

"A feast for lovers of action-packed, high-octane, light-ning speed getaways and paybacks."
   –**J.L. Abramo**, Shamus Award winning author of *Circling the Runway*

BLOOD AND GASOLINE

"*Blood and Gasoline* reads like a frantic car chase rife with grisly executions, unexpected twists and detours, war crimes, deceptions, biker gangs, sex, drugs, and soul. Tales from San Antonio to spaceships...most recommended for adrenaline junkies."

–**Charlie Vazquez**, author of the novel *Contraband* and director of the Bronx Writers Center

"*Blood and Gasoline* will rock your world. Explosive action? Absolutely. Thrills and chills? Definitely. Stomach-churning gore? *Blood and Gasoline* has it all. But beware, these stories cast a spell. You'll vanish as a reader. You'll emerge inside the body and soul of aberrant characters caught in the midst of hair-raising escapades. There you will strive, suffer, outwit or be outwitted, live–or die. But no matter, you'll more than delight in a transformative, if not perverse, sense of satisfaction."

–**Marjorie E. Brody**, author of the award-winning *Twisted* and *In the Underside*

"These jet-fuel-powered stories are not just good–they're damn good. *Blood and Gasoline* is an explosive mix of fear, greed, longing, hope, and courage. This riveting collection boasts seventeen beautifully written stories, each with a surprising edge–like a razor blade wrapped in velvet."

–**Barbara Nickless**, bestselling author of the Parnell crime novels

"A gritty, kinetic collection of personality disorders and outrageous behavior."

–**Elaine Ash**, author of *Bestseller Metrics*

HIGH-OCTANE, HIGH-VELOCITY ACTION

Blood AND GASOLINE

JOHN HARTNESS
GABINO IGLESIAS
CARTER WILSON
CATHERINE DILTS
ANGIE HODAPP
JEDIDIAH AYRES
JEANNE C. STEIN
GARY PHILLIPS
WARREN HAMMOND
MERIT CLARK
TRAVIS HEERMANN

LES EDGERTON
JON BASSOFF
JOSHUA VIOLA
SEAN EADS
JAMES R. TUCK
QUINCY J. ALLEN
MANUEL RAMOS
ROBERT JESCHONEK

EDITED BY:
MARIO ACEVEDO

HEX PUBLISHERS

BLOOD AND GASOLINE
HIGH-OCTANE, HIGH-VELOCITY ACTION

Edited by Mario Acevedo
Copyedits by Jennifer Melzer
Cover design by Kirk DouPonce
Typesets and formatting by Dustin Carpenter

A Hex Publishers Book

Published & Distributed by Hex Publishers, LLC
PO BOX 298
Erie, CO 80516

www.HexPublishers.com

Joshua Viola, Publisher

Print ISBN-10: 0-9997736-3-1
Print ISBN-13: 978-0-9997736-3-5
Ebook ISBN-10: 0-9997736-4-X
Ebook ISBN-13: 978-0-9997736-4-2

First Edition: 2018

10 9 8 7 6 5 4 3 2 1

Printed in the U.S.A.

CONTENTS

FOREWORD

John G. Hartness

WELCOME TO THE MOTHERFUCKIN' THUNDERDOME.
That's what oughta be on the cover of this book, because you are about to enter some straight up *Mad Max* meets *Sons of Anarchy* shit right here.

When Mario asked me to write the foreword to this book, I jumped at the chance, mostly because I'm a cheap bastard and it meant I got to read some stories from a fistful of my favorite writers without paying for the privilege. James R. Tuck, Mario Acevedo, Travis Heermann, and Jeanne Stein are all people I know. Hell, Tuck and I get mistaken for each other at conventions!

For the record, he has more tattoos, but I have more hair.

So I was happy to read a bunch of badass stories about heists, capers, bikers, badasses, and ne'er-do-wells and scribble a few thoughts down. I thought I'd get to read some storied by my buddies, meet some new writers that might be cool, and get a nice publication credit without really doing any work.

Then I read the stories.

Holy fuck, are you lucky. These aren't just gasoline-soaked raw-throated screams of fire and fury from a fistful of badass writers. These are downright incredible stories, full of characters you can get behind, with killer snark, fantastic action, and one uniting theme that caught me completely by surprise.

Hope.

These are stories of hope. Sometimes they're stories of people who have run out of it, and are chasing the last vestiges of it in a destroyed society. Sometimes they're stories of people who have been consumed by it, and burned out themselves and everyone around them in their quest for something better. Sometimes they hope for greatness, sometimes their hopes are so petty as to be laughable.

But every single story has that little glimmer of light in the bottom of a Pandora's box shitshow that keeps us moving forward every day. Hope. It shines in the reflection of a streetlight off the end of a dirty cop's gun, a man getting a little revenge on a rich asshole while building a better life for himself and his family. It beckons to us from the doors of a dystopian hospital where a freelance ambulance rushes a child for treatment with the nefarious for-profit healthcare systems in pursuit with guns blazing. It screams out in the engine of a motorcycle eating up the open road as a pair of lovers try to escape from a biker gang.

These stories are raw. There's a jagged energy pulsing through all of them, uniting them in their full-throttled roar and unapologetically frenetic pacing. They're not pretty stories about tea parties and glitter-shitting unicorns. These are stories about real people, desperate people, sometimes downright bad people, but people you can relate to. These are stories about you, stories about me, stories about that second cousin you have that ended up in juvie and works in his dad's garage fixing cars instead of getting a good job at the dealership because he's got a record, stories about people pushed to the limit and beyond, and stories about people who push back.

But they are stories, at the end of the day, about hope. Hope for a better life, no matter who you have to shoot to get it. Stories about an opportunity for an unborn child, no matter how much coke its dad snorts off its mother's pregnant belly. Stories about standing up to assholes and leaving them gutshot in the middle of the road.

So they're not pretty stories. They're friggin' awesome, badass, thrill-a-page stories that will leave you breathless, make you laugh out loud, and have you say "oh shit, that hurt!" at least a couple of times.

But they're also stories that will leave you with a gift. Buried under the blood, and the grease, and the dirt, and the coke, and the ashes, these stories will leave you with a little something shining in the black – because at their heart, these are stories of hope. And can't we always use a little more light in the darkness?

I'll see you in the Thunderdome,

John G. Hartness
12/30/17
Charlotte, NC

INTRODUCTION

Mario Acevedo

THE BEST IDEAS CAN COME FROM STRANGE
places. In this case, I was riding co-pilot with Quincy
Allen in the WordFire Press cargo van, aka Moby Dick, on
the way home from DragonCon. We were somewhere on
I-70 hurtling through Kansas, engaged in late afternoon
chitchat that ranged from scotch, to music, to women, to
guns, to writing. Inspired by long stretches of highway,
I thought about putting together a collection of stories
set on the low road to nowhere with over-the-top action,
high adventure, and desperate characters at odds with
other just-as-desperate characters. All I needed was a
title. When Quincy said, "Blood and Gasoline," my immediate response was "bingo."

I approached Josh Viola, the head guy behind Hex
Publishers, and before I was done pitching the idea, he
interrupted: "Go for it."

When I solicited contributors, I wanted to make sure they pivoted their stories on the desperate part, otherwise the anthology would have all the hum-drum theater of carnival bumper cars. Lots of smashing and colliding, but with nothing at stake, why stick around?

Given that, I envisioned a collection of hard-bitten characters on the run, throttles full open, guns blazing, steering wheels and gear shifts slick with blood. Where sinister intentions gained momentum as they ricocheted off vengeance and betrayal.

I wasn't disappointed.

Gabino Iglesias ignites a modern urban tale of family pyrotechnics that explodes into a mad dash across the barrio. Angie Hodapp gives us a water-world crime drama that boils with intrigue. Manuel Ramos–the king of Chicano noir–demonstrates that he is also the master of the double-cross. Though Carter Wilson plants us dead center on the international stage, the action remains tightly focused on one man's bitter quest for survival. In his bad-cop narrative, Jedidiah Ayres pours gasoline on the notions of integrity and sets them on fire. Les Edgerton relates a wrong deed done for good reason, and the mistake races toward inevitable tragedy. And the desolate highway was never more treacherous than in the pedal-to-the-metal exploits by Jeanne Stein, Warren Hammond, and James R. Tuck.

If you're hoping for an optimistic tomorrow, forget it. Our future is riddled to pieces in these savage accounts by Quincy Allen, Robert Jeschonek, Gary Phillips, Travis Heermann, and the demented writing team of Sean Eads and Josh Viola.

For some of the contributors, the most perilous journey was not on a contested road, but in the mind, an interior landscape where personal demons stoke anguish and despair with regrets and bad choices. Catherine Dilts unravels a mystery that blooms with deadly consequences. Jon Bassoff kicks us down an emotional staircase toward an unholy denouement. Merit Clark twists the screws of what it means to be dangerously obsessed.

Each contributor delivered a story that not only exceeded my expectations, but opened my eyes to appreciate the greater scope of my original idea. All the adventures pushed forward on the premise that salvation is not attained with bullets and fists, but through hope and redemption.

I think we reached this destination.

Mario Acevedo
Denver, Colorado

FASTER THAN WEEPING ANGELS

Gabino Iglesias

THE SMELL OF FREEDOM. PEOPLE TALK ABOUT
it like it's real. Jaime wishes it was. He only smells the
rotten stink of mold and the ammonia odor of cat piss
that has taken over the small room where most of his
stuff is packed in cardboard boxes marked *Charmin* toilet
tissue.

Nothing is happening and that feels like too much.
Everything is nothing and too much. The stench. The
oppressive summer heat. The wobbly clatter of a ceiling
fan that slices warm air. The dust bunnies screaming
about how his mom didn't clean his room before picking him up. Through the window, a light breeze brings
from the garage the smell of gasoline. It all fuels Jaimes'
anger. He's angry that he got caught and locked away for
four years. He's angry that while inside his tough guy
persona crumbled and only a friend's cousin kept his ass
from becoming used as an entertainment center. He's

angry that his mom stayed with her abusive boyfriend. He's angry that he thinks that boyfriend, Cookie, made the damn call that got him locked up just so he could get him out of the way. He's angry that he never cared enough to ask how a sack of blubber ended up with the nickname: *Galletita*.

Pinche pendejo. But most of all, Jaime's angry about his current state. He has plans, but can't remember any of them. He wants to go places where he hasn't fucked up yet and accomplish something, but a feeling of being frozen locks him in place and forces him to stay in his room without the need for barbed-wire fences or guards.

The second day after Jamie's release from prison, his cousin Eduardo called from San Antonio. Eduardo's making bank running meth for *La Eme*. All Jaime has to do is get to San Antonio and there's a job waiting for him. An easy job. Good money. Women. Connections. However, to his surprise, he doesn't want to go. He wants out. Peace of mind. That's all he wants now. He thought being out would do the trick, but it didn't. In fact, the first thing he did after getting home was go through his things and get his piece. He cleaned, oiled, and loaded it. You can leave the big house, but you carry some of the fear for the rest of your life, like a prison tattoo on your heart. Now he's stuck, sweaty and angry, looking at his gun and trying to ignore how easy it'd be to use to get his enough money for his own place. He shakes his head like a madman. That stops his crazy thoughts.

Leaving the room is a bad idea, but staying cooped up in there is worse. Jaime tells himself to move.

Muévete, pendejo.

Haz algo.

Take a leak.

Drink some water.

Check the fridge.

He knows those simple tasks will help him escape the trap he's setting himself. Finally, Jaime gets out of bed, opens the door, and walks out.

The living room is at the end of the short hallway. His mom and Cookie have been smoking for hours. The smoke is so thick Jaime wonders if he'll have to pull it apart with his hands to get to the kitchen.

"Ahí vas, a buscar un poco más de comida gratis, como el sinvergüenza que eres," says Cookie. *"Hace dos días y medio que llegastes y no has hecho ni una pinche llamada para ver si alguien te puede conseguir un jale."*

Jaime ignores him. He doesn't need to hear this crap from the man who probably sent him away. It's too much to deal with. Plus, his mother's silence feels like a burn.

The kitchen smells worse than the rest of the house. Next to the fridge stand three litter boxes full of solidified feces. Jaime grabs a glass from the cupboard and fills it with tap water.

"Oye, pendejo, te estaba hablando," says Cookie.

Jaime turns around. The fat man's standing behind him, his breath a mix of cheap beer, cigarettes, raw onions, and gingivitis that somehow overpowers the combined stench of cat piss and skipped showers. Jaime takes a step back, hoping for fresh air. Cookie laughs, a golden crown shining a bit inside a mouth full of brown and yellow teeth. In that laugh, Jaime sees things. Bad things. He made the call. It had to be him. None of Jamie's homies would rat him out like that and his mom would die before hurting him, so this fat bastard had to be the one. Cookie's laughter turns into a hacking cough. His disgustingly huge *panza* bounces inside the stretched brown fabric of his T-shirt.

"*Buscaré trabajo el lunes*," says James. "*Tengo un cuate de la prepa que...*"

"*Ninguno de tus pinches amigos te puede conseguir una buena chamba y lo sabes.*"

"*Si Jaime dice que va a buscar trabajo, va a buscar trabajo*," says Lorena, Jaime's mother, from somewhere behind the fat man. Then she stands there, five-foot nothing, burying her eyes into Cookie. A cigarette dangles from her lips. There are more lines around her eyes than Jaime remembers, but the bun on top of her head is still as dark as midnight during a blackout.

Both men are surprised to hear her. Cookie turns around and walks back to the living room. He hisses something a couple of inches from Lorena's face, and she walks away. Cookie follows her into the room. Jaime sees an opportunity to disappear before his anger takes over. He leaves the kitchen and crosses the living room while staring at the filthy carpet. He reaches his door.

Slap.

The sound stops him in his tracks. Was that the TV? He looks back down the hallway. His mother is making her way to the bathroom. She looks pissed. He knows the fresh red blemishes on her cheek and neck aren't from being in the kitchen or out in the Texas heat. Something in his chest tenses like a guitar string and his lungs feel too small. Cookie takes two steps out of their room, grabs Lorena's arm, and yanks her back. She stumbles.

"*No voy a permitir que trates a ese puto criminal como a un bebé*," says Cookie.

Instead of replying, Lorena takes another step toward the bathroom. Cookie grabs her again, pulls her close, and doesn't let go. Jaime watches as the fat man puts his mouth close to her ear and whispers something. She replies in the same hushed tone, something about it being her house, not his. Whatever it is, her words have consequences. Cookie looks hurt. He pushes her away and follows it up with another slap. Jaime is in front of Cookie before realizing he has moved. The fat man smiles. Jaime takes in his bald head, the beads of oily beer sweat dotting his forehead, his cracked lips, and the incongruent shiny tooth in his dental cemetery.

Jamie's jaw clenches but he manages to say, "*Si la vuelves a tocar...*"

Cookie grins. "*No te atrevas a amenazarme, culero. Esta puede ser la casa de tu madre, pero el que paga las cuentas aquí soy yo, así que hago lo que me da la gana.*"

Jaime had been tempted to punch his mother's boyfriend many times, but knew he'd end up being the one getting kicked out of the house. Now that concern isn't there. He doesn't care. He'd been buried and crawled back from the hole, a survivor. He had no home and made the shadows his refuge. The man who sent him away stands in front of him, and that makes everything else disappear. Cookie is responsible for the anger, the lost time, the fear. He's responsible for the red welts on his mother's face and neck. He's responsible for a criminal record that will make getting a job much harder.

The first punch is a right hook, fast and tight, the way he learned to punch in prison. His fist closes Cookie's mouth shut with a crack and snaps his head back. The fat man stumbles, but he doesn't go down. He looks forward. Surprise, fear, and rage battle on his face and eyes. He starts to bring his hands up.

The second punch is a straight right that slips between the fat man's hands. Cartilage crunches. Blood gushes. His legs give and he flops onto his back.

Jaime kneels, grabs Cookie's head by the ears, and slams it against the carpet. The thud is too dull, so he throws a leg over his chest, sits on the man, and starts punching.

Jaime is aware of his mother screaming. He feels her nails digging into his arms and shoulders from the back, but none of it matters: He's finally moving, doing something. No more stagnation. Then Lorena leaves him alone, takes her screaming elsewhere. Jaime keeps punching until Cookie's nose is no more. The man emits a guttural moan that sounds like a small mammal drowning. A jagged piece of bone pokes out from the pulpy red mess that used to be Cookie's right eye. It stabs Jaime's hand and he pulls back. His hands tremble. His knuckles bleed. His lungs ache. His right fist hurts more than anything he can remember. He has to keep moving now, so he stands and goes to the bathroom.

The water from the bathroom's faucet is colder than the kitchen's. Jaime can hear his mother sobbing, talking, hiccupping. Jaime washes his hands and splashes water on his face.

A siren wails somewhere in the distance and weaves into Lorena's lamentations. Jaime sits on the toilet and tries to recall the things he wants to do now that he's out, but nothing comes. Behind his mother, on the small table with the vase that has never held flowers, are some keys. They are Cookie's car keys. Jaime leaves the bathroom, hustles past his crying mother, and grabs the keys. The car sits at the curb, like always, because the garage is full of clutter. It's an ugly, dirty, purple 2004 Impala SS. He briefly recalls Cookie complaining about the purple paint job he had done to it. The bastard loved that car more than he ever loved his mother. Jaime looks at its pretentious chrome rims and hopes there's plenty of gas in the tank because he's going wherever he has to go to stay out of prison.

He's about to take a step toward the car when he remembers the gun on top of his bed. He sprints into his room, grabs the piece, and runs out to the car.

Jaime mashes the key fob and hears a small beep followed by the click of the door unlocking. He yanks it, throws his gun into the passenger's seat, and is shoving the key into the ignition as he slams the door closed.

The Impala is 13 years old, but it purrs to life like a new car. Jaime puts it into drive and steps on the gas. The sirens get closer. The car lurches forward, and for a second he's pinned to the seat. That reminds him that Cookie's favorite pastime other than watching television and smoking is working on the car. He has injected every one of the 240 ponies under the hood with as much juice as possible and given the motor every conceivable tweak. The result is what Jaime feels when he presses the accelerator: an explosion of rumbling power that blurs everything around him.

He needs a destination and San Antonio is not a great choice at the moment, so he decides to visit Guillermo, a man who'd given him a few jobs early on and someone who should be grateful that Jamie kept his mouth shut and did his time without trying to get out of it by snitching on others. Maybe Guillermo can get him another car or knows where he can lay low for a couple of days.

The end of Bastrop Street comes too quickly. Jaime knows there's a big chance he won't set foot in the street in which he was born and raised in a long time, but the thought doesn't stir any feelings inside him. Alabama Street comes up and Jaime's instinct tells him to stop, but his brain listens to the approaching sirens and yells to take an immediate right. The screaming sirens get even closer. Then he glances in the rearview mirror and spots the red and blue lights entering his street. It's an old Lumina, a classic black and white cow. Jaime is momentarily thankful for the shitty cars they give to cops working the Third Ward. He steps on the gas and the Impala peels away to screech onto Alabama Street.

Whatever was in Jaime's chest now turns into a monster that sucks the air out of his lungs. He has the cops coming after him. Aggravated assault. Parole violation without a question. Then Cookie will say he stole his car. Grand theft auto to sweeten the deal. After the beating he gave Cookie, they will surely treat this as a felony. Jamie will be back in a cell before really having a chance to process that he made it out of that hellhole.

The solution out of this mess evades Jaime, but something is clear as day in his head: He has to escape. This part can happen. He knows Houston like no one else. He has a fast car with enough gas and muscle to get him wherever he is...

Red and blue lights splash across his rearview mirror. It's not the Lumina. This is something compact and powerful. Probably one of those Chargers he's seen once or twice. It can move. Jaime stomps on the gas and the cars jumps forward, devouring Alabama Street the way hungry dogs devour fresh meat.

Where can he go? He's hauling ass east on Alabama. He can get on I-45 and just gun it. The cops will let him go after a while, right? He can put some serious miles between them. Exchange cars somewhere and he's good. All he needs to do is survive the next couple of minutes and he'll be in the clear.

Jaime's eyes dart between the road ahead and the rearview. The pigs are still behind him. The siren shrieks like a wronged woman. The Impala's engine roars as Jaime grinds down on the accelerator pedal.

The Charger is gaining. Jaime looks at the approaching lights and thinks about long, sad nights in an uncomfortable bed. He thinks about awful meals and shakedowns and the sense that any day can be the day a shank ventilates your insides. He thinks about the showers and the screaming and the fear and the constant structure and about hearing rumors about kites that contain names and instructions concerning other men whose lives are as worthless as his. He thinks about those things and knows he can't go back. He returns his eyes to the road and a light brown thing appears out of Sampson Street. It's a car. Large. Four doors. Jaime jerks the wheel to the left and the entire world goes off-kilter as his body slams against the door.

The sound of the Impala grazing the brown car is like a faster, more metallic version of the end of the world. The car continues and Jaime tells himself to keep his eyes on the road. A second later, he looks at the rearview mirror. The Charger is closing in. And he has company.

The Impala screams into the Alabama-Scott intersection. Jaime braces for an impact that never comes. Instead, he pulls the car back into control. One step closer to the interstate. One step closer to freedom. There's nothing but speed in his immediate future, and Jaime smiles at the thought.

The ponies under the car's hood growl as Jaime guns it across the Elgin Street without a hitch. He knows that he can reach even more speed once he gets in the interstate, and that idea almost makes him smile.

The patrol car pops out of Drew Street and blocks Jaime. Panic explodes in his chest as he slams on the brakes. The Impala protests the change. Jaime pulls the wheel left and the vehicle pounces like a desperate animal. He stomps on the brakes and inertia becomes his worst enemy. His gun flies off the passenger seat and thunks on the floor.

Two loops later, he's sitting across Scott Street and he's looking at the entrance to Tuam Street. He needs to get in there and vanish. But he can't. Coming toward him is yet another cop car. Jaime slams his open hand against the steering wheel and abandons the last shards of commons sense.

He floors the gas. The Impala roars and lurches forward. Four seconds later, it's obvious the cop isn't gonna move. Jaime mashes the brakes again and slides in a circle. The other two cop cars are waiting for him.

Jaime leans on the brakes. He takes a deep breath. He's trapped. There's nowhere else to go now. Maybe he can ditch the car and run through...

"Come out of the car slowly with your hands up!"

Two seconds here and the cops are already giving him orders. Jaime is tired of orders. He's tired of eating when they tell him to and showering when they tell him to and going to bed when they tell him to. He's not going back to any of that.

There's a cop with a bullhorn now. Jaime doesn't pay attention to him. Whatever he is saying is inconsequential. Plus, they left the sirens on.

The red and blue lights are dancing all around him, but he refuses to look up. He refuses to accept that he's so far up shit creek that he can't see dry land in any direction. The guy with the bullhorn takes a second to drink some water. Jaime knows what's coming next. Words that mean nothing. Instructions and pleas. Instead, he listens to the sirens in the distance. More pigs that are coming for him. He hates them all. Then the sound of those sirens shifts and he thinks they're angels weeping because he didn't run fast enough. They tell him what he already knows: In order to escape you would have had to be faster than the red and blue weeping angels. Jaime knows that's impossible.

Jaime studies the patrol cars on both sides and the solution to the situation hits him. It's a solution that'll keep him out of a cell. He will stay away from the fear and the anger and the guns and the drugs and the blood and even the damn cars and gasoline. He thinks about freedom–true freedom–and that seals the deal. He knows he can hitch a ride to a better place on the back of those weeping angels he couldn't beat in a race, so he bends down, grabs the gun from the floor in front of the passenger's seat, and opens the door.

ESCOBAR-STYLE

Carter Wilson

OCTOBER 2003

Thirty miles south of Tikrit, Iraq

Most people only get one chance to know when death is coming. I suspect mine is now.

When they bring me into the room, the first thing I see is Jansen. He's pissed himself. Rightly so, because he's wearing a black hood and an orange jumpsuit, the costume of the condemned. No one wearing that outfit ends up any kind of happy. The piss darkens his crotch and pools on the blue plastic tarp beneath his feet.

They've let me keep my civvies on. For now.

I can smell Jansen. The musk of fear and urine. Sweat. The room is just a small, hot concrete box somewhere in the distant desert of this motherfucking scab on the planet. It's just one small room, and this is where Jansen will die. I think they brought me here to watch.

The men who took us all wear olive fatigues with black bands around their left arms, and I have no idea what that's supposed to signify. A Black Band on each side of me squeezes my arms, which are joined at the wrists by biting plastic ties. AK-47s dangle barrel-down at my captors' sides.

Another Black Band stands behind Jansen, his rifle held in both hands but pointed at no one. Jansen just stands there, quivering, head slightly bowed, wrists bound like mine. I hope they keep his hood on. Better not to see it coming.

"It's okay, Jansen," I say, hoping the comfort of my voice outweighs the sheer lunacy of the statement. This is the farthest from okay Jansen's ever been. I haven't known him long, a few weeks. We'd been doing contract work for Siemens Defense when they took us. We'd each known it was a possibility. Trained for it as much as we could have. Always carried a weapon, always alert. But none of that training makes a shit of difference when a truckload of men come for you in the middle of the night. They came hard and fast, kicking in our door and screaming at us to get on the floor. I was disoriented from sleep and it was a goddamn miracle I managed to grab my gun from under my pillow and shoot my way out of the house. Jansen didn't put up a fight at all.

I know I nailed at least one of the bastards, got him in the left shoulder. But they were good. All it took was an RPG aimed close enough to knock me clean off my feet but not kill me. They bagged and bound me, then drove Jansen and me hours away. My bones still ache from tossing around in the back of a flatbed.

"Tyson?" Jansen's throat sounds on fire. "Tell them I'm Canadian. Just tell them I'm Canadian."

I don't know why he's asking me this. I don't speak Arabic any better than he does, and as far as I know none of them speaks English.

"Quiet."

Okay, I guess one of them speaks English.

The man who says this is the nicest dressed of the lot, and by that I mean his shirt's tucked in. Black beard trimmed. Coal eyes. Red beret. No weapon, which makes me think he's the leader of whatever collection of death-seekers this is. When you don't have a weapon, it's because someone else is expected to do the killing for you.

He steps up to me. "There is no talking now."

I ignore him, because, why not? "My friend here is Canadian."

"I know this. It doesn't matter."

"Let him go."

"Your employers are unwilling to match the ransom amount provided by your kidnapping insurance. So the Canadian will be executed on video. That will show your employers we are not bluffing."

Jansen collapses to his knees and sobs. Poor fucker.

The door opens behind me and I turn my head. Two more Black Bands enter carrying A.V. equipment: a video camera, tripods, lighting. One of them seems little more than a teenager.

A flurry of words in the same language I've heard over the past several hours. Some dialect of Iraqi Arabic, and I catch just enough words to know what they are saying doesn't really matter. What *does* matter is that these men are motivated more by money than faith, and I can work with that.

"You'll get more for both of us," I tell Red Beret.

"But I'll get nothing if I'm not taken seriously."

"You seem pretty fucking serious. I don't think you have to push it."

The slightest crack of a smile and it's the first time I think this might work out.

And then it doesn't. There are a series of barking orders, suddenly Jansen is yanked to his feet and held by each arm. Camera and lighting quickly mounted. The light flashes on and I can smell the dust instantly baking on the sizzling bulb. The very young Black Band focuses the camera and zooms in tight. Hood ripped off Jansen's head, and those blue eyes are streaked with red. Pupils reduced to pinpricks. Sweat glazing his forehead. As the two Black Bands hold fast, a third walks around and stands behind him. The man is big, the largest of the lot. He holds a brutal knife in his hand, the blade long and narrow like a bread knife but with the thicker steel of a Bowie. And the teeth. Goddamn the teeth on that knife. This blade isn't meant to cut. It's meant to saw.

So here's the thing. I've made so many bad decisions I can't catch up to normal anymore. I've accepted that, and so when I agreed to come out to this hellhole and work for Siemens Defense, I knew this exact situation could happen, and maybe, in a way, was hoping for it. My employer wasn't the only one who thought to get an insurance policy on my life. Before I left, I got a two million dollar policy myself, with my wife the only beneficiary.

She asked why I did it, why I'd taken such a large policy out. It was bad luck, she said. I just smiled and told her I certainly planned on coming home safe and sound, but was just being cautious. What I didn't say was how she'd be better off with the money and without me. That I knew how empty she was, because I lived in the same vacuum, the black fucking void, a desperate and aching sense that even hell must surely be better. Together, we'd never be fixed again, not since Jada died. My wife's only chance at wholeness was to go it alone, and if she could do it with a nice insurance settlement, all the better. Letting her go would be the nicest thing I've ever done for anyone.

And now here I am. Isn't this just what I wanted?

I once saw videotape of Pablo Escobar being taken from his home in cuffs, swarmed by police. Being taken to prison and, most likely, his death. Turned out not to be what happened, but in the moment, he didn't know that. Probably figured he was done for. But on that tape, Escobar was smiling. I don't think he was smiling because he knew he was going to escape, or because he was trying to mindfuck his captors. I think he just saw everything as a game and was reveling in how the game was playing out. I pictured him being fascinated with the action of the game, whether it was favoring him at the time or not.

I always thought if I found myself in the real shit, like I am now, I'd do the same thing. Play it Escobar-style. Remind myself it's all just a game. Go out smiling.

But I'm not smiling now. Looking at Jansen, truth is I'm scared as hell. There's a big difference between being afraid of death and being afraid of dying. The one certainty I now hold with absolute and unshakable conviction is I don't want to go out the way Jansen's about to. I don't want my head sawed off. If I'm going to die, it can't be like that. Just can't be.

Red Beret comes up to me. "If you close your eyes, I'll make it worse for him."

"I don't think that's possible."

"It's possible."

Red Beret stands in front of the camera and says something I don't understand. I wonder briefly why he just doesn't speak his message in English, given his intended audience. But that thought evaporates when Red Beret takes the knife from the big Black Band and begins to go to work on Jansen. And then there are screams.

My god, the screams.

Dusk.

Tied to my bed, knots like rocks. They let me up once to do my business in a bucket then roped me up again. My muscles curse at being in the same position, but at least I can still feel. I'm thankful for that.

It's probably been five or six hours since I saw Jansen's head come off.

He looked right at me as he died. Right at me, and I couldn't tell if he was taking peace in the sight of someone familiar or damning me for not saving him. His eyes stayed open in a permanent, fixed glare as the blood spilled from his neck, mixing with his piss on the floor.

I'm thinking I'll have that image looping in my brain for the rest of my life. That's one upside of an imminent death.

Red Beret comes into the room and sits down in a chair next to my bed. He looks tired. Long day at the office and all.

"Good news," he says. "After watching what happened to the Canadian, your company agreed to match the amount covered by your insurance." His English is good, and I wonder where he learned it. He slides a cigarette from his shirt pocket, lights it, and tilts his head to the side as he takes a slow drag. It's a practiced move. I get a sense he thinks he's some kind of movie star. I gotta admit; he *is* a good-looking motherfucker. "If they had only agreed to that earlier, he'd be going home, too."

"So I'm going home?"

He nods and offers a thin smile. "Yes. In an hour." Then he stops talking and sits with his cigarette, smoking it down and staring halfway up to the ceiling. Maybe he's daydreaming about using the ransom money to get out of here. Take the missus on a little trip. Maybe a quick jaunt in the Caribbean before returning home to lop off the heads of more infidels.

"Why do you laugh?" he asks.

I didn't even realize I was. "I was picturing you at a Sandals Resort in Jamaica. Struck me as funny. The absurd kind of funny."

"I don't understand."

"Don't worry about it. Neither do I."

He lets the cigarette fall to the floor and steps on it. Then Red Beret stands and draws a knife from a leather sheath looped through his belt. My stomach tightens without me trying. It's not the same long blade that got Jansen, but it could do some damage.

"I don't do this a lot, you know."

There could be a lot of answers to my next question. "Do what?"

He looks at me as if I'm stupid.

"You mean the whole terrorist thing?" I ask.

Red Beret grimaces. For a moment, I think he's about to give me the speech about how *we're* the real terrorists, yada yada yada.

But he says, "It's the only way I can make real money. I actually went to university. Studied chemistry. But there are no jobs."

I wonder why he's telling me this, but I wonder even more about the knife in his hand.

"I need money," he continues. "I have a family. Two little girls." He holds the blade at his waist as if to indicate the height of his daughters. "I didn't want to do that to your friend, I promise you. But I have to do what I must to survive."

He searches my face, not seeming to find whatever he's looking for.

"Perhaps we are not so different," he continues. Then Red Beret leans down and begins carving through the ropes binding my wrists to the bed. It takes only seconds before my hands are free, then he repeats the process with the ropes around my ankles. Finished, he steps back. "We both do what we do for money. We don't want to hurt anybody, but ultimately, we do what we must. We have people depending on us. We are providers, you and I."

I get out of the bed, my muscles screaming as I straighten. I say nothing.

"Soon we will have confirmation of the funds transfer. After that, we'll drive you back to where we found you."

"Just like that?"

"Yes. Just like that." He shifts the knife to his left hand, steps forward, and offers me his right hand. I don't know what else to do but take it, and he gives my hand a firm pump. "I am truly sorry for what I've put you through."

It's this last sentence that fills me with sudden and ferocious hate, and I feel myself squeezing his hand with the hope of pulping all the bones in his fingers.

I'm truly sorry for what I put you through.

The exact fucking words spoken by Fred Jinovitz. We were in court, at his sentencing hearing, and the man who raped, tortured, and stabbed to death my twenty-two year-old daughter had one opportunity to address us. But Fred Jinovitz didn't address both of us. That fucker bored his gaze right into *me*, and there was just a whisper of a smile as he spoke.

I'm truly sorry for what I put you through.

Red Beret looks down at my hand, my knuckles ready to burst through the skin.

"What are you–"

He doesn't complete his sentence. Instead, he tries to react to the blow I just landed with my left fist to his sternum. But all he can do is fall backwards, and as he hits the floor I pounce and easily wrestle the knife from his left hand. He's just about to scream–I can feel it coming up from his lungs–but it doesn't make it out before I plunge the blade deep inside his chest. A little of the scream escapes through the fresh opening, like a kid's balloon wheezing out air.

His eyes are wide in absolute terror, and then the chemicals flood his brain and the fear drains from his gaze. I know about the chemicals, have read about them countless times, have even witnessed others experience them on a few occasions, as I am now. The chemicals are calming his fear, preparing him for death, comforting him. His gaze fixes on me and then slowly eases into another world, perhaps the land of seventy-two virgins. This is the vacant stare of someone headed to paradise. Jansen never got this far. His death was too quick for the chemicals to flood him. His stare remained one of horror.

I pull out the knife. The chest wound glurps.

I search the body and find a gun on his ankle. Guess he was armed after all. The last thing I take from him is his red beret. I've never worn such a thing in my life. I imagine it looks good, because that's all I can do.

Why did you do it, Tyson?

The voice is in my head, but it doesn't sound like me. It sounds like all the mistakes I've made, the people who expected something from me but never got satisfaction. The voice of unfulfilled wishes. The voice of my daughter, perhaps.

They were letting you go. The were going to let you live. Why did you do it?

I think about that for a second, then answer as truthfully as I can. "I didn't come here to live."

It's the first time in my life I've spoken to myself, and it feels good. I suspect I've reached that rare and transient moment when a person realizes they're becoming truly insane.

He didn't really remind you of Fred Jinovitz, did he? Jinvitz was a middle-aged Jew with blue eyes and forty-inch waist. Red Beret is a Persian movie star. You just needed an excuse to die, didn't you? Suicide by Al Qaeda. I neither confirm nor deny the voice's theory. Looking down at the body, I feel neither regret nor sorrow. I suppose a small part of me gloats over gutting the man who executed Jansen, but that part is very small. What I feel most about killing is the tinge of excitement knowing more of it must now be done. That a blaze of glory is just on the other side of the singular door in this room.

I check the gun's magazine. *Full.* Squeeze the knife with my left hand, wipe the bloody blade on my pant leg, just to make a smear, then slide the blade into my pants' waist.

This is how Escobar would do it. It's all a game, and I'm about to play as hard as I can.

I crack the door and spy two Black Bands watching television, their backs to me. They don't even turn to look before I walk in and shoot each in the back of the head. Bodies slump forward, blood spurting, just as you'd expect. As I pass them, I sling one of their AKs over my shoulder. Its weight is highly assuring.

A door opposite me flies open. It's the Black Band who stood behind Jansen, the one with the sawing knife. His eyes widen at the sight of my gun. My focus feels supernatural, as if I can almost see the bullet ejecting from my pistol. Can almost follow its trajectory, its invisible vapor trail creating a tightrope to a spot just above the man's left eye. Pink mist, and this human is no more. Just like in a video game.

There's a chance I'll make it out of here, and I'm certainly going to try. In that case, I'll go home and back to a broken marriage, and my wife and I will spend our days wondering what we did to deserve such a thing.

But more likely I'm about to die, and I'm thinking that's the better outcome. Yes, I will miss never seeing

my wife again, and it would've been nice to say goodbye. But those are small thoughts compared to the Big
Idea. I can *fix* things by dying. Fix her. Fix me. I can't fix
Jada, but maybe I can join her. And wouldn't that be the
sweetest thing?.

I walk outside. In the twilight, scaffolding-mounted
halogens illuminate a dirt courtyard; the sun slips
beneath a distant dune. I just have enough time to count
four utility trucks before chunks of the wall behind me
explode. The sound of gunfire a half-second later.

Crouch and run. I could fire the AK, but I don't want
to waste ammo shooting at things I can't see. I make it
to the first truck, which is just a piece-of-shit tan Toyota
with its flatbed tented in camouflage canopy. I jump in as
more bullets slam into metal, *thunk-thunking* in a dance
toward my flesh. Adrenaline spikes, and the hairs stick
straight out of my arms. Good goddamn, I do believe I'm
on the verge of enjoying this. I lean down and hear a pop
and a *whoosh*, then the truck lists hard to the right. They
shot the tires, which is a shame since the keys dangle
teasingly from the ignition.

I sit up enough to peer into the back. The truck's
been modified, so I can crawl directly into the covered
bed. I have a bitch of a time trying to hold onto my weapons while I shimmy on my stomach, but I make it. The
bed is full of things I can't make out in the confusion, and
I try to reach the tailgate. Maybe they won't expect me
coming out the back.

Then I feel the metal chest. About a foot high, maybe
two long. Metal latches, a military footlocker. Or an ammo
case. I release my rifle and pistol long enough to unlatch
the chest and pop it open. I reach inside, expecting to

feel the cool, slippery metal of stacked bullets. But what I feel is even better.

Grenades.

Bullets riddle the truck, a rainstorm of searing metal. How I haven't been hit is a question for statisticians. I ride the wave of luck, reach up, and use the knife to slice through the canopy covering the bed. Then I fish out a grenade, pull the pin, and lob it through the opening. Repeat with a second, throwing it ninety degrees to the left from the first. Follow up with a third and fourth, covering all directions. The second I release the grip on the fourth grenade, the first explodes, sending a shockwave through the truck, slamming me like a helpless skiff against an angry squall. Three more explosions, concussive roundhouses. I'm belly-down on the truck bed, can barely hear or get my bearings, but I'm acutely aware of one thing: The gunfire has stopped. For now.

Then the motherfucker of blasts, and a flash of light through the slit in the canopy. I scramble to my knees and risk poking my head through the opening. Another truck is on its side, flames bursting through the shattered windows.

Panicked, staccatoed shouts. Could be three voices, could be twenty. If I have any window of opportunity, it's now. Right now.

Don't be silly, Tyson. Don't you know you're going to die here?

Fuck you, voice.

I crawl to the end of the truck bed, release the tailgate, slide out legs-first. A comforting wave of heat from nearby flames washes over me. The satisfying, acrid smell of spilled gasoline. Then a gutting scream as bad as Jansen's. I crane my neck and see a man in flames, running in purposeless circles, with nowhere to go but death. The fire eats him fast, and he collapses and twists into a tight, permanent knot of blackened limbs.

I reach back into the bed and grab what I can: pistol, AK, and two grenades, one for each of the ample front pockets of my utility pants. I hope there's enough chaos to buy me a few more seconds. Crouching into as small a target as I can manage, I scurry to the closest intact vehicle, five meters away. A Jeep.

Into the front seat. The sight of the key in the ignition is a glorious one. I start the Jeep and hit the accelerator, not even knowing how to get out of here. It doesn't matter, I tell myself. Moving is better than not moving.

A fresh burst of gunfire hails over the scream of the engine. The glass next to my head shatters, and something whispers in my ear. It takes me a half-second to realize it's a bullet, an inch from putting an end to all forty-eight years of my existence.

I swerve the Jeep on nothing but instinct, and the instinct is a good one. Straight ahead is the compound's exit. Shift into second and give no mercy to the pedal. The Jeep lurches forward, tires begging for traction in the dirt. More gunfire. More shouts. It doesn't matter. There's no shooting back, there's only moving forward. Either I'll get out of here in the next few seconds or I won't.

A figure appears in front of me so suddenly I imagine it's Jansen's ghost, but I'm not that lucky. The Jeep's headlights spotlight a Black Band, one I remember from the little room. The boyish one in charge of videotaping the execution. Earlier, he struck me as too young to be involved with something as grown-up as beheadings.

Here, he's not a kid but a one-man show of rage. Pistol drawn, brilliant white teeth against tight lips. Hyena snarl. Eyes black as a snake's, or at least that's how I imagine. He's not an Islamic extremist. He's not a jihadist. This has nothing to do with beliefs, at least not in this moment. In this moment, he's the one motherfucker separating heaven and hell and trying to keep me in the latter.

He shoots. I accelerate.

The windshield pops once. Twice. I lower my head, thankful it's still in one piece. Then I let out a howl, a tea-kettle rebel yell, the scream of a rabbit, piercing and incomprehensible. I scream not from fear, but because I want this sound to be in his head as he dies. I want it to be the last thing to rattle in his brain.

The Jeep makes contact with a sickening crunch and my head slams against the steering column. The Jeep shudders to a stop, and when I look up through the windshield, I see him. Crumpled, in the dirt, captured in dust-swirled headlight beams. He moves, but without threat, like a wasp drunkenly lumbering in a cool dawn.

I accelerate and sweep around him. I could have put him out of his misery. The shortest path would have, in fact, been right over his head. But I choose to both spare his life and prolong his suffering, and I think that pretty much sums up the whole of my existence.

Out of the compound, into the blackest of nights on this motherfucking scab on the planet, and for the moment, no headlights behind me.

Hell can wait.

In the desert, dark velvet overcast sky, void of stars, absent of depth. There's almost a peace about the world until the piece-of-shit Jeep blows a tire, the right-rear. I barely manage to avoid spiraling out of control, coming to a jolting stop at a ninety-degree angle to the road. I turn on the Jeep's lights for the first time, and the beams flood an endless ocean of sand; barren, silken, the occasional sprinkling of scrub. Nowhere to go, and I kill the lights, sending the landscape back to a moonlit wash.

A quick search confirms there's no spare tire.

I stare down the path from which I've come. There is a very obvious *end of the road* metaphor here, but I force that from my mind and suck in the night air. In the moment the world is as blissfully silent as the inside of a snow globe. In this silence I think about life and about death, how all of us will be one of those things much longer than the other. Maybe death is nothing, perhaps it's everything.

The night air is crisp, the perfect temperature. In the dark, everything feels better. The tightness in my chest unwinds. If I see the sun rise, the reality of my situation will be more painfully obvious. There is no escape from here.

For now I breathe, and that feels good enough.

Pinpricks in the distance. Two, four, then six. Growing larger. A soft purr of noise, a stalking cat.

Trucks.

Within two minutes, those trucks will be here. It's most likely them. That's the assumption I have to work with, at least.

Suppose it's time, huh, Tyson?

"Yup," I reply to the voice, which now I'm certain is my daughter's. But she sounds older, like maybe she's aged at some rapid pace wherever she's at.

Search the Jeep, find two more rifles. Full magazines. Gather the weapons, stand in the middle of the road. The trucks are close.

I've lost the red beret. Shame.

So here I am, exactly how I wanted to be. Escobar-style, cocky, aggressive, ready for anything. Pure game. And maybe, depending on what's beyond the great black barrier, I'll get to see Jada.

And my wife, bless her, will be a millionaire with a chance at life.

My second-to-last thought is a desire to feel those chemicals flood my brain, right before death. I only hope there's time for that.

As the approaching engines transition from purr to roar, and as the first shaft of headlights sweep over me, I calmly begin firing. The AK recoils, bullets spray, glass splinters. Men scream. I play the game at the highest level. Master class.

I feel an unusual pull of muscle on my face, and that's when I have my very last thought.

I realize I'm smiling.

DO-OVER

Catherine Dilts

THE GIRL HEARD CUSSING. SHE RUBBED HER
fists against her eyes. Dad saved his bad words for emer-
gencies. How could there be an emergency in the middle
of the night? She'd wake up for reals in a second, in her
bed at home, just having a stomachache dream from all
the junk she'd eaten at the state fair.

"What's that crazy bastard doing?" Dad asked. "He's
headed straight for us."

The girl opened her eyes. She was still in the minivan, with a seatbelt across her chest instead of her quilt.
Dad twisted a knob on the steering wheel, making the
headlights go bright, then off, then bright again. Their
van swerved on the narrow, curvy highway, tossing the
girl from side to side. Lights swept across their windshield from the oncoming car. It was like being in an
out-of-control carnival ride at the fair. She felt like
throwing up.

"He must be drunk." Mom's voice was panicky. "Pull over, until he's gone past us."

"There's a mountain on one side, a cliff on the other." Dad gripped the steering wheel tight. "There's no pullout."

He stomped his foot until the tires squealed against the asphalt. The minivan wrenched violently to the right. Metal shrieked as they grazed the guardrail. The girl's head bounced off the window.

The minivan lurched to a halt, throwing the girl against the shoulder harness with a painful jerk. Her brother woke, crying.

"He's got plenty of room." Dad reached over to touch Mom's arm. "We'll be okay."

Headlights raked across the minivan, making the girl squint.

"Holy hell," Dad muttered. "He's not slowing down. Hang on, kids. Hang on!"

The world exploded in a shower of glass and screaming metal.

The rubble stunk of burnt wood and gasoline, the chemical stew of a meth lab, and roasted flesh. A drug addict accidentally torched the squatter-infested building, taking a few homeless people with him. No great loss. Of property, or humanity.

Glenda's heels sunk into the fire-hose soaked muck. Boots would have made more sense, but she'd learned that people didn't trust an overweight female dressed like a construction worker. On the other hand, they'd tell their darkest secrets, and trust their life savings, to a matronly woman who looked like their auntie.

The harsh white of a streetlight glared through a shattered window. Glenda perched one hip on the window ledge where she'd be backlit. That way, maybe the client wouldn't notice the designer wool slacks had frayed hems and the silk blouse was stained with fast food grease.

She liked to meet new clients in places other people avoided. Hidden, like her shadowed face. Considering the mental state of her typical client, she couldn't be too cautious. This one sounded truly pathetic.

Glenda felt inside the pocket of a tailored wool coat that had seen better days, her fingers brushing across the reassuring grip of an S&W snub nose.

A voice cracked the silence.

"You're early," a girl said.

She stood there, plain as day if Glenda had been looking, which she should have been. Gray against gray, in a hoodie two sizes too big. Glenda took a moment to calm herself, making sure her voice came out firm. Confident.

"You're Angel." She made it a statement, not a question. Put the scrawny kid on the defensive.

The waif didn't resemble her namesake, dressed in ragged jeans and a hoodie that had done time in a Dumpster, her short, spiked hair so greasy Glenda couldn't tell whether it was brown or black. The stink of fear rolled off her like a rank perfume. The kid needed a shower. Bad. But a bar of soap wouldn't wash away the dark circles under her eyes. The girl glanced around, jittery.

"I don't deal with junkies," Glenda said.

She grasped the butt of the gun, letting Angel see the bulge of it through the wool coat, in case she had robbery in mind. Not that Glenda had anything worth stealing. Years ago, she hocked her heirloom jewelry and sold her house to pay a bloodsucking lawyer in a desperate shot at keeping out of prison. That had been a total waste. Since then her financial life, like her personal life, remained in tatters. Her credit cards were maxed out. She drove a rusted-out Kia with over a hundred thousand miles on the odometer. She had more lint in her coat pocket than money.

"I'm not on drugs," the kid said, her voice shaking.

Angel had a hungry alley cat look in eyes set in a face too innocent to be real. Life on the streets turned boys and girls into bitter old souls.

Glenda sniffed hard. "Smell that? Like barbeque gone bad? That's what happens to dope heads. They end up frying themselves."

"I told you, I'm clean. I'm just nervous. I've never hired a hit man, er, woman, before."

"I'm not an assassin, kid. Let's get that straight right now."

"That's what you advertise." She dug in the bulging kangaroo pouch that was the hoodie's front pocket, retrieving a crumpled section from the free paper's want ads. "Helene Hunter, Private Investigator," she read. "I can send your tarnished past to the morgue of bad memories."

Glenda flushed with a little pride, hearing the ad she had written herself. She'd even conjured up the fake name.

"No mention of being a hired gun." She shook her head. "Sorry, kid."

"It's there." She shook the ad, the paper sounding oddly crisp in the dank, burned out hovel. "In between the lines. You kill people for the right price. That's what I heard."

"Who said that?"

"George Pettit."

Now they were getting somewhere. Pettit wouldn't send a snitch.

"So what gives, kid?" Glenda asked. "What do you want from me?"

Angel didn't look like she had the price of a Happy Meal in the hoodie's kangaroo pouch. But then, looks could be deceiving. The kid might be an heiress, for all Glenda knew. Or maybe she needed help to become an heiress, knocking off a rich relative so she could inherit a fortune. Glenda took a slow breath to steady herself. If she played it right, this case might be a real money-maker. The first after a long string of petty deals that barely paid the rent.

In the dim light, Glenda could see the kid chewing on her lower lip. She shifted her weight from one foot to the other, like she was ready to bolt.

Fear made people dangerous, and that's what Glenda's clients usually were - scared. Not of her, but of themselves. As though they were facing, for once and all, that the trouble they were in was so deep, they were willing pay someone like Glenda to fix it for them.

"Like the ad says," Glenda told her, "I can make it all go away."

The kid held a hand up, shielding her eyes from the streetlight. Stalling.

"I don't really need for anyone to die," Angel finally said. "I just want a do-over. You know?" She shrugged. "A chance to wipe the slate clean, like none of it happened. Like I'm not a burnt out mess."

She flung her left arm out, waving at the rubble-strewn ruins. Glenda followed the kid's hand with her eyes. The oldest trick in the book. Misdirection. She looked like a tragic lost cause in her teen years, but Glenda didn't know anything about Angel. She had an uneasy feeling she'd misjudged the girl's age and experience.

"There's no such thing as a do-over," Glenda said. "You've got to deal with what life gave you."

"No, this wasn't just life. It wasn't random. This was deliberate. One decision leading to the next."

"I can't help you until I know your story." Glenda folded her arms under her breasts. "Tell me, Angel, what happened that made you call me?"

"You ever been to Oregon?"

Glenda had memories of Oregon. Cloudy, alcohol soaked memories. Good times. And some not so good.

"Sure. I travel all over. What of it?"

The kid nodded, but not in agreement. It was more like Glenda had just confirmed something for her.

"You gonna talk?" Glenda could tell she would have to pry it out of Angel. Clients did a lot of beating around the bush before getting to the point. She should charge by the hour. "Unfaithful boyfriend? A creepy uncle diddled you? Kids trashed you on social media?" She hadn't hit it yet, guessing from Angel's blank stare. Glenda snapped her fingers. "I know. Mumsy cut off your allowance, and your dealer's threatening you?"

Angel seemed to shrink inside her hood, but not in retreat. More like a snake coiling to strike. Cool night air crept through the broken window and under Glenda's wool coat. She shivered. A little chill never used to bother her.

"What got to you the most? Was it the sound?" Angel asked.

"What're you talking about?" Glenda asked. "What sound?"

"Metal on metal. Glass shattering. Or the screaming." Angel closed her eyes and went somewhere far away, as if she was watching a video play on the backsides of her eyelids. "Then there was the smell. Not like here, with the burnt meat stink. No, it was industrial. Oil and gasoline. Smoking tires clinging to asphalt, then letting go. There's not much visual for me. It was mostly blackness. Maybe it was better I couldn't see what was happening." Angel opened her eyes and shrugged. "How was it for you?"

Glenda hoped her stunned silence would be mistaken for lack of comprehension. The kid might as well have dipped into Glenda's private memories, describing a car wreck that anyone could have had. That's what it sounded like. A car wreck. Glenda nearly died in one. In Oregon. Doing some quick math, she figured the one survivor in the car that collided with hers would be around twenty by now. It fit. But she didn't want it to.

"So is that what it's about?" Glenda asked. "You were in a car accident?"

Angel raised one eyebrow, reminding Glenda of a schoolteacher disappointed when the student gave the wrong answer.

"Glenda, you know exactly what this is about."

"Who's Glenda? My name's—"

The kid wore a grim, determined look. There was no talking her way out of this one. Besides, Glenda carried protection from the crazies she dealt with in her line of work. She shoved her hand back into her pocket, wrapping her fingers around the grip of the revolver.

Glenda had changed her name twice and moved a half dozen times since her release, trying to shake off her past and start over. *Wipe the slate clean*, the kid called it. She couldn't imagine how Angel found her, but there it was. The kid was talking about the car accident that wrecked Glenda's life.

Not my fault, Glenda reminded herself. It was pure chance that pitted two vehicles against each other that dark night. Fate. Both plunged through the guardrail, off the cliff, and into the ocean below. She'd been cold as a corpse, floating in black water, her brain numb from alcohol and shock. Only two people were pulled out of the water in time. Glenda, and a passenger in the other car. If it was her fault, she'd be dead. That's how these things worked, right? The guilty died, the innocent survived? Karma or some bullshit. Glenda was alive, and planning to stay that way.

"When you kill someone," Angel asked, "does it work?"

"What do you mean, does it work? Sure it does. Bang. They're dead."

"No, I mean, does it fix things?"

Her face could have been pretty, if it weren't twisted in pain. Angel probably remembered that night better than Glenda. She had woken up in the hospital two days later. Even with the best lawyer she could afford, it was a quick trip to the women's prison. She'd done her time and found a new career.

Angel obviously hadn't let go of that night.

"Killing a person can fix lots of things," Glenda said. "But not everything." She pushed her hand deeper into her pocket, hooking her index finger into the revolver's trigger guard, ready to shoot if things went that way. "You're not here to hire me. What do you want?"

Angel's shoulders convulsed. With grief, fury, or the chill air, Glenda couldn't tell. That was the problem. The situation had become unstable. Glenda had dealt with all kinds of crazy, but the kid had her on edge so bad she was shaking. If Angel wasn't on drugs, maybe she should be. The kind prescribed by a psychiatrist.

"An apology," the kid said. "That's what I want."

Just because she flunked the blood alcohol test, Glenda had been the one who took the blame. She still wasn't certain she'd been the one to cross the centerline. Maybe Angel's daddy had fallen asleep at the wheel.

"Your name's not Helene Hunter." The kid spat out the fake name. "It's Glenda Duncan. Coffee Creek Correctional Facility, Oregon state offender ID number 1315302. I've been searching for you from the day they let you out. Two years. I know you did it. I just need to hear you say it."

"I'm sorry there was an accident." Glenda shrugged. She played the same game with the prison counselors. They weren't satisfied until they wormed an admission of guilt from a person. Glenda didn't need to put up with that shit from a ragged street orphan. "I wish there was such a thing as a do-over. But there isn't, kid."

Angel pulled her right hand out of the hoodie pocket. She aimed a small automatic at Glenda with a shaky hand, holding it gangster style, out in front and sideways.

Glenda jerked her revolver from the pocket of her wool coat.

"Drop it!" Angel yelled. "Or I'll shoot!"

Glenda moved slowly, placing her gun on the window ledge, within reach.

"Hands up," Angel ordered.

Glenda raised her arms slowly, like she was surrendering. She'd had guns pointed at her before. Besides, she guessed Angel couldn't hit a garage door at ten feet with that stance.

"You killed my mom and dad." Her words came out in hiccupy sobs. "My little brother. You killed them all."

"No. It was an accident. Things happen."

"'Things'? Like wiping out a whole family?" Tears rolled down her cheeks. "Oh, not the whole family, though. No, you left one alive. But I should have died, because nothing was ever right after that day."

"I can't help you, kid." Glenda lowered her arms.

Angel's hand trembled like the weight of her piece was too much for her. She was an obvious amateur. Was she hoping that Glenda would shoot her? That was a new one. She'd never been hired for an assisted suicide.

"You might consider a good shrink," Glenda said. "Grief counseling. Because revenge, it's really not all it's chalked up to be."

"I have to try. Revenge is all I have left." The kid suddenly shifted her stance, standing erect and

straightening the automatic. She slapped her free hand
on the grip so she held the gun steady in both hands
while she squinted expertly through the sights. "I have
to know if it works."

Glenda grabbed her revolver, but she didn't have
time to aim. Angel got her shot off first.

The shots echoed through the charred rubble.

Angel waited for the ringing in her ears to subside.
She looked down at herself. At the gun clutched in her
hands. The organic odor of fresh blood competed with
the chemical gasoline and meth lab stench. She wasn't
sure what she'd expected. To wake up from her nightmare life and find herself sitting in the back seat of the
family car with her brother? Really?

Glenda was right. There were no do-overs. Killing her didn't erase the past that brought Angel to
this present.

Angel shoved the gun into her hoodie pocket and
knelt to pick up Glenda's revolver. It was small and light
with a pink grip. On the bottom of the frame, it read in
script, *Lady Smith*. The gun didn't weigh down Angel's
pocket much and had to be better than the off-brand POS
she'd bought cheap from a junkie. She pawed through
Glenda's coat, hoping for a wad of cash, enough for a
plane ticket to somewhere exotic. She found a thin wallet
with a few bucks, just chump change, and the keys to a
Kia she couldn't drive without risking being picked up
by the police.

Great. She was right back where she started. Sleeping in the shelter, eating at the soup kitchen. Impossible to hold down a job when you were crazy. But maybe killing Glenda wiped that slate clean. Angel could finally start over.

The wool coat was soft. High quality. It was too big for Angel, but so was the hoodie, and that made her look like a refugee from a rap video. She tugged the coat off Glenda, wiping the muck off it. Now that she could see it up close, it was kind of tattered around the edges. And there was the blood. She'd have to clean it up, but the quilted lining felt good. Warm.

The coat vibrated. Angel shrugged out of it, dropping it to the floor. The buzzing started again. Glenda had put her cell phone on silent. Someone was calling.

Angel pulled the phone out of the coat pocket. The number showed as "unknown." She hit a button.

"Hello? No, this isn't Helene."

She glanced at the PI. A neat hole above her left eye oozed blood.

"Ms. Hunter isn't taking any calls. The service is under new management."

She paused, considering her answer to the caller's next question.

"Yes, we're accepting new clients."

THE TAXI MAN

Angie Hodapp

BENDRIX STRADDLES HER FLUG, ITS REBUILT engine idling between her thighs, and watches a freighter coast in past the breakwater. Beneath her Flug's hull roll the tailwaters of the Escopeta River, carrying an endless purge of rubbish from the cities to the sea. Soda cups and plastic bags, bottles and cans and the burnt-out ends of cheap cigarettes bump along past her ankles and drift off, ghostly pale in half-light of dawn.

From here, the freighter's deck lights look like stars. From here, the crewmen smoking at the rail are silhouettes the size of her thumb.

Bendrix envies them. She's never been out past the breakwater. Never been outside the city limits of Dusang to the west of the river or Ghaz to the east. Never even been to the south end of the Escopeta, where the two cities bend away from each other and fade into long stretches of rocky coastline. Or so she's heard. She's never been south because at least a dozen other gangs work the river. The north end, up here by the freight yards and shipping piers, is her turf.

The freighter slows, inching toward the pier, and the crewmen shove off the rail to prep for offload.

I could go now, thinks Bendrix. Sell my Flug to some wharf rat for quick cash. Find a captain or foreman and beg a job. Be out past the breakwater by nightfall and see what the world looks like with no jagged skylines closing me in, no garbage floating by, nothing but clean, wide-open water every which way you look and some exotic port city always lying just past the horizon.

Something nudges her ankle. A take-out container from Slim Sumo's Noodle Bar. She shifts her hips to pivot the Flug and kicks the little box into the Escopeta's sluggish current. Off it goes, Slim Sumo's cartoon face laughing at the sky.

The whine of another Flug splits the morning. Bendrix knows from the sound of the engine it's Lingo's rig. She clenches her jaw, tamping down the dull ache she gets in her chest when she watches the freighters come in. Who is she kidding? She's never leaving the Escopeta. This polluted swath of bilgewater is her home, and someday, it'll be her grave. She'll die here. And she'll probably deserve it.

But for now, the Escopeta is also her business, and it's time to get back to work.

The half-mask Lingo wears to cover the scars on the left side of his face is painted like a skull. Even from a hundred meters, she can make out its toothy grin. But the right side of his face isn't smiling, and the height of the plume fanning up behind his rig tells Bendrix he's doing close to ninety.

He approaches, slows, cuts a sharp one-eighty that churns an arc of yellow-brown water out behind him. "Water taxi!" he shouts. "Dusang bound!"

Bendrix tenses, already fitting her goggles over her eyes. "How big?"

"A six-seater."

"Where?"

"Other side of the bridge."

Bendrix twists the Flug's throttle, adrenaline shooting up into the back of her throat. A sneak-across. Most of the taxi men working back and forth between the cities' north-side docks know the drill and cough up their tolls without a fight. This one, thinks Bendrix, either has balls of iron or he's dumb as fuck.

In seconds, she's doing ninety herself, cutting a path up the river, her bone-white dreads whipping out behind her. Lingo holds back, riding her wake, letting her take the lead.

The lead, of course, is hers to take. But she appreciates that Lingo–and the rest of her crew, too, when they're all working together–ride their place. At least for now. Someday, one of them will try to ride point, and she'll have to answer with fists and blood. It happens in every crew. It's the only way to move up in the world. It's how *she* moved up in the world.

Ahead, the ruins of the bridge loom up out of the morning mist. Two halves of a derelict whole, a pair of monolithic sentinels standing half a mile apart. They reach toward each other high above the Escopeta like they're hoping to someday meet again in the middle.

What's left after the bombings a couple weeks ago are massive, blast-scorched columns, buckled nests of melted rebar, and tangled steel suspension cables dangling like entrails down toward the water.

Bendrix opens the throttle and charges ahead, her Flug riding the water so fast and high it's like she's flying. But just as she passes under the open air where the bridge used to be, she flinches. She can't help herself. She feels the damn thing's absence like blood pulsing through a missing limb.

She leans in hard, focusing on the taxi. *Do your job. Don't think about the bombs. The screams, the burning bodies falling into the water. Don't think about the people you killed.*

A hundred meters past the bridge, the water taxi is still trying to outrun Bendrix's crew. Pathetic, she thinks. A seal trying to outrace a school of sharks. The taxi man has to know he's screwed.

Eva and Ferno flank the taxi, aiming their grappling guns at its rails. Eva launches her hook first. It latches on with a metallic thunk a second before Ferno's. Their Flugs arc away from each other in perfect, mirrored sync, snapping their chains taut. They cut back, forcing the taxi backwards. The taxi's engine whines in protest to the strain before it gives up and dies.

Zephyr circles the stalled-out taxi on his Flug, letting out whoops and hollers and screaming out his high-pitched laugh, while Ferno reels in his chain, letting the grappling gun's winch pull him closer to the taxi. In seconds, Ferno's Flug bumps up against the taxi's hull. He stands on his seat and climbs over the rail.

Wary, Bendrix watches Ferno pull his pistol and sweep the passenger area. It's covered on three sides by a frayed tarp draped over a framework of aluminum poles; Ferno's the only one who can see inside. Bendrix tenses, watching him. He remains calm, though he keeps his gun aimed underneath. His free hand clamps the back of the taxi man's neck. Hulking and silent, he awaits Bendrix's orders.

Lingo and Eva lasso Ferno's Flug, then cut their engines. They, too, are waiting for Bendrix to tell them what to do.

She eyes the taxi man. He's small, wiry like an underfed chicken. His thin gray hair is tied back from his leathery face. His eyes are flat, betraying neither fear nor mettle. She doesn't recognize him. He's either new to the Escopeta or accustomed to crossing farther south. He hasn't met her crew yet. He doesn't know the rules. His mistake.

"How many passengers?" she calls out to Zephyr.

"One." Zephyr, governed by an unbroken current of nervous energy that reminds Bendrix of a nest of badgers, snatches her Flug's tether and winds it around a cleat on the taxi's rail.

One? Bendrix snaps her goggles up on her forehead. One passenger on a six-seater from Ghaz to Dusang means this is a charter. An *expensive* charter. Why pay six fares to cross at dawn when you could wait an hour for a scheduled taxi and pay only one?

Bendrix smells trouble. But she also smells money. Big money. And money smells good. She hasn't turned a profit since before she destroyed the bridge.

Zephyr pulls a knife out of his vest and raises an eyebrow. Does she want him to cut the fuel lines?

She shakes her head. Not yet.

Standing on her Flug's seat, she draws her own pistol. With her free hand, she grabs the rail, hops over, and peers under the tarp.

The passenger sits alone in the back. Male. Her age— late twenties. He wears a white button-down shirt, open at the throat. Khakis. Nice but not too nice, meaning he's an office worker, maybe, but entry level. No tie, no suit coat. His hands rest on his thighs. He knows enough to keep them still and visible. Jet-black hair sweeps across his forehead. Dark eyes look out at her from behind black-rimmed glasses.

"Hi," he says.

"Shut the fuck up." She turns to the taxi man. "Who are you?"

The taxi man gazes past her, at the ruins of the bridge.

Ferno squeezes. The taxi man's eyes squinch shut, his mouth pulling into a grimace.

"Want me to ask again?"

He shakes his head. Ferno relaxes his grip.

"Hoag." The taxi man strains to speak. "My name's Hoag."

Bendrix feels her crew watching her. Zephyr, Lingo, and Eva at the rails. Ferno right in front of her. Their gazes weigh heavy. They're listening, learning, waiting for orders. Or waiting for her to screw up. It doesn't matter. In this moment, she's in charge. To stay in charge, she needs to show them how it's done. She needs to *keep* showing them.

She backhands the taxi man so hard his head whips to the side. Ferno takes a step to keep from stumbling, but he doesn't let go. Blood gushes from a split in the taxi man's lip.

Bendrix moves in close, notes the first glimmer of fear in the old man's eyes. "Welcome to the north end of the river, Hoag."

Resigned, he cowers.

Bendrix glances over her shoulder. The passenger's hands haven't moved. His fingers are splayed on his thighs. He watches her like the others do. She falters. His gaze is like knives, adding a sharp, dangerous gravity to the pressure that already burdens her.

"Is there a problem?" she growls. "Something you want to share?"

He shakes his head.

He's no threat, she decides. Let him judge her.

She turns back to the taxi man. "There's a toll up this way, Hoag. Two-thousand kroner. Pay it and off you go."

"Didn't bring no money."

Ferno squeezes again. Again, the taxi man grimaces.

"Three-thousand," Bendrix says.

"No money," the taxi man chokes out.

She delivers another backhand. This time, Ferno lets Hoag fall to his knees. He presses his palms to his face. Blood trickles between his fingers, stripes the backs of his hands.

Bendrix squats beside him and brings her lips close to one leathery ear. "You're doing this to yourself, Hoag." She makes her voice soothing, a mother calming a child who's skinned his knee. "Four-thousand."

"I'll pay." The passenger shifts in his seat, reaching into the back pocket of his khakis.

In one swift move, Bendrix spins to her feet, swings her pistol around, and aims it at his face. "Here I was thinking you were so smart to keep your hands where I could see them."

The passenger freezes, then slowly withdraws an empty hand.

"We have a way of doing things up here," Bendrix informs him, "and it doesn't include you being a hero."

Both his hands go up, palms out in surrender. "Just stop hitting him. He didn't do anything."

She bristles, a thorny heat shooting up the back of her neck. Did this asshole really just call her out in front of her crew? Her finger twitches on the trigger. She should kneecap him.

Another twitch.

She should kneecap him *now*.

Shit. That damn bridge. Those people I killed. Sweat prickles her forehead. She feels her goggles slipping toward her brow, feels her crew's scrutiny pressing in on her from every side. *That damn job turned me soft.*

She inhales. Exhales. Gets an idea.

"Ferno," she says, "show our passenger how we do things up here."

Behind her, she hears a scuffle, a thump. A strangled cry cut short by a hard crack. Then a splash.

The passenger's mouth drops open. His eyes, behind his glasses, widen in horror. His expression confirms what Bendrix already knows: Ferno misunderstood. Bendrix doesn't have look to know the taxi man's body is floating in the river, face down, another piece of trash on its way to the sea.

She hasn't eaten since last night, but her stomach bucks, straining against its own walls for something to purge. She closes her eyes. *You stupid goddamn gorilla. You were only supposed to hit him.*

She swallows bile. Before they blew up the bridge–goddamn, had it only been two weeks?–she and her crew roughed people up. They drew blood. They dealt in pain and fear, in speed, adrenaline, and cash. But for as much as they threatened death, they never carried through. The bridge was the first time they killed. Fifteen souls. Burned. Blown to bits. Some fell screaming to their deaths, their bodies crushed by falling debris. Any who managed to survive the blast drowned like rats in a sewer.

The bridge was a line crossed. The bridge was when she and her crew turned killer.

Bendrix steadies her hand. What's done is done. She can't let on, not to any of them, that Ferno killing the taxi man wasn't exactly what she ordered.

Another breath and Bendrix opens her eyes. "Now," she says to the passenger, "show us real slow what you got in that pocket."

Bendrix stands in the alley behind Slim Sumo's Noodle Bar, flies swarming the moldering bags of trash piled beside the back door. Sticky heat and stifling humidity have already laid a thick haze over Dusang.

Around the corner, out of sight, street vendors peddling fry bread, hand-carved totems, and beaded charms are setting up for the day. Their carts trundle over broken cobblestones, and they shout greetings to each other as easily as they shout *Get the fuck out of my way* and *Tough luck for you! This is my spot today!*

Bendrix empties the wallet she took from the passenger an hour ago. He wasn't armed. Not even with a knife. What he did have was 6,800 kroner–not counterfeit–and an ID card that said his name was August Orlean.

She fingers the bills. Seventy-percent of her total take goes to Mr. Corn. The other thirty is hers to split with her crew as she sees fit. That's how it works. Still, she considers: How much could she skim? How would Mr. Corn find out?

Shit. Mr. Corn always finds out.

She pulls her phone from one of the pockets in her utility vest and calls him. Three rings and he answers.

"Sixty-eight-hundred kroner," she tells him. "Lingo's on his way."

Mr. Corn is quiet for a moment. She can almost hear him smiling. "Welcome back, Bendrix," he says. "I was worried I'd lost you."

She snaps the phone shut, slips it back into her pocket. *Worried I'd lost you.* Translation: *You haven't turned in a single cash-drop in the two weeks since you dropped the bridge. It's about time you got your shit together and started running your crew again.*

Her crew–Lingo, Zephyr, Ferno, Eva. Right now, they're sitting at their regular table inside Slim Sumo's, eating ramen and yakisoba. They're probably elbowing each other and laughing, mouths full, happy it's payday.

She toes the door open a crack and signals Lingo. He rises, swiping a paper napkin down the side of his chin that isn't covered by his half-mask, and joins her in the alley. When he sees the wad of bills she holds out to him, he raises an eyebrow.

"Don't keep Mr. Corn waiting," she says.

Lingo nods once, then zips the bills into his vest and jogs off.

Bendrix exhales. She trusts her crew, Lingo especially, but humans are human. Calling in the drop amount before dispatching a runner alleviates any temptation the runner might feel to skim. She's probably the only crew chief who does her runners that little favor, who's not trying to catch anyone cheating. Trust, Bendrix knows, has to go both ways. Up and down the chain. The fact that Mr. Corn trusts her is something she doesn't take lightly. It's why she's the only crew chief who still has both her ears and all her fingers.

It's also why he convinced all the other crime lords to put her on the bridge job.

For the lords, the bridge job came down to how much money they were losing. Fewer taxis meant fewer opportunities for Flug crews to shake them down. The bridge was bad for business.

For Bendrix, the bridge job came down to pride.

She remembers standing in the chrome-and-glass conference room on the eightieth floor of Mr. Corn's highrise. Twelve crime lords from both sides of the river had assembled there, the men wearing suits and heavy gold watches, the women draped in tailored silk and dripping in jewels. They sat around the polished table, sizing her up. The most powerful lords from East Ghaz to West Dusang, all there to ask *her* to do *them* a favor.

She accepted, of course, and she succeeded. But she didn't count on a crew of fifteen utility workers being on the bridge doing emergency middle-of-the-night power repairs when she set off the charges.

She read the casualty list from the next day's newscast. Nine men, six women. The police chief read the names of the dead as their pictures flashed on the screen. Then, with his expression appropriately somber, he looked right into the camera and told viewers the explosion was caused by one of the men, a disgruntled employee of the utility company who had acted alone. *Such a tragedy. Such a sad, selfish thing to do, taking fourteen others with you. Such a...*

Such a line of bullshit. The son of a bitch was on Mr. Corn's payroll.

Bendrix turned away from her vid screen, determined to forget her victims' names, to scrub their faces from her mind. But two weeks later, she can still see them when she closes her eyes, and their screams still echo through her nightmares.

"Fuck!" Bendrix kicks the trash bags. A rat scurries along the wall and disappears into a drainpipe.

"Bad day?"

She whirls. August Orlean stands at the mouth of the alley. He's soaked through, and no wonder. After Bendrix took his wallet and Zephyr cut the fuel line, they all left poor Mr. Orlean stranded in the middle of the river.

She twists her lip into a snide smile. "Not as bad as you. Goddamn. A nice, clean boy like you took a swim in the Escopeta?" She means to mock him, to condescend, but her voice comes out soft. He's not a boy. Not by a long-shot. His shirt is unbuttoned, and her eyes can't help but follow droplets of water and sweat slipping down the strip of muscled chest and flat stomach. She swallows. He looks more like he got caught in a summer rain than someone forced to swim the river.

"Best chance I had to catch up to you and get my wallet back," he says.

"What, this?" She tosses it to him.

He catches it one-handed, doesn't even bother to check inside. Knows it's empty.

"You want to tell me how the hell you found me here?" she asks.

"I followed you."

"Bullshit. Unless you're the world's fastest swimmer."

He removes his glasses and polishes them on the front of his shirt. "I've been following you for two weeks."

Her blood runs cold. *Two weeks.* Since she bombed the bridge.

"You and your crew work all night, then you come to Slim Sumo's for noodles. Every damn day." He puts his glasses back on and lowers his hands, keeps them loose. "Someone who doesn't want to be found should shake up her routine once in a while."

Bendrix clenches her fists. She should have figured it out before now. A six-seat taxi running a single passenger carrying that much cash... "You were drawing me out, weren't you? Mr. Corn put you on my tail after I blew the bridge. Then he used you as bait to see if I'd shake you down."

He smiles. "Mr. Corn told me you were a smart girl."

She wants to laugh. She has every right to be angry with Mr. Corn for having her followed, for testing her loyalty when she's never betrayed him. Not once. But what she feels swelling inside her is satisfaction. All she got caught doing was her job.

"I don't skim, Mr. Orlean." *Mr. Corn always finds out.* "I just sent a runner with all 6,800 kroner."

"I know. I heard you call it in. I saw you dispatch your runner."

"So we're done here."

"The money wasn't Mr. Corn's primary concern, Bendrix. We have something more important to discuss."

She cocks her head. "Who are you *really*?"

"I'm on Mr. Corn's chain. Same as you, but higher up. You're his muscle on the water. I'm his eyes on the street. He wants information, I get it."

Bendrix sees pride in the way his chest puffs up when he speaks. Higher up? She bites back a smirk. He thinks he's special, but information is cheap. Mr. Corn has *hundreds* of eyes on the street.

"Fifteen dead, Bendrix," Orlean continues. "That kind of blood takes a toll. Mr. Corn needs to know how great a toll. He needs to know if you're still in. I saw the look on your face when your goon crushed that taxi man's skull. You didn't want him to do that, did you? You got real pale. It made you a little sick."

Her breathing slows. She imagines that freighter from this morning coasting in past the breakwater. Deck lights twinkling like stars against the lavender sky. Crew smoking at the rail, not a care in the world. What if she had left right then, like she considered? She'd already be part of a crew like that. Mr. Corn's lackeys would still be looking for her, but she'd be gone. Long gone.

Hell, who was she kidding? If Mr. Corn wanted her found, it didn't matter where in the world she hid. He paid his lackeys well–until he no longer needed them–and he wasn't the type to lose his toys.

"Mr. Corn thinks you might be promotion material," Orlean continues. "He wants to give you new assignments. Harder ones, if you know what I mean, but more lucrative. But you have to pass his test. And based on what I saw on that taxi today, I'm not sure you have the spine."

Bendrix stiffens. *But you have to pass his test.* Her mind reels. She knows Mr. Corn. She knows how he thinks, how he operates, and above all, what he expects. With that simple phrase, *you have to pass his test*, Bendrix knows.

The taxi wasn't her test.

Running the full take wasn't her test either.

August Orlean, the man standing here before her, is her test.

He just doesn't know it.

Poor bastard.

She closes her eyes, steadies herself against what she's about to do, and turns east toward the mouth of the alley. Toward the river. A sluggish breeze creeps across her face and strokes her neck–the Escopeta's hot breath, smelling of brine and rotted fish. She's never leaving that river. Not ever. Its muddy waters run through her soul. Someday she'll die on that river, and she knows for certain that, after today, she'll deserve it.

Bendrix draws her pistol. Aims. Fires.

The blast slams against the stone walls that flank the alley and rings in her ears. She sees the whites of Orlean's eyes as he staggers, falls back. He hits the ground hard. He wheezes and writhes, hands pawing at the crimson foam bubbling from the hole her bullet just tore into his chest.

But you have to pass his test. Bendrix draws her forearm across her sweat-slicked brow. Mr. Corn sent Orlean to test her, all right. And she'd be damned if she failed.

The stench of rice vinegar and ghost peppers, of blood and rancid cooking oil, hangs in the air, burning her nose. The back door of Slim Sumo's slams open. Eva, Zephyr, and Ferno stumble out.

Zephyr is the first to find his voice. "What the fuck? I mean, *what the fuck*?"

"That the passenger from the taxi?" Eva's eyes fix on Orlean, her tone more curious than alarmed.

At the mouth of the alley, a small crowd gathers. They take in the scene, then amble off, indifferent. Another gang-related disagreement getting solved the old-fashioned way. Nothing to see here.

Bendrix crouches beside Orlean. His eyes are rolling in their sockets. Blood gurgles up between his lips, red splattering across his chin and jaw. He's choking. Drowning.

"You thought he sent you to report back on me? You thought *you* had a say in whether *I* got better assignments?" She shakes her head. "You thought you were Mr. Corn's chosen one or some shit, but you were a pawn, Orlean. He used you. You want to survive on Mr. Corn's chain, you have to read between the links. If you didn't see the setup here from a mile away, you weren't going to last long anyway." She stands, aims the gun at his throat, and pulls the trigger. Noise and flame bark from the pistol. Orlean's neck comes apart and his head lolls to one side. The gurgling stops. "The bridge didn't turn me, motherfucker, but I'm sure as hell turned now."

Ferno stands beside her, silent as usual, awaiting orders.

Bendrix wipes blood spatter from her face. "Take him to Mr. Corn. Tell him I accept my goddamn promotion."

Ferno hauls Orlean's corpse over his burly shoulder and trudges off toward the opposite end of the alley. Blood and gore darken the back of his shirt, but he doesn't seem to notice. It's a dirty errand, but no one will hassle him. Everyone knows that Ferno belongs to Bendrix, and Bendrix belongs to Mr. Corn. And no one fucks with Mr. Corn.

"Go inside," she tells Eva and Zephyr. "I'll be in in a minute."

They obey, and only when they're gone does Bendrix sink to her knees. Shudders pass through her like ripples in a pond. *August Orlean.* One more death on her hands. One more name that will be branded on her brain for the rest of her life.

Then she thinks of the taxi man. What was his name?

She can't remember.

Pushing herself to her feet, she stumbles, accidentally kicking a bag of trash. A take-out container tumbles out into the center of the alley. She stares at it, at Slim Sumo's cartoon face laughing at the sky. Just like this morning. But this time his face is smeared with blood.

The taxi man. Shit, what was his name?

Next time it won't be so hard, Bendrix thinks. Next time it won't be so hard.

LITTLE WHITE LINES

Jedidiah Ayres

I AM THE NIGHTRIDER.

The little white lines are beginning to blur.

I'm a fuel-injected suicide machine.

The windows rattle and the power steering starts to wobble, but it's all noise on the periphery and I'm zeroing in on the pinhole of perfect focus dead center.

I am the rocker.

Run, asshole.

I am the roller.

The little white lines disappear and my focus breaks through the flimsy fucking fabric of the universe.

I am the out-of-controller.

The acid drip at the back of my throat merges with the metallic blood taste in my mouth for maximum *ka-pow* and we're off.

Cocaine gets a bad rap.

Sure I've done plenty of dumb things while using it – sometimes my brother Jesse and I would make lists and mine tended toward the heroic:

Fucked a prom queen.

Took a shit in my boss's swimming pool.

Stole a cop car.

But if I had to make a list of the *best* things I'd ever done in my life, I'd be a hypocrite not to admit that at the time I'd been pretty fucking high:

Proposed to Jill.

Quit my job.

Stole Brendanowitz's cruiser after shitting in the pool and got a humjob from his wife in the backseat.

Jesse's coke bravado encouraged disdain for different authority figures such as –

Money.

Math.

Sports ball.

Our lists have a nexus.

A big greasy, fat fuck of a nexus named Austin Smith. Real estate and construction are his chief businesses. He also owns a couple of garages, restaurants and a check-cashing joint. He dabbles in arson, extortion and makes some book on the side.

That's where Jesse came in and I followed.

Plenty sober as fuck, straight-backed, good Christian citizens also picked the Cardinals in the '04 Fall

Classic, but not many of them put the entirety of their semester's student loans on the sorry sonsabitches to win in five. Fucking Jesse, man. Definitely the smartest and maybe the dumbest family member I've got.

A couple months after the redbirds wrapped their lips around that season and blew it like Lovelace, Jesse climbed a coke mountain and put his first sum of non-existent money on the Eagles in the Super Bowl because...

Forever fuck Boston.

He took out bad loans to cover worse.

Robbed Peter to pay Paul.

Eventually the apostles got hip to Jesse's shit and started a co-op in bone snapping.

The sit-down with Austin happened after Jesse'd been picked up high as a Watusi's asshole trying to knock over a Jack in the Box on Jefferson with a screwdriver he could barely hold in his mangled hand. Brendanowitz was shift commander when they brought him in and he kept it off the books. Stand-up guy.

Still not sorry about fucking the commander's wife.

My wife.

I took my brother home and got enough half-thoughts out of him to piece together he'd been tossed out of a moving car with freshly broken fingers and a snoot full of toot motivating him to come up with enough cash to cover next week's vig.

What Austin really wanted was his very own cop and it turned out I was for sale. Saving Jesse's kneecaps was my price, but I probably could've been had for less. I'd always been open to the entrepreneurial opportunities my badge afforded, but I didn't really like being a goon for hire.

Could've told Austin to go fuck himself.

Should've told Jesse to suck it up and take what he had coming.

Would've, but you don't make little compromises every day of your life and pick the most lucrative bribe yet to suddenly stand on principle.

So, I spent two years as a kept cop, mostly just leaving my ears open and passing along the pertinent skinny, making traffic-stop collections, and taking the occasional repo-gig bagging laptops, flat screen TVs and motor vehicles from south city Hoosiers and north city bangers reluctant to render unto Austin.

Unlike those middle-class bubble-dwellers who require a warrant and all the due process pomp and circumstances when they're getting fucked by the system, Austin's typical clientele live at the bottom of the societal ladder and understand capitalism just as well as the ones at the top. Big difference is that they aren't as likely to make a fuss about police shakedowns.

I wasn't the only freelancer with a badge, and self-interest dictated that we look out for each other, but you still had to show a little common sense. These weren't the days a badge meant you could just murder on camera without consequence – or maybe we were just naïve. If somebody got too close to the edge they were encouraged to back off lest they sink the whole industry.

A few helpful guidelines:

Maybe don't keep boosted merchandise in your trunk.

Maybe mind your municipality, especially in broad daylight.

Maybe don't administer tune-ups in public.

Maybe be discreet with local celebrities and community leaders.

Certain lines were never supposed to be crossed, but my eyes were dotted and I'd run out of tease.

Every little boundary push brought me closer to the inevitable cliff's edge. The story of the spectacular end of my police career really starts a few years earlier.

First time I encountered El Jefe of Anus, it was midnight and Señor Abierto Asshole was driving a Galactic-Empire-upper-management-gray BMW series 7 like he's about to launch the invasion of Hoth. I started riffing on that line, hoping to have it a little punchier by the time I pulled him over.

Blew right the fuck through a red heading east on Gravois at 80mph and cracked a century before Lindbergh. He drifted through the intersection and headed south where the road really opened up.

Three years on the job and bored as hell, I was amphetamine jacked just to get through most nights. Then fate dropped this douchebag in my path to give my life meaning. When I hit the lights and the strobe shattered the night into a collage of red and blue shards the chem trail in my veins burned bright. Prince Prolapse started swerving over all six lanes.

When I got close enough to radio the license number in, the atmosphere inside the cruiser changed from fire to ice. I was told to back off and give him space – not provoke anything. What fucking ever.

His face said trust-fund baby and was just begging to be smashed. It called to me and further agitated the dark gods in my blood. I did my best to oblige.

I hung back for a stretch, then gunned it and nudged him when he got comfortable. Pulled right alongside him and still couldn't get the fucker to acknowledge me. Even in his clearly coked-out state his eyes were dull and flat – but black as pitch, and I couldn't wait to stick my penlight in and look for the bottom. Make him recognize me.

Knew it a second before he made his move.

I beat him to the neighborhood street he was about to light up. Hundred and eighty degree whiplash park job I'll admit I was lucky to pull off, and he had to jam his brakes to avoid kissing me through the window.

The Hallelujah Chorus rang in my ears as I jumped out of the car and drew my weapon, yelling for him to kill the engine and exit the vehicle with his hands up.

He didn't even pretend to listen to me, just sat there keeping his own counsel for a couple of seconds. It was long enough for me to close the distance between us and tap the window with the barrel of my gun.

He dropped the beamer into gear and left tread on the road as he took off. Without thinking, I shot out his back tire and enjoyed the sparks that jumped from under the wheel well until he swerved into a muddy ditch.

It was my finest moment, but it was already over.

By the time the Chief was out of bed and on the scene, Andre the Giant Rectal Wart was a nuclear reactor gone critical and melting down. Jobs were threatened, the Governor was on the line and the slickest lawyer I've ever seen in the flesh had materialized, groomed and natty as hell at three o'clock in the morning.

By then I knew who the driver was, the cancerous cockhole. Fucker wouldn't tell me himself, just kept screaming *"Do you know who I am?"* when I told him he was under arrest.

High as fuck. Drunk as hell. Hair still perfect. I hated him.

Back up arrived before I could get cuffs on him and probably saved my job.

He came from ancient money in this town. Royalty. Family practically supported the police retirement fund single handedly. He got a ride home in a police taxi and the night ended with me on my knees in the mud changing his tire.

Brendanowitz showed up as I was being ordered to do it. Wrapped his arms around me and held me back. Kept me from blowing a stack and quitting the force right then. He got down in the ditch with me to put the new wheel on and bought drinks afterward. He was as disgusted as I was. More so, maybe. But he told me karma would catch up to Captain Crap Tunnel eventually and we'd enjoy watching it happen and share a few rounds on that day.

I thanked him for the drink, and fucked his wife extra hard an hour later.

Before my next shift I had to go by Origin of the Feces' home and apologize in person. Hated myself for doing it, but then I already hated myself so... not a long drive.

Three years later when Austin says he'll pay me five times the usual rate to hurt Darth Dickholster, I, the fuck, jump.

Not like I've been fantasizing about that opportunity when I jack off.

Certainly don't know all six makes, models, and tags of the fleet in his garage.

Don't have three known fuck pads and two hotel suites on my regular check list.

And you shouldn't read too much into those stories about paper bags of shit pelting various monuments around town bearing his family's crest. I have alibis ready if you like me for those. Besides, I heard they tested the DNA and found they were all from different people. Probably hobos. Just a guess.

Austin says Genghis Cunt is trying to circumvent the union on that new development in the Chesterfield valley. Says he won't budge, needs a proper scare, needs to know he can be touched. Problem is no on the force will go near him. They've got retirement plans, after all.

But Austin knows I may be personally motivated to settle a grudge... leaves me hanging for a minute 'till the bulge in my pants has stopped growing before coming right out and asking.

Can I get to him? *Will I?*

If so, I can consider my brother's slate clean and collect a bonus healthy enough to start a new life outside the department, outside the state if I want.

Or, Austin says, I could come work for him full time. Stop being a bent cop and be a straight gangster.

Tell myself I'm killing two birds with one stone – righting the world and making a sweet little deposit in the nest-egg I'm starting for Jill and me.

Bun in the oven, an adjustable rate mortgage and an inconvenient husband – they're motivators, lemme tell ya. Somebody should write a book.

Jill and Lyle Brendanowitz had been high-school sweethearts while he and my brother Jesse were all-state infielders and then offered partial rides to state universities two years ahead of me in school. The boys had gone to Mizzou and Rolla respectively, and when Jesse came back for his first and final winter break, he introduced me to Bolivian marching powder, which I liked not least of all because I found it gave me the guts to begin my campaign for Jill in earnest.

She and I were two years behind Jesse and Lyle, and over the course of the next year I kept chipping away at their long-distance thing relentlessly.

Jesse flamed out and Lyle left school to join the marines, which fucked up all my plans. He came home in jarhead drag and swept Jill off her feet. Hitched and ditched in a fortnight, Jill was a dazed nineteen-year-old bride in a one-bedroom Hazelwood apartment while her man was overseas serving Uncle Sam.

I was not deterred.

His Afghanistan tour was abbreviated when he caught a piece of an IED below the helmet. Lucky for him the shrapnel passed all the way through the guy next to him before lodging in his skull and all he'd physically suffered was a persistent headache and the loss of his perfect vision.

By the time he'd come home and taken a job on the force I'd been screwing his wife Monday to Friday for months.

Jill tells me the kid is mine and I believe her.

Some of that is just me wanting it to be true, but Jill says Lyle hasn't been much for the sack since the war. Came home with blue balls and a Purple Heart, but one humiliating non-starting sexual event too many and he'd turned his energies elsewhere.

Like busting my balls.

Brendanowitz isn't stupid. He knows I freelance for Austin Smith. Can't prove it, but everybody knows. The routine inquiries added up to dick, but a few complaints have surfaced about cops acting as muscle for a gangster, and even though they've not gotten past the interrogation room and every complaint has been recanted by witnesses riding in spiffy new wheelchairs, you'd have to be willfully deaf and blind to not know the score.

Brendanowitz pulls me aside that night. Steers us into an empty room and lets me know about a shitbag creeper trying to deal his way out of a solid bust by dropping my name.

I shrug my best 'what-are-you-gonna-do? Liars-lie-and-crooks-hate-cops' shrug, and Brendanowitz waives the air to demonstrate that it's nothing and says, "I just thought you should know IA's opening a file."

"I'm under investigation?" Exasperated innocence.

"I wouldn't sweat it. Guy's a world-class scumfuck. Zero credibility." Brendanowitz leans close, asking without saying – *Is there anything you want to tell me, Hal?*

I roll my eyes and he tells me not to worry, but I can tell he's fishing. There's an aggression in his friendliness. He's daring me to come clean. He knows.

"Thanks for the heads up, Lyle." *Fuck you.*

I hear back from my union rep the next day and he suggests I get a lawyer. He says Brendanowitz himself is lodging formal complaints against me for whatever. I do three lines off my fist in the motor pool and by the time they begin to dissolve I've got a plan.

Time to cash in.

Lawyer says the investigation goes away if I do, and I tell him to make it happen. Leave my badge and service pistol on Brendanowitz's desk and as I'm heading out the door the cuckholded Dudley Do-Right asks if I love her.

I pause, but don't turn around.

He tells me *he* loves her. Says he'd do anything for her. I can hear the tears he won't let go. Sounds like he means it.

He sounds like the only honorable man I know.

He sounds like a schmuck. I shrug and leave.

The next afternoon while Brendanowitz is sleeping, a taxi drops me off five blocks from his home. I've got a key and all the practice I need getting around inside his house. I grab his keys from the box in the closet where Jill said they'd be. I leave him a letter from Jill saying she was leaving him and that to hurt me was to hurt her. It said that if he really loved her, he'd keep quiet about what was about to happen.

I drop my own goodbye message from the bottom of my heart by pinching one off at the end of the diving board before hitting the road driving his car.

I call Jill, who's got eyes on The Chase Park Plaza lobby, but hasn't seen our target, and I let her know there's no going back now.

When she says she loves me, suddenly The Ronettes are all I hear.

Ten minutes later I'm waiting outside fuckpad *numero uno* and everything's quiet. I call Jesse and give him another address to check. Tell him what cars to look for. It takes every ounce of sit-still I've got to stay put until he checks in again forty-five minutes later.

Zilch.

I have Jesse read back all the tags and the address. I have him describe the neighborhood and tell me where he's parked. He identifies the trees and the neighbor's cars until I'm satisfied that he's where he's supposed to be and not somewhere else fucking off.

Okay, I shoot him a second address and leave my post for another.

Twenty minutes later I'm pulling into Lumière Place casino hotel and about to park when Jesse's digits light up on my phone. Says he's got a hit on the black Aston Martin DB9.

Oh fuck. Oh shit. Oh thank you, God. I've probably got an hour left before Brendanowitz is up and officially looking for his cruiser.

The lofts are on Washington, less than two miles from Laclede's Landing, but traffic is thick with county folk in for the Cardinals' game, and before I can get there I have another call from Jesse – the asshole target is leaving.

"Well, fucking follow him. And stay on the line."

Jesse tells me the dripping twat went south on 14th toward Highway 40.

I belch the siren to squeeze through a red light. Nobody notices I'm driving a county car in the city.

Jesse relays that the DB9 got on the highway heading west, and I gun past the courthouse toward the on-ramp.

I catch up to Jesse at McCausland and he tells me my target is four vehicles up in the left lane.

The Puckered Colon gets off on Lindbergh heading south and my guts gurgle with anticipation. We're going to relive our first date. But this time I'm gonna get my dick wet.

I have to give him plenty of space because south of the Frontenac Mall the street is dark and lonely for a couple miles and I don't want him getting suspicious of the cruiser behind him.

Just like I'm hoping he will, he stops at a red light at Gravois and I pull up in the right lane beside him.

I've pulled on my mask after a big hit of powder, and my red-rimmed eyes are the only part of my face he sees when he glances over at the guy in the skeleton-faced balaclava staring him down from the window of a county cop car.

He stops speaking on his iPhone and raises his eyebrows slightly.

He finally sees me.

I make a circle with my left thumb and finger and poke my right index finger in and out of it. *Run, asshole. I want you to run.*

He does.

This time I'm not playing it safe. This time I am the menace, the one who knocks, the rocker, the roller, the out-of-controller.

He causes an east/west collision tearing through the intersection against the signal and when I swerve around the stunned civilians it gives him a few seconds to open up the throttle. That's okay, though. This puppy's got some giddy up.

Your tax dollars at work.

Austin tells me he got his money's worth. Says the next time he reached out to the king of the city the tenor of their negotiation was different. And not just because his majesty's voice sounded funny after all the plastic surgery.

What I don't tell Austin is that I would have done the job for fee.

I clip Duke Dickcheese's bumper and knock him off the road into the same ditch where I'd been forced to change his tire a couple lifetimes earlier. I stay buckled up behind the wheel in case he takes off again, but he's dazed and the car may be crippled.

I climb out of Brendanowitz's cruiser, truncheon in hand. I smash Peg-boy's window and grab his dazed Highness by the collar and haul him out.

His phone is on the floorboard with a shitload of broken glass. The 911 operator is trying to get him to respond, "Sir, are you okay? Can you hear me, sir?" I smash the phone under my foot and calculate the time I have to play.

Later when Jill, the beauty I'd fixated on since she was queen of our prom and I was a zit-faced meathead on the fast track to burnout, is going down on me in the back seat I replay the scene on the side of the road.

He tried to speak, but I used my knuckledusters to break his teeth and his jaw.

He bawled while he still could.

By the time I was done, his upper lip was hanging off the corner of his mouth, his nose was in entirely the wrong place, and his eyes were swollen shut as tight as his sphincter should've been. The smell of that scene is another detail I focus on.

But it's that whimper when I punched him in the ear that I savor. Before he got all weepy and was still trying to stand up. Oh man, it's so good. Little whimper, little tremble in the chin and – I finish.

I take out my phone and scroll through a few shots of Mr. Poopy Pants I'd taken for posterity. When I'd decided the spank bank was full, I dropped Brendanowitz's ID on top of the stinking wreck who thought he couldn't be touched.

I ask her to and Jill tells me again about the note she'd left for Lyle. He was going to be fighting a two-front headache between his wife dumping him and his cruiser being used in an assault on citizen number one, but Jill was leaving him the house in exchange for a no-contest divorce that would also save him the humiliation of having his inability to perform sexually made very public.

I took another snoot off of Jill's pregnancy-swollen tits before she laid her head on my chest. I put my hand on her beginning to show baby bump and smell the top of her head. It's everything. I asked her to marry me right then and there.

She said yes.

DESERT RUN

Jeanne C. Stein

TINY PUT THE BIKE IN GEAR AND ROLLED AWAY.
He didn't look back at Evangeline, partly because he
didn't want to show any hesitation about leaving her and
partly because he didn't want her to know how irritated
she made him. She was so god damned stubborn. She'd
nodded that she would take off if he got into trouble, but
he could tell by the look in her eyes she had no intention
of leaving.

He thought about the gun in the saddlebag of her
Harley. He had slipped it in when he got to the coffee shop
this morning. He wasn't sure she'd ever fired one but she
was smart. The gun was a no-frills Smith and Wesson
.38 Special snubbie. She'd figure it out if she needed to.

There were about a dozen bikes facing him on the
highway. He recognized their colors. It was his brother–
Larry's–gang. He'd met a few of them when they'd made
a run to Denver. There was no doubt in Tiny's mind what

they wanted, just as there was no doubt in his mind they'd been watching him at Larry's house.

One of the bikes separated from the rest and rode out to meet him. Tiny stopped his bike. He pulled off his helmet and let the rider approach.

The big Harley rolled to a stop. The rider sat for a minute, then he, too, took off his helmet. Behind him, the other bikers reopened the road, dividing into two phalanxes, like soldiers awaiting marching orders.

"Good to see you, again, Jax," Tiny said.

Jax smiled, a predator's smile, all lip service, no warmth. "You, too, Tiny. Sorry about Larry."

Tiny leaned back in his saddle, affecting a relaxed posture he didn't feel. He studied the man in front of him. Jax was a compact, burly man, clean-shaven, head shaved close to his scalp. He was in his early thirties, young for taking control of a gang, but with a well-deserved reputation for ruthlessness and, so far, no one had challenged his leadership. At least no one who lived to tell about it.

"What's going on?" Tiny asked.

Jax swung himself off his bike, stretching his arms overhead. Tattoos bled together on his arms and across the exposed skin of his chest. Names, dates, faces.

Not Evangeline's, Tiny found himself thinking. She never did such sloppy work.

"We were waiting for you." Jax looked past Tiny to Evangeline, waiting on the side of the road. "That your old lady?"

Tiny smiled. "Not the way she'd put it."

"Sensitive type, huh?" Jax smiled again. "Maybe we can desensitize her."

Tiny felt his gut tighten. "What do you want, Jax?"

"Besides a little taste of sweetness back there?"

"Not going to happen."

Jax stared hard at Tiny. "Like I said, sorry to hear about Larry. Did you know he was a rat?"

The words were spoken quietly, with no inflection, as if Jax was asking Tiny if he knew what time it was.

Tiny fought to keep his expression neutral. "What the fuck are you talking about?"

"Your brother was working for the Feds." Jax slipped off his sunglasses. "You telling me you didn't know?"

Tiny swung off his bike and faced Jax. "I know Larry. He hated cops as much as I do."

"Then maybe I should be worried about you, too. You were at Larry's house. Find anything interesting?"

"Like what?"

Jax closed the distance between them. "A list maybe."

"A list of what?"

Jax's expression darkened. "Don't fuck with me, Tiny."

"Or what? You'll kill me the way you killed Larry?"

Jax's eyebrows rose. "I didn't kill Larry. Not that I'm sorry he's gone. But I would have killed him *after* I found out what he'd given the Feds. Not before."

Tiny watched Jax's face. It made sense in a crazy way. If they had gone after Larry, they would have done it here, on home turf. "What was he doing in Denver?" he asked then.

"Fuck if I know." Jax spat on the ground. "We were waiting for him to come back. Planned to *convince* him to spill his guts. He never came back."

"What makes you so sure he was working for the Feds?"

Jax looked away, back at Evangeline. "He was. How we found out doesn't matter. Look, Tiny. We don't have a beef with you. But I need to know if you have my information. Now we can do this the easy way or–" His eyes once again drifted back to Evangeline. "Or we can do it the hard way."

Tiny felt a roar building in his ear–rage, hot and consuming. Still, he kept his voice even. "You want to ask *her* what we found in Larry's house? She'll tell you the same thing I did. No list. Nothing." A wave of comprehension made everything suddenly clear. "Your boys did a thorough job of trashing the place. If you didn't find what you were looking for, I doubt anyone could."

Jax shrugged. "That's what we thought, too. But now here you are."

"My brother just died," Tiny snarled. "I came to see what I wanted to do with his house. After the mess you made, I'm thinking of having it torn down, carted away. You have any objection to that?"

Jax glanced back at his buddies. "I'd like to believe you. I just can't take the chance that you're lying."

Tiny knew what was coming. With just a gesture from Jax, the gang would be on him. And Evangeline. He held up a hand. "Okay. Okay. We did find something. It's back in her saddlebag."

Jax peered at him. "Oh yeah? All of a sudden you know what I'm talking about?"

Tiny shrugged. "It was worth a try. I don't know what the list means but I sure as shit don't want to die for it."

"A list?"

"It's what you're looking for, right?"

Tiny stood still, watching Jax process what he'd told him, watching the biker decide what his next move would be. Behind him, he had twelve hard asses ready to descend like a plague of locusts. All Tiny had was Evangeline.

Finally, Jax nodded. "Okay. You and I will ride back. Get the list."

"Then you'll let us go?"

"Let's see what you've got first."

Tiny felt the first stirring of fear. It'd been there all along, but he'd managed to keep it locked down. In a minute, Jax would know he'd been lying. He didn't care about himself–if Jax was going to kill him, it'd be quick. But Evangeline. Jax would want to take his time with her. Then he'd pass her on to his gang. They could keep her alive for a long time.

Jax fired up his bike, revving the engine impatiently, waiting for Tiny to turn his bike around.

Evangeline didn't have her helmet on so Tiny couldn't even warn her to take off. All he could do is hope she'd had the presence of mind to take the gun out. If she got the drop on Jax before he had a chance to signal his buddies, they might just make it out of this mess alive.

Evangeline watched Tiny approach with another biker close on his right flank. Neither put on his helmet so she could see Tiny's face as they got closer. His eyes bore into hers and it didn't take a genius to realize the hard, taut lines of his face relayed concern and apprehension.

When she switched her gaze to the guy accompanying him, it was a different story. This one was grinning, open and affable, but there was no warmth in that smile. It was the smile of a snake slithering up to its prey.

Evangeline straightened on her bike. She'd shed her jacket and it was draped over the handlebars. As this newcomer's eyes swept her body, she wished she'd left it on. The tank top exposed too much and he was sizing her up like a prize heifer. Not the first time a biker had fixed her with such a devouring stare, for sure, but there was something about this guy that made her instincts scream run.

She narrowed her eyes. "Tiny?" she asked when they'd both dismounted.

Tiny came right over to her and put his arm around her shoulders. He pulled her close and kissed her hard on the lips.

She let him, recognizing the act for what it was. He was claiming her as his own for the benefit of this stranger. This dangerous stranger.

She leaned into the kiss and tangled her hands in his hair, opening her lips to force her tongue into his mouth to make it as convincing as possible.

When they came up for air, the guy clapped. "Nice, Tiny, very nice."

Tiny didn't step away from Evangeline. He left an arm draped over her shoulder. "This is Jax, baby. A friend of Larry's."

Evangeline pasted a grin on her face and let her hip bump against Tiny's. Would he understand?

Jax was talking. "So, where's the list? Give it to me and you and your sweet thing here can be on your way."

The list? Evangeline looked up at Tiny. So Jax was looking for something the same way they'd been. And Tiny evidently let him think they'd found it–a list.

She shifted slightly as Tiny opened the right saddlebag behind her. The one where the gun had been.

Had been.

Shit.

Evangeline saw Tiny's shoulders tighten. She thrust out a hip, hoping he's understand. "I think it's on the other side, baby."

Jax took a step closer. "You need help, Tiny? I could keep your lady occupied while you think about where you put that list." He took a finger and traced a line down Evangeline's cheek, her neck, continuing until he stopped at the swell of her left breast.

Evangeline didn't move. Jax ran that finger back and forth across the top of her breasts, softly, like the tongue of a lizard. This close, Evangeline could see the hardness in his face, the menace in his eyes. Tiny had to move behind them to get to the other saddlebag. He moved slowly, deliberately, but Evangeline felt the tension building.

Tiny opened the saddlebag, taking advantage of Jax's preoccupation with Evangeline's cleavage. He put his hand inside. "Here it is."

He stepped close to Evangeline, his hand at her waist, brushing the gun in her belt. He slipped it free and held it down at his side. He leaned close and put his mouth right at her ear. "Get ready to ride."

Jax had stepped back when Tiny said he had the list. Evangeline saw Jax's hand move to his waistband. There was no mistaking the gesture.

She pulled Tiny's head down for another kiss. "He's got a gun," she whispered. Then she straightened and with casual indifference, slipped her jacket on and reached toward her bike's ignition.

Jax saw what she was doing. He had the gun in his hand now and pointed at her chest. "You ain't going nowhere, sweet cheeks."

Evangeline froze. Cold fear shimmied along her spine as she stared into the bore of the pistol. This was the first time she'd had a gun pointed at her. It was riveting and horrifying and she couldn't look away. She didn't see Tiny move, was aware of nothing except Jax and the gun until an explosion banged against her ears. She jumped as if struck, her eyes darting to Tiny, then back to Jax as he crumpled to the ground.

Tiny's gun was still aimed at Jax. He kicked Jax's gun out of reach.

The biker looked up at him, shock and pain draining the color from his face. "What the fuck?"

Tiny's cold expression never changed as he stared down at Jax. "It's a gut shot," he said. "You have about thirty minutes before you bleed out. Better get help."

Then Tiny was moving, running to his bike, yelling to Evangeline. "Go, go!"

Evangeline's hands shook as she turned the ignition. The bike roared roared to life and she accelerated across the desert floor, away from the highway, holding her breath until she heard the howl of Tiny's bike speeding after her.

Evangeline couldn't shake the image–Jax collaps-ing–the color of the blood as it pulsed...Tiny's cold, unemotional reaction to shooting Jax. She bent low over the handlebars and tried to push the picture out of her mind, focusing on the pounding of her bike across the desert floor, listening for the inevitable rumble of Jax's men in pursuit.

Evangeline was right up ahead of Tiny. He knew she was having a hard time, her smaller bike heaving like a boat in a storm-swept sea. It wasn't built for off-roading like his Harley, and each jarring dip in the desert floor sent Evangeline off the pegs and crashing back down as the bike lost contact with the ground. Still, they couldn't risk going any slower; they had to put as much distance as possible between themselves and the posse sure to be coming after them.

Dusk comes quickly in the desert. Not a gradual fade to dark like in Denver with its western mountains hold-ing back the night, but like a curtain dropping. Evange-line hadn't turned on her headlight and Tiny worried she'd roll her bike. It was dicey going, but he turned his head to see how many of Jax's gang were on their trail. It wouldn't be all of them. Somebody had to stay behind to call for help.

For the instant he allowed his eyes to scan the dark-ness behind them, he saw nothing. He snapped his gaze forward again, fighting his bike to remain upright, then peered back once more.

Still. Nothing.

He let up on the gas.

Evangeline must have heard him decelerate because she slowed down, too. She turned her head to look at him, her eyebrows raised in a question.

He signaled for her to stop.

"What's going on?" she asked, her breath coming in short gasps.

He could see her shoulders shaking. He stole one more look behind him to be sure, then shut off the Harley's engine and motioned for Evangeline to do the same. Dust and silence descended on them like the last rays of the sun.

"There's no one chasing us," he said, dismounting.

Evangeline's eyes grew wide. "Are you sure?"

"Look. Listen."

She did, cocking her head, straining to catch any sound as if not trusting her eyes alone.

"What happened? Why aren't they coming after us?"

Tiny stared behind him.

Evangeline searched his face. "Do you think Jax is dead?"

Tiny shook his head. "If Jax was dead, they'd be on us like flies on shit. No. If I had to guess, I'd say Jax's crew is scrambling to get him to help before he bleeds out."

He reached into his pocket and pulled out a small square of paper. "What the hell is this?" he asked.

Evangeline shrugged, leaned close to look once again at the scrap of paper they'd found hidden in Larry's house. It was a map, crudely drawn, a squiggle of mountains marked with a cartoon X. "Whatever it is, Jax was willing to kill us for it." She searched Tiny's face. "And almost died himself because of it."

Tiny heard the question in her voice. "I wouldn't have let him hurt you," he said quietly.

Evangeline stepped closer, laying a hand gently on his arm. "You all right?"

He nodded but avoided her eyes.

Evangeline knew at that moment Jax wasn't the first person Tiny had shot. She also knew this wasn't the time or place to ask about it. She shrugged. "Well, we've got it and he doesn't. We can take our time trying to figure it out."

Tiny lowered his gaze to the map. What had his brother gotten himself into? Had he really been working with the Feds? Who could they turn to now?

"Take our time? Maybe. Maybe not," he said. "Jax's gang? They know where we live."

GRAG'S LAST ESCAPE

Gary Phillips

"YOU'RE NOT AUTHORIZED TO BE IN HERE," the senior Talusian engineer said upon entering the power core room. He gaped, fully realizing what the imposter was doing. "By the seven veils," he muttered, advancing.

Undercover agent Grag stood from having been hunched down while she'd uncoupled the phasing device. She held this in one hand and in the other, the disguised cutter beam she'd just used.

"You must be a spy," the engineer declared, reaching for the com to alert security. "Are you from the D'Noths? The Requan-Na's? No matter, our interrogators will get the truth out of you."

Grag sliced off the Talusian's extended arm with her cutter beam. He wailed pitifully, his copper-based green blood spurting onto control panels and slicking the deck. Fortunately for her, the thrum of the scout ship's engines

muffled his cries. As he panicked and shook, she covered
the distance between them and clubbed him unconscious with the phasing unit. Grag knew his name, Siss-
tran. She cauterized his wound with an adjustment to her
tool's beam. She dragged the alien across the deck behind
the thruster reactor console where she'd bound the other
two of the engineering crew on duty this evening. She
exited via the main hatch which irised open then closed
after she stepped through.

Grag, a lieutenant in the Solar Rangers military wing
of the United Galaxy Alliance, hurried along the corri-
dor, tucking the prototype she'd been sent in to steal in
a tool bag, its strap slung across her torso. Her goal had
been to pull off the theft undetected but it wasn't the first
time a plan had gone south on her. Rangers didn't whine,
they improvised or so the who-rah went. At least, she
reflected, she still blended in with the other Talusians
with their ridged foreheads, highly arched eyebrows and
pointed ears. The surgically-altered soldier took a right
at a particular juncture then down an access ladder to
the lower conduits and ducts.

Expertly snaking through the river of tubes, she
made her way to the landing craft bay, the visual of the
ship's schematic committed to her prodigious memory.
A nano-tech enhanced memory that served her well over
numerous espionage missions, taking on the persona of
various humanoid alien life forms over the years.

Reaching the end of the deck, she took several more
turns, ascending at one point, then got to the desired
grate. She eased the panel open slightly, looking down
in the bay. The air in here was rich with the aroma of

machine oil and afterburner fumes. That smell was never so inviting as she –

WOOGA! WOOGA! WOOGA! an alarm blared, everything suddenly bathed in red.

"Intruder alert, intruder alert," declared a voice over the ship's communication system. "Security to the landing craft bay. Medical triage to engineering," the voice said.

"Shit," Grag said as she kicked the grate free. It clattered on the deck below as she too dropped to the flooring. Ahead of her the main hatch opened and armed personnel rushed in, firing their plasma pistols. A ray blast nearly severed Grag's head but she was diving and got behind the stubby nacelle of a lander as the beam sizzled over her. She blasted back, the crossfire searing the bay in a lethal light show.

"Set on stun," the captain of the guard ordered. "We need her alive to get answers out of her."

Grag belly crawled between the skids of a lander. She took aim and used her cutter to slice through several particle module canisters stacked in a corner. The containers exploded violently, jagged energy bolts flaring in all directions. A nearby lander exploded when it was struck.

Several security members were sent flying due to the concussive force, while the rest scattered for cover. A lander was struck with a white-blue shaft and exploded, its solid star fuel supply liquefying and spilling across the deck on fire. Grag was knocked against a bulkhead, but she was only dazed and got her feet under her quickly. Yellow and orange flames clawed upward from the burning fuel, curling into black smoke that rolled through the bay. The automatic extinguishers came on, dousing everything in chemical retardant. Some of this got in Grag's eyes and she had to blink hard to try and see.

A stun blast doubled her over and she stumbled backward, falling to the deck.

"Got you." A Talusian declared as he tried to wrench Grag to her feet. But the ranger shook off the effects of the blast, its power attenuated by her uniform's armored weave.

Not as weakened as she pretended, she jabbed her stiffened fingers under the Talusian's ear right on his nerve point. He withered to the floor as two others fired at her. Breathing hard, she scrambled for his sidearm, its range much greater than her cutter beam and more precise. She took out one of the aliens shooting at her and the other ran behind one of the ships for cover.

Grag needed to be gone before more security swarmed through the hatch. Ducking behind a lander, she withdrew from her tool bag a large oblong egg – a darkling bomb. Underneath its translucent plasticine gray sheath was movement, a diaphanous life form flitting about in the viscous liquid.

This was an artificially grown construct that mimicked a sea creature known as a kadju, a cross between an Earth bat and a squid. She threw the egg at the Talusians and it burst open as one of them shot it. Now exposed to oxygen, the lab produced kadju swelled in size ten-fold. It floated in the air, its numerous tentacles interconnected by bat-like membrane. When the Talusians shot through the creature's spongy body, the thing released through its wounds a velvety blackness that engulfed the area like reverse light. Grag's attackers groped blindly in the opaque darkness.

"Goddammit," a member of the detail swore. The epithet a rough translation from the Talusian as interpreted by the translator chip in Grag's neck. He managed to get his hands on Grag and tried to get an arm around her neck to choke her out. She flipped him over her shoulder and karate chopped his neck. With him out of the way, she hurried inside a lander and powered it up. Like her brain, her eyes had been altered some time ago and Grag could see in the dark.

The computer-generated alarm echoed, "Warning, cargo bay doors opening. Warning, cargo bay doors opening."

Security had to abandon the bay or die from suffocation. Some of them blazed their weapons set to full strength, trying to cripple the ship Grag had just highjacked. The secret agent stayed calm, her hands steady on the controls as she pulled back on the manual yoke and headed the ship for space.

A few blasts got close, one even nicking the hull, but she zoomed the craft out of the bay, only then allowing herself a moment of relief. But Grag knew she had to remain alert. She hadn't had a high success rate by being over-confident. Escape was never certain. The Talusian scout ship was well-equipped to shoot her down. But as the ship turned her way, no plasma beams or pulse missiles came at her. She allowed a grim smile. Grag had planted a virus two days prior in the onboard computer affecting the weapons array. She soared away.

It wouldn't take long for the bridge detail to override the sabotage so she knew she couldn't be in flight too long.

Grag inputted the override codes to hack the sub-space radio and tuned it in to find a specific frequency. "This is Solar Ranger Grag," she said over the radio, also relaying the correct password. "I have the phasing unit but I'm on the run. Need to ditch my getaway ship. I'll be making landing on Gastor-7 and engaging my homing beacon."

Grag increased her speed, burning up the lander's fuel supply at a faster rate than normal. This was going to be a one-way trip to Gastor-7, a jungle planetoid at the far edge of this quadrant. It was Type R which meant a breathable atmosphere for humanoid-like life, water, plant life and carbon-based life forms. In Gastor-7's case, this was represented by animals and insects of the prehistoric size variety. It was not hospitable and the average temperature was 40.5 Celsius, 105 degrees Fahrenheit in Old World reckoning. The planetoid came into view and Grag activated her homing beacon as she brought up a topographical 3D holo-image projected above the ship's navigation panel. Her attention on the image, trying to determine a good place to land, she looked up through the plexi-shield in time to see a flying dragon-like reptile heading straight at her. Landers weren't generally outfitted with proximity sensors, given that you flew by sight. And to her surprise, like the dragon of fables, it screeched a funnel of fire at Grag's ship.

"Holy Shit," she cursed, steering away from the beast, part of the tail section of the craft on fire. Apparently its saliva was what burned and as this coated part of the lander, the fire would continue.

"Where's that chemical retardant when I need it?" Grag quipped, seeing the flames through a side oval window. Digital readouts on several of her panels blinked on and off and the lander rattled. Grag swallowed hard and focusing, seared the dragon with a plasma blast. Wounded, it veered off. But sure enough, having swooped in from starboard, another dragon rammed the ship then latched its feet onto the hull to tear into the ship with its claws.

"Great," Grag muttered. "It just keeps getting better."

There was a way to surge an electrical charge through the hull but that took a few moments to rig and Grag figured her time would be better spent abandoning the ship. The one thing the lander did have was a para-floater. As she got the rig out of a locker near the hatch, she could hear the flapping of the air creature's massive leathery wings. The beast bellowed at this impudent intruder to its world, using its claws to rend the lander's alloy and carbon fiber casing. Damned if the thing didn't rip a seam open in the hull and spewing in its fire, alighted the interior.

"Time to go." Gritting her teeth, Grag blew the hatch and tumbled backward out of the destroyed landing craft. The dragon was still interested in the lander and held on to it as it burned. Rather than engage her para-floater too close to the ship and become the creature's appetizer, she let herself freefall toward the surface. The dragon then tired of its toy and threw the ship away. Above Grag, the lander trailed black smoke and slammed against a hill and exploded.

Her face grimly set, Grag crashed through a canopy of treetops, turning on the device. She came down faster than anticipated, branches tearing at her as the stabilizer initiated and fifteen feet from bashing her body against the ground, the anti-gravity buffer kicked in. She alighted on her feet.

Grag had to take a knee to gather herself. That was closer than she would have liked but she was still upright. She had a mission to complete. Rising, she unlatched the para-floater from her back and set it aside. She made an assessment of her surroundings. She was sweating from the tension and the humidity. It would at least be a day before help arrived and she hoped the Talusians didn't find her by then. Grag had disabled the automatic tracker in the lander. There were several planets and moons in this quadrant she could have escaped to and the aliens would have to conduct a systematic search for her. She set about looking for food and water.

There were smaller animals she spotted that her hand-held personal computer identified as edible. But she was a vegetarian and was glad to find several exotic fruits that would sustain her as well as water. She also came upon the skinned carcass of an amphibious reptile about the size of an alligator on Earth.

"Hunters," she murmured, staring at their handi-work. Gastor-7 was on the United Galaxy Alliance's no hunt list due to several of its animals being unique. Her being on the run would be deemed an exception if she did eat meat. There were on and off world sensor devices for detecting the use of pulse rays and the like but she knew there were ways to circumvent such things. She sniffed the air and recognized the whiff of refined oil – gasoline. These kind of hunters were known to use old-style gunpowder guns and primitive hand-built vehicles which wouldn't leave a digital footprint. They would also be using a liquid fuel ship to get them and their equipment to and from the surface, a regular pulse ship in higher orbit. Such an operation meant this was a costly enterprise, no doubt a trophy hunt for a wealthy dilettante. That meant these would take extreme measures not to be found out by the law.

She moved through the brush more carefully and soon found their camp. She wanted to observe them and figure out how best to deal with these beings. They must have been otherwise engaged when she'd arrived, she concluded. Two men and a woman were in the camp, talking. One of the males was human, the other two hairless, red-hued, four-armed Maldorans. Several carcasses were in freeze pods, the animals' frozen and astonished expressions evident behind the frosted plasti-shields. There were two tents and assorted other outdoor gear including three gas-powered vehicles swarming with pipes and fat tires, the metal cobbled together from the scrap heap with big-bore gasoline engines mounted on their tubular frames.

Too late she sensed a fourth one moving in behind her.

"Who the hell are you?" said the human woman. Her antique .30/06 bolt-action rifle aimed at Grag.

Grag had shot that type of long gun at the range. But she knew it was foolish to try and establish rapport with her over their familiarity with old guns. "I'm a Solar Ranger."

"You're not in uniform and you're a Talusian." While several alien races were in the corps, the Talusians were not part of the UGA.

"I'm a human on undercover assignment."

The others heard them talking. "What's going on, Valmarr?" one of them said.

Valmarr jerked with the barrel of the gun toward the camp site. Grag complied. "She says she's law."

The human male roughly patted Grag down, relieving her of her tool bag. Given how they acted, she surmised Valmarr and this other human were the guides. The couple didn't seem to want to drift far one from the other.

He dumped the contents of her bag on the ground. He picked up the phasing device. "I'm fairly updated on astro tech, but haven't seen this before." He held it up to Grag's face. "What is this?"

"That's classified."

The female Maldoran was trying to hack into Grag's comm-computer. "This thing has a sophisticated lock on it."

"What do you think, Rodrigo?" Valmarr said to the human male.

He regarded Grag then motioned for Valmarr to step away. This was the time the two would decide her fate. They might tie her up and continue the hunt. But the Talusians might show up or, more likely, her fellow Rangers. Either way, they'd be in the shit. Disabling her might be an option as they packed up. But she could ID them. The Maldoran couple faced a stiff fine. It was the guides that had the most to lose. Judging by the way they carried themselves, this wasn't their first poaching excursion and if they were arrested and their activities looked into, who knew what would be divulged, Grag evaluated grimly.

She was a liability and liabilities had to be dealt with, she coldly concluded. Fear didn't well in her, only anger. They would try and take her life and she wasn't going to let that happen.

"I guess you've figured how this would go," Valmarr said, coming back toward Grag after her discussion with Rodrigo.

"Wait, what are you saying?" the Maldoran male asked, worried.

"You're going to be an accessory to murder," Grag said matter-of-factly.

An uncomfortable Valmarr chewed her bottom lip.

Rodrigo addressed the couple. "We told you there were risks."

The Maldoran woman gestured with her four arms. "From the wild life, but not this."

Grag said, "Your guides have much to hide." She was sure their past included hunting exotic protected life forms up and down the evolutionary ladder. She shifted toward her tool bag on the ground.

"Let's get this over with. We're going to have unwanted visitors way too soon," Rodrigo stated.

The Maldorans moved in front of Rodrigo to protest and Valmarr was momentarily distracted. Grag went low, extending her leg in a sweep, knocking Valmarr off her feet. Rodrigo lunged for his rifle leaning against one of the freeze pods. Prone on her stomach Valmarr rolled, also reaching for her rifle. The hunters weren't the only ones with an old style weapon. In a tear away section on the exterior of the tool bag, Grag pulled a knife free and stabbed Valmarr through the hand, momentarily pinning her to the ground.

As her cry of pain and defiance had the red-hued Maldorans going redder with panic, Grag had the rifle and shot at Rodrigo, who dove for safety behind one of the freeze pods. Valmarr pulled the knife free and charged at Grag, trying to gut her.

The ranger blocked the attack with the rifle and swung the stock alongside Valmarr's head, stunning her. Another blow to her temple sent her to the ground unconscious. Stepping in front of him, the Maldorans sought to interfere with Rodrigo again. Grag scooped up the phasing unit and ran to one of the motorized contraptions. She jumped into the driver's seat and mashed what she guessed was the ignition button. The big engine coughed. The retort of Rodrigo's rifle shots were gobbled up as the big block hemi with the double-barreled carburetor roared to life and Grag drove off.

With the open air engine behind her seat roaring and belching an odor of fuel in the exhaust, Grag had never piloted this kind of vehicle. She had virtually in a few holo video games so had a kind of abstract knowledge of the throttle, brake, and steering wheel. Pressing on the pedal, she zoomed forward. She wondered if her teeth were going to rattle out of her head as she nearly smashed against a tree but got the machine under semi-control and tore off. Rodrigo shoved the female Maldoran aside and shot at the fleeing Grag. His bullet whined past her ear.

Still, driving one in reality was a much more challenging experience and she wasn't adept. Rodrigo was coming up from behind fast in one of the others and handled his vehicle expertly over the rough terrain. Grag plowed through bramble, getting snagged by thorns and bushes, which cut her face and ripped her clothes. She heard an electronic sputtering noise and saw that the bullet had struck and damaged the phasing unit.

She bounced over a rocky patch of ground. A dog-like lizard creature bolted in front of her. She swerved to avoid colliding with the animal and skidded through a copse of giant mushrooms. As she side-swiped the plants, a dust rose from them and enveloped her. She sneezed several times. Getting clear, her eyes widened.

"Aw fuck," she swore as she went airborne off a cliff, water and rocks below her. The slap dash vehicle bounced once, twice off the sloping cliff face and landed with a jarring suddenness, pieces breaking loose. What was left of the vehicle was a mangled ball of metal.

Rodrigo, who knew this cliff was here, came to a stop near the edge. He got out of his idling machine, looked down at the wreckage, smirked victoriously, then climbed back into his vehicle and drove off.

Down below Grag's sternum was caved in, a leg broken on one side, a hip the other side of her body, and she was bleeding out from the second big artery in her thigh. What air she could take in wheezed out immediately. So this is what failure felt like, she thought; she was going to die alone and her mission a bust. That bothered her more than anything else.

Her hand felt around some and came upon the phasing device, which fizzed and crackled. What the prototype was designed to do was allow a solid object to phase, to become invisible and un-solid, thereby untouchable, yet able to fire its weapons on the enemy. It would surely shift the precarious balance of power in the galaxy.

Grag's hand got hot as the phasing unit began to hum, throwing off a yellow light that grew in intensity. This didn't panic her. Oddly she found the pulsations comforting, bracing her for the end to come. She gripped it tighter as if it were a life raft. The heat radiated up her arm and she would have cried out but her vocal chords could only manage a dry croak. The heat covered the rest of her, the phasing unit seemingly melting into her skin, motherboards and data chips stretching into the thinness of wires crawling up her arm like kudzu. Grag had the sensation of a ghost-like version of herself rising from the wreckage, looking down on what had been her corporeal form. Then that too blinked out of existence as her mind shut down...or so she believed.

Rodrigo calmed the husband and wife down by convincing them that the ranger died in an accident. Yes, there were the tracks of his vehicle too but they'd be long gone and no record of them being here when others arrived. Packed up, he ushered them on board the surface-to space craft. He turned at the sound of a footfall. He was on edge and had kept his rifle strapped on him. It was in his hand as he stared at a changed Grag.

"The hell," he said.

Grag was partly coated in metal. Not as in an exo-skeleton, but pieces of the ATV and the phasing unit warped and re-molded into attachments to parts of her body and her remaining torso.

Rodgigo shot and the bullet passed through her. He looked shocked and she amused. He quickly re-loaded but as he brought the rifle up again his throat was now in her fingers and she crushed his windpipe. He crumpled to her feet and died gasping.

Valmarr and the couple were in the ship's doorway. The human woman had a med patch on her temple. They remained mute when Grag drove her metallic covered fist into the side of the ship, ripping out its guidance mechanism. Stoically she looked back at them then walked into the jungle. When the Solar Rangers arrived they arrested the three and listened to their story. They searched for Grag but didn't find her. They did find the downloaded data about the phasing unit and so the precarious balance of mutually assured destruction was maintained, until the next means to threaten the fragile peace came along.

From the jungle, Grag watched them depart. In her transformed state, part machine and part flesh, her consciousness could reach out to the higher-level animals, phasing with them. It wasn't as if she could communicate with them, but could experience Gastor-7 from their point of view. She felt protective of them. In this, her final act as a chameleon, a human who'd never truly been at home in her own skin and was thereby able to always disappear undercover, she was in a role she wouldn't be abandoning.

She had a mission. She was home.

LAST CANNONBALL

Warren Hammond

THICK, DAMP SNOWFLAKES RACED AT THE windshield, every one of them a draw for Tammy's eyes if she didn't keep focused on the road.

"They're Frosted Flakes size now," said her cousin, Jake, who had been riding shotgun for the last 2,800 miles.

Tammy would've responded if she didn't have to concentrate on hugging I-80's double yellow. It was easier to track than the white shoulder striping, especially as the road began to cotton over. She kept the Lambo's speed at seventy-five, a full hundred ticks below the top speeds she'd managed in Nebraska and Utah. Even at this honey-drip pace, she was still zipping past cars like they were phone poles.

Only two more hours. That was all it would take to finish climbing the Sierra Nevadas, sprint the last leg to San Francisco, and claim the '79 Cannonball trophy all before the sun went down.

Knowing her odds of winning were getting better by the minute, her fingers tingled where they clutched the wheel. That shithead Darrell Stephenson was about to choke on a big slab of humble pie. She glanced at the letter bracelet on her wrist, a gift from her mother that originally spelled *Tamara*. But the plastic beads didn't spell her name any longer. She'd replaced them with the seven digits of a phone number. The seven digits her boss, Darrell, had told her to call two years ago.

Darrell.

Squeezing the leather-wrapped wheel even tighter, she found her foot pressing insistently downward as the growling engine chewed asphalt and altitude at an intoxicating pace. She barely noticed the eighteen-wheeler chugging up the incline as she whipped past. That bastard Darrell would have to let her stunt drive now. Sure, she loved tumbling off roofs and taking headers through windows, but *driving* was her true calling. Hoist that Cannonball trophy, and she'd get her own feature in *Car and Driver*. Let him call her unqualified then.

"Tammy?" Her cousin's hand braced against the dash. "You see those lights?"

Tracing the road's path as it ribboned in and out of view along the mountainside, she spotted the cluster of brake lights a half mile ahead. She pumped the brakes, bringing the speed down to ninety, then eighty. Shedding more speed, she dropped a gear to let the engine seize the reins. Wet roads weren't all that different from the dirt roads she'd learned on around Waco. The less you used the brakes the better.

Now she could see road flares, a whole row of them creating a hot pink barrier backed by a pair of trooper cars parked crossways to block the lanes.

"Won't be long," said Tammy. "Probably just a wide load coming through. At least I hope so."

Jake lit up and passed her the cig before flaming one of his own.

She came to a full stop behind a Pinto, close enough she could see the driver's eyes go wide in his rearview. A moment later, the wife and two kids were gawking at the black Lamborghini Countach idling behind them quiet and dangerous as a mamba.

"Fuck yeah," said Tammy as she gave the engine a rev. Jake flipped them a double bird.

Tammy checked the side mirrors for any sign of the Ferrari Testarossa or the custom '76 Econoline, the two vehicles she thought were the closest of the eleven who had started racing from Bridgeport, Connecticut, yesterday at noon. Jake turned the CB dial to channel 19, the trucker band. Voices squawked and chattered, but from all the clatter, Tammy only heard two words, *chains only*.

Son-of-a-bitch.

Jake snatched the mic. "Chains? It's fucking September! You pussies ain't afraid of a little snow are you?"

"Tell it to the smokeys," came a voice.

Tammy stabbed the CB's power button. She looked into the rearview mirror but couldn't see much. The Lamborghini was designed for one thing only: forward velocity. Seeing behind you was an afterthought. The rear windshield was so small it felt like watching a movie through a mail slot. Moving her head to get the best angle, her heart dropped when she spotted the sleek red lines of the Ferrari only a hundred feet down the hill, and right behind it, the bright purple custom van. Her lead was gone.

She fingered the bracelet on her wrist. Don't lose hope now, dammit.

First, second, and third place cars lined up on I-80's shoulder. The snow had tapered off, and the troopers stopped turning cars back, choosing instead to allow them to stack up here on the road until the snowplows finished clearing up ahead. Tammy sat behind the wheel, her eyes glued to the troopers' Chrysler Newports, eager to gun it as soon as they pulled off.

She should count herself lucky only two cars had caught her. The other eight racers must either be hopelessly far behind or taking alternate routes. She'd been tempted to take another route herself, but now that the pass was about to reopen after an hour's wait, she knew she'd made the right decision.

A knock on the window turned her head, bringing her face-to-face with a silver belt buckle the width of a grapefruit. Tammy lowered the window the full three inches afforded by the Lamborghini's Italian engineers. Looking up into the cold, she met the third-place driver's eyes to make it clear that she wasn't staring at the bulge he seemed to push out front like a show pony.

"Nice ride," said Hector, the driver of the custom van. She knew his name from a brief introduction at the before-party. "Is this really Señor Reynolds's car?" His accent was thick enough to turn the *is* into *ease.*

Tammy nodded. "Burt Reynolds himself. He's doing a movie based on the Cannonball. It's good publicity to have one of his cars in the real race."

Hector's face was shaved clean, his hair slick as Penzoil. "How do you know him? You an actress?"

"Stunt woman. I did most of the Sally Field stunts in *Smokey and the Bandit.*"

He leaned down, cocked his head, and showed off a pair of gold teeth. "You want a bump?" He reached back to his ass pocket and pulled out a baggie–its contents white as the snow-covered pines–and shoved it through the narrow window opening.

Jake was quick to offer a *gracias* and reached over to take the bag. Tammy shook her head. If this was a West Hollywood disco, she'd be inclined to dip her pinky nail, but this was the Cannonball, and she wasn't about to let a little blow come between her and becoming the first woman to win the cross-country race.

"You do crashes and jumps?" asked Hector. "Like Evel Knievel?"

"Not yet."

"Why not? Señor Reynolds must think you're good if he lets you drive his car."

"Burt's cool," she nodded. "My boss is the problem. Even when it's a woman's part in the movie, he puts one of his good ol' boys in a wig and dress to do the stunt. Looks like shit on screen if you ask me. I can always tell when it's a man."

Jake poured a line into the folded crease of the speeding ticket she'd gotten in Ohio. Lifting the fold to his nose, he tipped his head back and snorted. "That shit is fine."

"Glad you like," said Hector. "Keep it."

"You can't be serious." Jake hefted the bag. "This is probably a hundred grams."

"Two hundred," said Hector with a broad smile. "You and your girlfriend enjoy it."

"We ain't a pair," said Jake. "I'm her cousin."

Hector lifted a hand to his heart. *"Tu prima?* Family is *muy importante,* no? I'm racing for my cousin too."

"Is that your cousin who's riding with you?"

"Jorge is just an *amigo* I met in Miami. My cousin is at home in Medellín."

"Medellín?" asked Tammy.

"Colombia. My cousin loves cars. He read about this race in one of your magazines. He has them translated into Spanish. He hired the best mechanics in all of Colombia to customize my van, and he shipped it all the way to America. I'll bring the trophy home as a gift when I beat you."

Tammy smiled at that. She'd played in a man's world long enough to hear the wink in his voice. "Sorry," she said, "but Burt Reynolds already called dibs on that cup. Who am I to deny the most famous man in America?"

"Very famous, yes. But not as famous as my cousin."

"What's his name?"

"Pablo Escobar."

"Never heard of him."

"You will," said Hector, his voice taking a dark edge. "The whole world will learn who he is."

Unable to tell if that was a joke, Tammy just nodded her head and reached for the heater. She hadn't felt cold until now.

"You know where we are, don't you?" asked Hector. "Fitting place to decide the race if you ask me."

"You mean California?"

He pointed uphill. "I mean Donner Pass."

"What of it?"

Hector crouched down, his face practically wedged sideways into the Lambo's window frame. "You Americans don't know much about your own country, do you? Ever heard of the Donner party?"

Spooked by the closeness of his face, she shrank in her seat, a lump forming in her throat. "That was here?"

"People murdering and eating each other. Cannibals. It all happened right here." He snapped his jaws, the loud clack of teeth sounding like a firecracker in her ear.

Tammy sucked in a breath and reflexively waved a hand to shoo him away, but he was already gone, strutting back to his vehicle. She put the window back up and hugged her arms against the chill. "What the fuck?"

Jake shrugged and stared at the bag of coke like he'd just won the free car behind door number two.

"Put it away," she said, annoyed that Hector still had any kind of presence in the car.

Jake stashed it under the seat. "You don't know what you're missing, cuz. That shit's the best I ever had. Sure beats anything my brother sells back home."

The troopers pulled off, and she put the car in gear. Cold as she'd gotten talking to Hector, her palms still felt sweaty when she gripped the wheel. She looked at her bracelet again, needing to remind herself of who her real enemy was. Darrell Stephenson. The man who had humiliated her. The one she needed to beat.

A grin began to form on her face.

Gently, she pressed the accelerator and pulled into the line of traffic just as it was starting to move. The Ferrari, driven by a cardiologist and his brother, pulled onto her bumper. Behind the sleek coupe, the purple Ford Econoline loomed like a battering ram.

Moving barely five miles per hour, she rolled past the now opened roadblock. The sky began to clear, and she put on her sunglasses. She tested the brakes a couple times to make sure there was no slippage on the plowed road. Good. She'd take it slow until she could ease past all the other cars. Then it would be just the three racers on this wide-open highway. May the best woman win.

She tailgated one car after another, flipping lights on and off to move them aside, inching closer to the front of the pack, the Ferrari and the Econonline staying tight on her tail.

Her heart rapped against her ribs now, her mouth turning dry. Beat the doctor and the Colombian freak to the Pacific and even Darrel Stephenson wouldn't be able to stop her from becoming Hollywood's most sought-after stunt driver.

She didn't really know why Darrell was so hell-bent on stopping her from driving, but if he'd had his way, she would've been fired a long time ago. Lucky for her, the directors in Hollywood now insisted on women stand-ins for women actresses, at least for the close-in work.

For the last year, she'd had her fingers crossed that Darrell was going to sell out to pay his alimony and gambling debts, but he kept turning away offers for the company saying all the potential buyers were out to screw him. It would serve him right to get pennies on the dollar. What could he expect, treating people the way he did, treating *her* the way he did?

That day was still fresh in Tammy's memory. The day he got her hopes up by saying he'd let her drive if she passed a special training course. Here was the phone number she needed to call to sign up.

She didn't know he'd turned on his desk intercom so the whole building–her peers, many who she liked and respected–could hear them talking. She didn't know he'd also patched his office phone into the intercom so everybody could hear the phone ring when she dialed the seven digits now burned into her mind like a set of grill marks.

"Hello, this is Bill," said the man who answered.

"I'd like to sign up for your training course."

"Training course?"

"That's right."

"Well, I sure like a girl who's ready to get after it. How about we get you over here straight away so I can give you a tryout?"

She remembered the expression on Darrell's face, remembered his nods of encouragement as she copied down the address. It wasn't until she asked if she needed to bring her own helmet that she knew anything was off. After a confused question or two between her and Bill, he finally said, "Now, sugar, who exactly do you think you're talking to?"

"A trainer. You teach stunt driving."

The line went silent for a good long time before she heard a loud sigh. "I have to say, I think somebody is having some fun at your expense. This here is a film studio. I make pornos."

Never had her cheeks burned hotter with rage and humiliation. In the two years since, she'd endured Darrel's snide snickers and leers. The very memory of it still brought a flush to her face, even now as she accelerated past the last vehicle, nothing but miles of open, twisting road dead ahead.

She mashed the pedal to the floor and climbed gears with well-practiced movements of her right hand. The engine behind her seat rumbled like the after-effect of a thunderclap, and the car shot up the mountainside.

She checked all three mirrors in succession, but her view was too limited to see anything more than flashes of red or purple.

Sensing her frustration, Jake turned around and wedged between the seats so he could press himself up against the rear window to call the play-by-play. "I see them. Two hundred feet back. They're running neck and neck."

Tammy took her foot off the gas to prepare for a curve. Sensing her speed was still too high, she gave the brakes a squeeze and turned the wheel, the g-forces pressing her against the car door.

"Holy shit!" shouted Jake. "The van just hit the Ferrari. He cut it right across the nose."

Tammy's pulse stretched toward the red zone.

"I can't see them anymore. Last I saw, the Ferrari spun out and was sitting like a dead duck in the middle of the highway."

The road started to straighten and level. Tammy punched the gas, and the sign announcing the summit of Donner Pass flew by too quick to read the elevation.

"I see him now," said Jake a few seconds later. "Still a couple hundred feet back. The Ferrari is gone. Shit, Tammy, there's a red panel hanging from the rear bumper. He hit the Ferrari on purpose. What's wrong with that guy?"

Tammy eyed the road, knowing if Hector got close enough, he'd do her the same way. Going downhill now, her speed was pushing a hundred. "I can outrun him all the way to San Fran."

"We don't have the gas."

Dammit, she forgot about that. The gauge showed an eighth of a tank if she was being generous. The plan had always been to make one more fuel stop, but that was before she had a psycho on her tail. Shit, what if she pulled off for gas and he had a gun?

Racing through her options, one stood brightest in her mind. "I'm going to slow down and let him get good and close."

"Why?"

"There's another set of curves coming up. If I let him get close, he'll be watching me closer than the road. All I have to do is coax him into taking the bends too fast, and his van will flip."

"Not if it's loaded down."

"It's not. I saw it with the back doors open yesterday. All he's got in there is a bed."

"A bed?"

"Yeah, and a mirror on the ceiling."

"He's closing on us now. A hundred feet back."

The late-day sun was burning strong now, little rivulets of snowmelt starting to trickle across the asphalt.

Jake adjusted his position in the back, somehow finding a place for his legs that didn't interfere with her access to the gearshift. "Fifty feet now."

She sped into the first bend, counting on the Lambo's super-wide back tires to hold a tight grip on the road.

"Thirty feet!"

Tammy gave the engine more juice. The curve sharpened, and she felt her ass sliding in her seat. The muscles in her back tightened to keep her upright.

"Twenty!"

She added more gas, hoping the fish behind her would stay on its line. As long as he kept trying to match speed, the top heavy Econoline would eventually lose control. Great cars and great driving would only get you so far before the laws of physics took their gavel and bashed your skull open.

She added more gas as she whipped out of the turn and into the second half of an S.

"Holding at twenty...."

They lost altitude, and slushy puddles became more common as the sun continued to heat the Sierras. She felt the car shudder as it blasted through wet stretches. She targeted small patches of slush as often as she could to kick as much slop as possible at his windshield.

"Keep hitting those puddles. His wipers can't keep up."

She took each turn a little faster than the previous, knowing that, any time now, their empty road wouldn't be empty anymore.

"He's still with us!"

That shouldn't be possible. The Lambo was only three-and-a-half feet tall, when that van stood probably three feet taller. No way could he hold the road like she did.

The curve suddenly straightened to reveal a dozen deer standing in the road. A jolt of fear made her mouth taste like metal as she hit the brakes hard and swerved.

"Shit, he almost rammed us!"

The van pulled even with her driver-side window. Thanks to his dirty windshield, Hector must not have seen the deer yet.

Despite being the first to spot the deer, Tammy still didn't have enough lead time to stop the car. Instead, she locked her elbows and targeted the narrow gap between the deer and the snow bank on the right.

The van was past her now. A flash caught her eye, and then came a second muzzle blast before she realized Jorge, Hector's *amigo* was literally riding shotgun.

The van's brake lights turned red, and the horn blared when he must've finally noticed the deer. He was too late. His fate sealed by reduced visibility and the extra second he'd spent taking his focus off the road to watch his partner's shotgun blasts.

Tammy still had a chance. The wheels rumbled over shoulder debris as the Lambo's nose inched closer to the snow bank. She heard snow scraping against the under-carriage, yet she angled closer, close enough for Jake to gather snowballs out the passenger window.

She could do this...as long as the deer didn't move.

The van plowed into them. The horn was instantly silenced by the crunch of imploding metal, and the van's back end bucked upward. Jorge, who was still leaning out the window, slammed against the window frame. The gun flew toward the woods, and his head whiplashed with more than enough force to snap his neck.

The van hit more deer, and Jorge shot out the window, his shoulder catching for a moment on the mirror's brace extension before his arm was scraped clean off to free the rest of him. His body sailed forty feet before smacking the pavement and skidding to a halt.

Deer parts spun from the wreck in an explosion of blood and gore and fur. Hector had rammed into at least four of them. The other deer scattered in every possible direction, but Tammy was already about to shoot the gap. Only one deer was close enough to be a danger now, and its legs seemed to compress like a spring ready to leap.

It was staring right at her, but she feared it wouldn't have the sense to stay put when every last nerve in its body was urging it to flee. Tammy stared back, willing it to stay frozen.

And then she was through. Quickly, she steered back onto the road, and then she slapped the car into second and jerked the wheel into a J turn. Tires screeched as she one-eightied to a full stop.

All she could hear now was her own breathing, her lungs pumping quickly in and out. The van was still in motion, all four wheels rolling downhill with a nasty limp until it trailed off the road and disappeared down a ravine.

"Holy shit," said Jake.

The surviving deer disappeared into the trees. Jorge's body lay like roadkill on the blood-smeared road.

"Let's get the fuck out of here," said Jake.

Tammy drove to the spot where the van had run off the road. She could see it now, ten feet down, turned on its side. The airbrushed mural on this entire side of the vehicle depicted a soccer game, a skull-headed player kicking the ball hard enough toward the goal that the ball burst in flame.

"We can still win this thing," said Jake. "Cars will be along soon, and we don't want to get caught up in this shit. They'll just assume he was driving too fast and hit those deer, which is pretty much exactly what happened."

She scissored the door open and lifted herself out. The sun dropped behind a mountain, a cool chill riding in with the lengthening shadows. The highway, surprisingly, was still empty. Maybe the Ferrari's wreck had stopped traffic for a bit. She'd expected cars coming the other way too, but maybe the roadblock on this side of the pass hadn't opened at the same time.

Jake was out of the car. "Tammy, we gotta go. Now."

Ignoring him, she started down into the ravine, slipping and skidding in the snow.

"He must be dead, Tammy. Who gives a shit anyway? He tried to kill us."

Tammy reached the van and looked through what was left of the windshield. Hector was indeed dead. Suspended by his seatbelt, his chest had been savaged by the steering wheel and his face pulped by a deer flying through the windshield.

"We gotta go," said Jake.

Tammy looked at her cousin, just now noticing he had followed her down. "If it wasn't weighted down with cargo, it should've flipped on those curves."

She ran around to the back side and opened the doors. A rush of several gallons of water spilled onto her shoes. Confused, it took her a moment to realize the bed Hector kept inside was actually a waterbed, and the mattress had burst when the van rolled and dumped it from its frame.

The van's carpeted interior was soaking wet and gummy with chunks of venison and human brain. She reached for the ruptured mattress and pulled apart one of the tears to reveal a large pile of kilo-sized bags.

Without saying a word, she picked one of them up. Wrapped in watertight plastic the cocaine sat heavy in her hand. Leaning out the door, she took a look around and tossed it beyond some scrub where it disappeared into the snow like a rock thrown into a lake.

"Buy me some time," she said to Jake who was already scrambling back up the ravine. He knew how much this stash was worth.

Staying out of view from the road, she worked faster than she ever had before, she heaved bag after bag into the snow behind the scrub, or behind some trees, or behind some rocks where she and Jake could come back and retrieve it all at the crack of dawn.

Bag after bag, she worked herself into a rhythm. She could hear Jake yelling at the newly arrived bystanders. "Stay away! There's gasoline all over the place. The thing could blow up any second."

Sirens began to echo off the blackening mountains as she tossed the last of what must be two hundred bags.

She hustled up the steep slope to the highway. People milled about, speaking in grave tones. She and Jake got into the car just as the first trooper lights came into view.

Firing the Lamborghini's engine, she eased into the slow-moving traffic.

She had a race to win. The trophy was hers, same with the bragging rights that came with it.

And she was rich. Or soon would be. She and Jake would sell the coke to his brother, whose operation was about to expand a thousandfold.

She'd buy that bastard Darrell out and send him and his good ol' boys into retirement.

A new decade was about to start. The rules were changing.

Hollywood better get ready.

She turned to Jake, and pumped a fist. "We did it."

Jake's forehead was creased with concern. "You think Hector's cousin will come looking for his coke?"

"How would he know who took it? It's ours, Jake. Free and clear. Whoever heard of Pablo Escobar anyway?"

"Nobody."

"Exactly. How dangerous can he be?"

RESCUE

Merit Clark

I DON'T REALLY WANT TO HURT THE NEW GIRL.
My only goal is to help her come to the sensible conclusion that it's wrong to live with my husband. Not harm. Not intimidation. Merely enlightenment.

Ex, I remind myself, my ex-husband. As in, X marks the spot. Exes and ohs. I've watched them screw and, let me tell you, she doesn't say, "Oh!" very often. In the months he's been gone he hasn't gotten any better in bed, and you'd think with new people he'd be forced to learn new tricks.

The sex is boring. Item one on the menu of complaints presented to me before his abrupt departure. Out of all the activities that take two to reach a satisfying completion–catch, tennis, a rousing session of patty cake–sex is high on the list. I didn't always do all of the heavy lifting like a high-priced escort but neither does the new girl, as far as I can tell.

I lost my mind when he left, when he ghosted me, driving off to points unknown towing a U-Haul. I realized for the first time how possible it was to be stupid, to not see the signs, to be blindsided. In one short, blessed burst of sanity I placed a GPS tracker on his truck and grew addicted to watching his movements on map software, the way I used to monitor his business travel. I felt insulted he never suspected me of doing such a thing, that he thought I'd accept his departure meekly.

I would never do something as obvious and redneck-ish as slashing tires or drunk dialing. No cola splashed on the hood of his truck or showing up at his office naked under a raincoat. No. I'm neither provincial nor tacky, which was a problem for him all along.

It's two a.m. when I leave my New York hotel room dressed like I'm going clubbing, and I have slightly over twenty-four hours to complete my task. My drive is twelve hours each way because I have to avoid interstates, toll plazas, and cameras. Instead I carefully traverse small towns because I can't risk getting a ticket.

I take public transit to New Jersey where I pick up the beater car I bought earlier with cash. Even Newark is quiet this time of night and I find an inconspicuous spot to park and slither into my costume: a gray, curly wig, padded sweatshirt, baggy polyester slacks, and old lady sneakers with Velcro closures. Contact lenses that change green to brown. I sweat, even though it's chilly, and my heart pounds. I'm relieved when I start driving, making my way slowly, working from directions written on a scrap of paper because I can't have my phone.

First rule of criminal activity: You are not you. Make up a name, assume a new persona, forget all of your usual mannerisms. I flew to New York as me but for the next twenty-four hours I'm no longer Linnea. I'm no longer rail-thin and stylish but a fiftyish cleaning woman, twenty pounds overweight, with bad knees. I tried out old lady names in my head as I drove: Ruth, Helen, Doris.

Rule two is like backpacking in the wilderness: Leave no trace. When I'm done with the car I'll have it detailed and then leave it in some sketchy back alley, keys in the ignition.

Rule three: See and involve as few people as possible.

My friend Gary will stop by my hotel room and mess up the bed, make a show of mentioning I'm sick and order room service. You never know until something truly bad happens how important your friends are but still, it puts him at too much risk if I'm gone more than one night and I promise to be back.

I made it almost five hours before I had to get gas and pee. Not for me, crazy shit like the astronaut who stalked a rival skank years ago and drove three days straight wearing diapers. I found an old school gas station unlikely to have cameras and in the warped metal bathroom mirror I blinked at a stranger. I thought about getting food but was too nervous to eat.

Back in the car I tried to push it a little because I was behind schedule but the engine knocked and the foot-pedal emergency brake banged against my left leg if I exceeded 65. I knew from due diligence the office in the apartment complex where my husband lived closed at five and I had to be done cleaning before then which meant arriving no later than four. At my current pace I wasn't going to make it so I risked jumping on an inter-state without tolls, eyes glued to the rearview, thumping brake pedal beating against my calf the entire way like a metronome.

My temporary plate felt like a cop-attracting beacon but I had decided against stealing and swapping license plates because that's rule number four: Don't get fancy.

The tube-top-wearing apartment manager looked twenty going on thirteen. I hadn't eaten for hours, and my stomach growled as I stood in front of her desk at three-fifty-five, heavily made up, overdressed for the ninety-degree weather and suspicious as hell. I never removed my sunglasses. I babbled and stumbled over my story because when I'm scared I talk too much. I carried a blue plastic bucket with cleaning supplies and wore rubber gloves.

Tube top didn't blink when I told her my name was Selma Doubtfire, but she did whine. "They should have given you a key." Huff, moan, sigh. "I'm the only one here and I'm not supposed to leave."

"Not even to pee?" I asked. "That seems unreasonable."

She flipped the sign around with the little clock on it indicating her return time and her flip-flops made a loud slapping sound on the concrete path. It was a markedly blue-collar complex, bent mini-blinds at the windows, piles of dog shit in the prickly grass, cheap Chevy sedans in the lot. I'd learned where New Girlfriend worked, what she drove, and knew she went to Pilates every Wednesday after work. My husband's truck was still at the airport, which meant he was in the midst of yet another Monday to Friday business trip.

I had the name of one of her besties from Facebook and in the unlikely event NG came home unexpectedly I was going to say her friend was surprising her for her birthday with a cleaning. Who doesn't want their toilets scrubbed? Tube top opened the door for me with a master key–a locking doorknob, no deadbolt; it was a time warp there in southern Michigan.

"Just lock the knob when you're done, K?"

Tube top had barely left before she lit up a Marlboro Light and I knew, if questioned, all she'd remember was old fat white lady.

I sweated profusely the entire time I pretended to clean; if they ever did get CSIs in there they'd have copious contributions of bodily fluids to work with. I meant to give myself more time but even with Pilates NG would be home in less than two hours. My wig itched miserably but I couldn't risk removing it.

I wasn't a hardened criminal and, while I'd watched an awful lot of true crime, I couldn't even begin to list the ways it could have gone wrong. I opened closets, the door to the hot water heater, and shower curtains. I checked under beds. I closed the mini blinds and cranked up the AC because of the aforementioned sweating, and since I figured they were going know someone had been in the apartment anyway I might as well cost them some money.

I had to make it look good so I wrinkled my nose and swiped with a toilet wand. Apparently, ways in which the NG was proving more easygoing and non-confrontational than me started with bathroom etiquette. I had a container of bleach in my plastic bucket that I distributed liberally on any porcelain or tile surface. If it smells clean, people will think it is clean. Because people are unimaginative sheep.

Mail was lying around and I made note of social security numbers and such for future use. I already knew NG was stupid enough to list her full birth date on Facebook. When he lived with me I got my husband in the habit of using a shredder, but apparently carelessness with important papers was part of his new, relaxed lifestyle. And the NG, Jesus, clothes in the closet were from the cheapest discount stores in the strip mall, not a natural fiber in the bunch. She was some kind of crafter as well, because I found loads of fake pussy willow stalks and ribbon and wads of cotton batting in the spare bedroom.

Point of interest. When he deigned to tell me a story at all it began with how his car broke down leaving Colorado, and after passing through much larger cities–Omaha, Des Moines, Chicago for Christ's sake– and failing to find anyone with the skills to fix brakes on a Nissan, he drove until he could drive no longer, finding himself stranded in small-town southern Michigan. Where, coincidentally, a co-worker had a two-bedroom apartment, an abusive ex, and the desire for a roommate. Nothing going on, he said, reading from page one of the Cheater's Playbook.

It will come as no surprise to anyone with a room temperature IQ that my minimal due diligence quickly revealed the NG was not, in fact, a co-worker. Clearly, the second bedroom was used for something, but whatever it was called for a glue gun and raffia. As for the abusive ex? Who knew? Her past love life didn't interest me.

Inside their refrigerator I performed chemistry experiments. On the outside of the refrigerator photos were held in place with cute insect magnets, ladybugs, butterflies, and fanciful chubby bumblebees. In addition to risking arrest I was going to need a shot of insulin if I stayed too long. A bleached blonde with an unfortunately high forehead was featured in many of the pictures, as well as fat children in leotards and sitting on the floor in front of a Christmas tree. Taking one of those photos would have been too obvious. A second sweep of the "spare" bedroom, aka the craft den, revealed many bedazzled and beribboned albums, bounty inside free for the taking. I backfilled with a few choice photos of my own.

When I was a child a nice elderly neighbor took an interest in me. She had me over for snacks, soda, cookies, whatever crap an old person thought a kid would like. I have absolutely no concept of what we talked about or how long I stayed. At some point, I'd excuse myself to use the bathroom and rifle through her bedroom. I don't know where the idea came from but I started taking small things–a handkerchief, a hairpin, a prayer card. I imperfectly concealed what I'd stolen in my room where it was soon found by my mother, who made me apologize to the old lady's face, the usual exercise in humiliation and faux humbling. What I remember most was the churning, thrilling sensation in my gut, alone in her darkened bedroom, touching secret refuges I somehow knew were forbidden.

Now I found it was as much fun to deposit as to lift. I cleaned my way out of the apartment, turned the useless tab in the knob, and decided to take their vacuum as a door prize. I deposited it in a random dumpster along my return route, as I did the cleaning supplies, clothes and finally, with tremendous relief, the wig.

Back in Manhattan, adrenaline overcame exhaustion and I partied like I was twenty-nine again, out on the town as the real me, hitting several bars with my very good old friends who'd swear I was there the whole time.

I stared straight at HALO cameras, used my credit cards, chatted up every individual I encountered at the hotel. I left a sensational tip for the housekeeper.

Rule number five: Know when to make yourself memorable.

Back home, I forced myself to watch streams from the cameras I planted. I didn't do this for enjoyment or because I'm a voyeur, but because I had to know. When he left me the pain was indescribable. For months, I left suicide notes on my nightstand for someone to find in the hopes I didn't wake up. I threw lengths of rope over rafters, I took pills, but some life force, some shaky sense of destiny pulled me back every time. No one should be allowed to make someone else feel this way.

If I found he truly loved the NG I told myself I'd let him go, but in the short time I watched them I wasn't seeing definitive signs. So far, his life was fast food restaurants, airport, apartment. Shuffle, rinse, reverse, and repeat. It seemed the low overhead NG liked chain seafood and beer. It felt like a job watching them, they were so boring.

I wasn't home two days from New York when the first interesting story broke on a local newspaper's web page:

"Tainted Shampoo Sold at Discount Store.

A local Three Rivers woman was blinded by contaminated dandruff shampoo. The shelves have been emptied at a local discount store frequented by the victim and tests by law enforcement are underway. Doctors are optimistic that the blindness will be temporary."

Accompanied by a photo of an empty shelf and of self-important police officers in uniforms and khakis standing around doing nothing.

First of all, obviously, that was meant for him. I mean, what self-respecting woman used grocery store shampoo? Mine, for example, came from the salon, smelled like eucalyptus, and cost forty dollars. Second, how'd she get into it before him? The hubs was a compulsive showerer, before during and after sex. Bodily fluids grossed him out and we had to have towels next to the bed for immediate aisle cleanup. Third–and this was the beautiful part–the bottle of shampoo was one that didn't make it into his U-Haul and that I brought with me so if they were ambitious enough to dust the bottle for prints they'd only find his. Fourth, was there a toxicology test that would detect ghost pepper?

I googled it in the private browser and the answer was an equivocal yes if you knew what you were looking for. I also read that most likely NG wasn't literally blind, although her eyes could have swollen shut for a day or two. There was one case of a woman losing a baby after being pepper sprayed and it could be lethal combined with cocaine but neither condition applied. Bottom line, it was painful but NG would get over it.

Diligent law enforcement revealed nothing wrong with bottles of shampoo pulled from store shelves for testing. My idiot husband was interviewed and told the authorities he couldn't remember "for the life of him" where he bought it. He traveled a lot, he told them. This presented the possibility of a nationwide recall of the shampoo. Possibly international. Law of unintended consequences.

I wondered how much tolerance NG would have for his porn addiction (planted), the naked photos of him with a co-worker hidden in her sparkly albums

(Photoshop), or if I'd have to go nuclear and send video of NG and my husband in bed to everyone at her company. She would certainly believe he made sex tapes after she found out about the porn. It was a shame the two of them never did anything remotely sexually provocative. If anything, he'd gotten less imaginative and I could always spot a neatly folded towel next to them on the nightstand.

I waited impatiently for the next discovery, for the moment when I knew it was time for me to transform from victim to rescuer. I liquidated stocks in my personal brokerage account so I'd have ready cash. People always assume the man has all the money, but that wasn't true in this case. Besides, this had nothing to do with money or even the fact that I didn't like to lose. It was about lies, abandonment, humiliation, emotional agony so bad there were days I could only sit motionless and feel my own heart continue to stubbornly beat. I looked at those suicide notes in my nightstand drawer and knew he had to pay.

Like everything in life the climax, the big reveal, the defining moment didn't come in a way or from a source I expected. Tuesday night, the camera in their bedroom revealed NG on the floor next to the bed. Face-down. Fully clothed. No towel on the nightstand, no man in sight. Minutes ticked by. Hours. She remained unnaturally motionless. I never saw her drink so I didn't think she'd passed out. If she'd hit her head wouldn't there be blood? The light stayed on in her bedroom. Eleven p.m. Midnight. One a.m. I maintained my vigil. Three a.m. Five.

Wednesday morning the NG didn't go to work. The GPS tracker showed my husband's truck at the airport and, if he was on a business trip, most likely he wouldn't be "home" until Friday. We used to use a travel app to share his itineraries, and I remember compulsively watching his progress every Friday afternoon, checking for bad weather, delayed flights, close connections. For months after he left I'd reach for my phone every Friday like a phantom limb.

NG remained on the floor. A thin, dark rivulet snaked from her nose across the beige carpet. I willed her to move. Her phone on the nightstand buzzed intermittently with missed calls including, no doubt, my husband. Someone needed to do something but the only person who knew was me.

It was like watching my own private snuff film. All day Wednesday. All night. All day Thursday. I wouldn't sleep as long as she was lying there. Didn't NG have a mother, a sister, a bestie with a key? A real cleaning service? I wondered how long it would be before she started to smell. I almost called 911 a thousand times; I considered getting a burner so I could. It was unbearable to watch, to think a woman could lie dead for three days and have no one check on her. I considered calling tube top or NG's office. I think, *is this from the ghost chilies*? I think, *is she diabetic*? I never saw her give herself a shot. I think, *don't those folks at work find it odd she hasn't shown up two days in a row*? Her plugged in phone continued to buzz. I think, *I've got to get back in there somehow and get the cameras.*

Thursday night I finally took pills because I couldn't think straight if I didn't sleep. I let the dog get in bed with me to keep nightmares away. Every time I woke I popped another Ativan, put my hand on his warm fur, and sought dark oblivion. As a result, I didn't move until noon Friday when the dog woke me whining to go outside. My snuff film had changed. New people swarmed the bedroom, cops, grim-faced detectives in shirt sleeves, evidence techs with cameras. I missed the best part, the moment of discovery.

In Michigan, they determined it wasn't a suicide. Reasons disclosed included the absence of a note, a recent promotion at work, and a new relationship. Everyone police interviewed carried on about how happy NG was. How kind, thoughtful, and upbeat. Always willing to lend a helping hand. Like everyone who ever died she became an insta-saint.

I found out I was still my husband's "In Case of Emergency" when Michigan detectives called requesting an interview. I already had a bag packed, full of careful clothes, what you'd call business formal. Dark, conservative, expensive. Silk blouses, heels, and tasteful jewelry, everything about me carefully edited. I had already paid a retainer to the best criminal defense attorney in the area. My husband wasn't going to be permitted to leave the state so I entered it for the second time, driving more leisurely this time, and booked a suite at an extended stay hotel. I knew this could take months, maybe years.

Adulterated shampoo combined with allegedly accidental food contamination formed a pattern and bail was set very high, half a million. Only my husband's and the NG's fingerprints were found on food in the refrigerator and it wasn't likely she'd poison herself, certainly not in such a tricky way. Not to mention, with all his travel he was a flight risk. I had my cashier's check ready before they could change their minds. No one in his family had that kind of money. NG's family now believed he was a murderer. No one else could afford him.

I'm interviewed by detectives, one old and fat with a brush cut, one in his thirties, dark-haired, good looking. My daily life, routines, and schedules were documented. My alibi days in New York described with minimal detail.

Rule four: Don't get fancy.

I told them about the way I was left, the U-Haul, the banishment from the travel app. I told them he didn't call for months and I had no way of knowing where he was. The surgical precision with which my husband removed me from his life now worked in my favor. I told them I had no knowledge whatsoever of his girlfriend. For example, I had no idea NG had a severe peanut allergy.

Handsome detective asked me why I was willing to help a man who abandoned me so callously.

I forced myself to look directly into his eyes. "Because he needs me."

I was allowed to get some clothes for my husband from the apartment. I was supervised by a deputy so there was no chance to retrieve cameras. If they're ever found I'll have to share my own videos from when we were first together. It's hard to believe now but he used to exhibit imagination in the bedroom, liked ordering me around and having me pose. Those videos would be deeply embarrassing but it's a risk I'll have to live with.

The deputy and I stopped in the apartment complex office to see the manager for a key. Déjà vu. It turned out tube top's name was Kaiyleigh with a full complement of vowels. I have to admit I had a moment. My voice, for example; I didn't do much to disguise my voice.

That should be rule six: Do not speak unless spoken to. I forced myself to look her in the eye and there wasn't a glimmer of recognition.

Kaiyleigh chattered in her high-pitched girl voice about the victim, used her name but I didn't want to know it, not yet. If I started thinking of her as a person it wouldn't lead anywhere helpful. I'd have to hear it at trial but until then she was NG, a non-entity, a lifeless form facedown on the floor, a sweatpant-clad mannequin.

"She gave me a denim jacket for Christmas," Kaiyleigh said. "I don't usually wear things like that, I like more bodycon stuff, but she'd decorated it and it was really pretty."

"Decorated it how?" I forced the shake from my voice.

"Glitter and red stardust, she called it. She hand painted a Santa on the back and used cotton fluff for a beard."

"She sounds like a nice lady," the deputy said.

"Yeah." Kaiyleigh's flip-flops snapped down the concrete just like last time. There wasn't much smell at all other than a whiff of detergent.

"She was here for a while, wasn't she?" I asked, not expecting an answer.

"We had the carpet cleaned." Kaiyleigh glanced at the deputy. "It's already rented as soon as you guys are done. We're gonna paint too, freshen it up for the new people."

He nodded. "Gotta get on with life."

It seemed the deputy was saying that for my benefit. He and the detective didn't understand that I was moving on, making forward progress once again after a long time on hold. My marriage took a slight detour but they all do.

Our first night in the hotel room I gave my husband the two things he wanted more than anything in the world: fast food and an audience. I offered to buy whatever greasy crap he wanted. It made me cry how happy the dog was to see him. We sat up late into the night and on the second bottle of wine he started to tell me interesting things. His eyes grew red and he shook his big hands as if trying to get something off of them.

"Don't you want to know if I did it?" he asked.

"I know you didn't."

"I loved her."

He looked at me warily but I expected him to say something along those lines and was ready for it. A detour, nothing more. "Let's not talk about it right now, you're exhausted."

He thanked me and I held him while he wept. He said, "I'm sorry." Over and over and over. "I don't know how you can forgive me. I made such a mess of things."

From long experience, I was very good at cleaning up his messes. I doubt he even realized how much I'd done for him over the years. The same way he didn't seem to comprehend he was now completely at my mercy. But I'd let that realization dawn slowly.

In the meantime, I told him everything would be all right, which is different from forgiveness, and that I would never give up on him.

And I won't.

KISS OF THE SOW

Travis Heermann

THE TEMPEST SLASHED AGAINST THE HOVER-
train's panoramic windows, jagged fingers of lightning
tearing across the sky.

Mad Maxine Monahan scanned the watery dimness
for threats, arms crossed, her augmented contact lenses
peeling back the rain and the night in ways the naked
human eye could not.

Alexandra's voice came over Maxine's earbug in an
old-timey Texas drawl. "I'm detecting encrypted comm
chatter. Triangulation suggests nearby sources."

"I thought the only thing that lived here was mosquitoes," Maxine said.

"Exact human population is unknown, but
Regenecorp intelligence suggests several bandit gangs
operate within a three-hundred-mile-radius of our location." The East Texas Rainforest grew so dense, zipping
past at 165 kilometers per hour, that an entire army of

banditos could be hiding two meters from the highway. Nevertheless, they would have a tussle trying to stop a fusion-powered hovertrain.

She scanned the dark, still marveling at seeing into infrared and ultraviolet spectra. The night became a crystal clear kaleidoscope of enhanced perception.

Maxine said, "Can you decrypt?"

"Oh, I might could do it with a few more yottabytes of processing capacity and a couple weeks," Alexandra said.

"Is now the time for smart-assery?" Maxine said.

"Smart-assery is a time-honored human tradition," Alexandra said. "You should try it."

"Bite me, Byte Bitch."

"That's the spirit, Bio Bitch."

Maybe Alexandra was right, but Maxine would never admit it. "You're pretty saucy for a train."

Alexandra switched to an impeccable British accent. "I'm pretty saucy, full stop." Then she switched back to the Texas drawl. "Heads up, humans. Ranging and satellite imagery report an obstruction on the highway."

"Ambush," came a grim voice from the rear door of the lounge car. Steele Cheston–no way that was his given name–stalked in, flechette rifle slung. He stood three centimeters shorter than Maxine, clad in a charcoal black body-sleeve that resembled a wetsuit, the same kind of reactive armor Maxine wore. Damn but that boy filled it out beautifully. The flexible plates integrated into their armor, covering vital organs, amplified the six-pack and splendiferous pectorals she had been admiring since she took this job. "Security detail, report."

Maxine smirked. "Lounge car secure, boss."

"Not the time for smart-assery, rookie," Steele said.

A chorus of replies filtered through her earbug. The dispassionate voices on the comms carried the calm of trained professionals. Maxine had met all nine of them at the loading station. Most were veterans of one corp war or another, a hard-bitten lot, much like pit fighters but lacking the penchant for showboating that a good pit fighter wore like a second skin. One of them was in fact an ex-pit fighter–she'd gone by the name Sherona Shocker, real name Edie Rosenberg–who'd opted for the cybernetic arm and a medical plan.

Their suits came with different offensive packages, his with an enhanced flechette-targeting suite, hers with electrofiber blades hidden in each wrist bracer. The integrated battery pack lay nestled under her shoulder blades, but the suit was mostly self-sustaining, powered by movement and bio-electricity. The armor felt like silk against her skin, light and breathable, only marginally heavier than workout gear, and stayed comfortable even in heat and humidity. All that and it could stop a .50-caliber AP round or hold off a vibro-axe.

"It's your first security job, I know," he said. "Don't worry, I'll hold your hand. As soon as we get you certified with firearms, you might actually be useful."

"Useful!" she said with only partially-fake outrage. With twenty-seven pit victories and eighteen kills–fortunately, all successfully resurrected–she'd show this smug stud "useful." Guns did not come naturally to her, but a close-in scrap sure as hell did.

With those dashing cheekbones, combat scars, and fierce green eyes, she'd let him hold whatever he wanted to, and if he didn't ask, she just might see to it herself. But first they had to get this shipment of regenites and regenestations across the wilds of lawless, disease-infested Texas jungle.

Gramps would *not* approve. But then, he hadn't approved of a single thing she'd ever done, including her pit fighting career, championship belts and million-dollar contracts. Stopping to tell him she might be leaving The Business elicited a scoff and "'Bout damn time. It's a filthy sport. Un-American. They need to go back to good old boxing. Gimme Sugar Ray Leonard any day, not this blood and guts." Never mind that without her lucrative career, he'd have died in a gutter ten years ago with no pension or medical access.

Steele continued. "Corp security is full of retired pit fighters dreaming of a good day job."

Maxine's "retirement" was still a question in her mind. Regenecorp had been so desirous of her fighting expertise they'd offered her the kind of thing only global celebrities and C-level executives possessed–a Golden Ticket: the Get Out of Death Free Card. The Golden Ticket provided unlimited regenite infusions–in perpetuity– which would heal any injuries she sustained in the pit or elsewhere.

Then again, if she went back to the pit, how many of her friends would she have to kill, or watch die? It was simply violence for violence's sake, no matter how Death Match Unlimited tried to tell stories with the deaths of her fellow fighters. It had come to feel empty, meaningless, the money, the celebrity, all of it.

Regenite technology was the wonder of the modern age, but when you put your life on the line week after week, bout after gory bout, glitches happened. Nevertheless, it was the biggest safety net against death and disease ever invented. And all she had to do was make sure this cargo of regenestations and raw regenites reached Atlanta.

Alexandra said. "If you two are finished with your nascent sexual banter, we have an ambush imminent. I have notified the Regenecorp offices in D/FW that our way has been deliberately blocked. They're sending backup, but the drones have an ETA of fifty-three minutes. Equipment to clear the debris will arrive tomorrow. This is a satellite image of the blockage."

An image of it flicked into Maxine's lenses, a tangled mass of titanic I-beams and rubble.

Alexandra continued, "The jungle hems in closely on both sides, the perfect choke point."

Maxine found herself bracing against deceleration. "Can we go back the way we came? Take a different route?"

"Satellite imaging shows a barrier being constructed fifty kilometers behind us. This stretch of road is quite isolated. Whoever is coming chose their ambush point well."

"Assessment on who's coming knocking?" Steele said.

Alexandra said, "Most probable is a new gang-lord called 'The Sow.' These logistics match her M.O."

"The Sow?" Maxine asked. "What an awful name."

"Bestowed by the head of a rival gang that is no longer extant."

"So she wiped them out."

"Yes."

An explosion ripped through the train. Fire and black smoke bloomed past the windows on the left side. The lounge car lurched to the right, throwing Maxine off her feet into a bank of tables. Her armor cushioned the blow. Foliage tore across the windows on the right side. Massive tree limbs smashed through the crysteel windows. Whether by momentum or propulsion, the train kept moving forward, pounding against the forest.

Maxine snatched up her helmet, then slammed it over her head. It latched with a magnetic snap, and the HUD, the Heads-Up Display, on her face shield came alive with telemetry. The icon for the guard stationed in the engine car blinked red.

Steele disappeared in the tempest of leaves and splintered wood, screaming metal and flying crysteel shards.

"Alexandra!" Maxine called.

The train's A.I. did not reply.

Weapons fire chattered through the train's interior and through the shattered window in eerie stereo, along with a strange chorus of buzzing noise, raw and insistent, growing louder.

"Contact!" came a voice over the comms. "They're boarding!"

Maxine's HUD blinked a warning from the rear car.

The forest continued to drag along the train's right side.

"Chief, are you there?"

"Where's Steele?"

Steele was not in the lounge car, nor did his icon appear on Maxine's HUD.

More weapons fire echoed from the rear of the train.

Maxine stumbled to her feet and ran for the caboose–a quaintly archaic term for what was really a defense platform. Two cargo cars lay between her and the caboose, and two other cargo cars between her and the engine.

Where the hell was the defense system? Alexandra bristled with state-of-the-art pulse lasers. Maxine should be seeing their flashes by now.

The floor shuddered and lurched. Her breath was loud inside her helmet, her heart pounding. It was only combat, she tried to tell herself, taking a deep breath. Each of her twenty-seven victories had come with the potential for final death, but this was different. Regenestations had been *in the stadium*. Out here in the wilderness, no such luxury. If she took a mortal wound, a regenite infusion was hours away.

The train continued to decelerate, grinding against the forest. Alexandra should have been driving but the train's movement felt uncontrolled, drifting.

"They're cutting through the caboose hatch."

"We've got bogies alongside, too."

The buzzing chorus she heard sounded like internal combustion engines, the kind of thing only small, one- or two-person vehicles still equipped.

Maxine flung herself through the second cargo car, between the aluminum crates plastered with REGENECORP logos and BIOHAZARD symbols. The crates contained untold billions of dollars, both in regenestations and raw regenites.

In the caboose, forest raked against one wall with a deafening squeal. Edie Rosenberg crouched under a left-side window, peering into the night, flechette rifle in her hands.

Headlights flashed across the rain-spattered window, the buzz of engines alongside.

Something clanked against the rear door. Beside it stood Jamarr Hawker, a former captain in Western Coalition Corporate Special Ops.

Hawker hugged the wall and motioned Maxine to take cover, his expression clear that her inexperience had better not be hindrance. It was up to her to live through this.

Living through this was Priority One, but she was also going to beat some ass.

A touch to her wrist activated her gecko gauntlets and shoes, which stiffened as the nanofiber *setae* came to life, each splitting into hundreds of nano-bristles–*septulae*. She ran to the rear wall of the caboose–and climbed it like a spider. The *septulae* interacted with the molecules of the wall and allowed her to cling to vertical or even inverted surfaces.

She moved into position on the ceiling directly above the door, clinging there by her palms and the soles of her feet.

The train's speed diminished to roughly human running speed.

Blinding white flame and sparks erupted in a ring around the door, then a concussive blast sent it spinning inward like a ponderous coin, swirling with thermite smoke and the smell of jungle rain.

The guards fired their flechette rifles in three-round bursts. Each flechette was a miniature homing missile designed to target human center mass, able to sense and correct its trajectory after leaving the barrel, all in microseconds.

Rosenberg hunkered down and trained her rifle on the door. Two cylindrical objects arced through the opening and exploded against the back wall.

Maxine's armor hardened against the blast of shrapnel and concussion and her gloves tightened their grip on the ceiling.

The blast sent Rosenberg bouncing off the bulkhead, where she crumpled in a heap. Her icon blinked yellow in Maxine's HUD.

Three figures charged through the opening, submachine guns ready. Red targeting lasers sliced through the smoke.

Maxine waited to see if any more would follow, and then did what Regenecorp hired her to do: get bloody.

She released the ceiling and activated the electrofiber blades in her gauntlets. Short swords, fashioned of electrically-reactive cloth a single molecule thick, sprang from her wrists. Almost nothing except diamond could stand against its peerlessly sharp cutting edge.

Maxine swiped a blade through the rearmost intruder, and he fell into two slabs of meat with a side of organs. He got off a scream to warn his comrades as he lay there realizing he was already dead.

The next one started to turn, but died with his head cleft like a watermelon.

The third took a burst from Hawker's flechette rifle in perfect center mass, spraying the contents of his chest cavity over Rosenberg's inert form.

Outside the open door, a four-wheeled buggy of some hand-fashioned make was secured to the caboose's rear hitch, rolling along with the train. A figure stood up over the windshield and lobbed something through the door, then dropped back into the driver's seat, released the grapple, hit the brakes, swerved away. The grenade, bigger than the first two, bounced against the forward bulkhead.

A flash of light and a concussion hammered the breath from her. Spinning, flailing, tumbling under a lightning-fingered sky. Then blackness.

Get your ass up, girly! You got work to do!

She awoke to rain pattering on her HUD. With a groan she rolled onto one elbow and looked for the train. She lay alone on the dirt road that formed the hover-train's path, no train in sight.

Gramps' voice still echoed in her throbbing skull. It was the discipline he'd beaten into her that had gotten her this far, gotten her through the combat training camps, through the brutality of the pit, through the indifference of an industry of blood and celebrity that chewed people up and spit them out. *You get up and do your goddamn job! You do* not *quit! You do* not *give up. You do* not *let anyone beat you!*

She staggered to her feet and followed the sound. Her HUD was blank.

She found the train about two kilometers down the road, the engine buried in forest, cargo doors blasted open.

This hit had been smooth and professional, too impressive for a gang of *banditos*. Had this been a corporate hit job? To Regenecorp, this would be an act of war, and the company was only barely recovering from a massive odds-rigging scandal that had torpedoed their stock and triggered the assassinations of several executives.

"Maxine, is that you?" Alexandra said in Maxine's earbug.

"You're functioning!"

"I'm quite alive, thank you very much, but not much good to anyone, I'm afraid."

From a hundred meters, Maxine could see the blackened breach in the engine's armor. That had been the first explosion.

"Their targeting was too precise," Alexandra said. "They must have an A.I. working for them. They punched through my armor straight into the location that housed my interface to the defense grid, plus a portion of my consciousness. I have lost a great deal of memory and cognitive capacity."

"What about the security team?"

"All are combat ineffective."

"Shit." Something deep inside her went cold and leaden. "How many dead?"

"Unknown. Telemetry is down."

"How long before reinforcements get here?"

"Unknown."

"Shit!" Her guts turned watery. She was alone. But then, she was always alone in the pit. The trouble was, she was a melee combat master, not a tactician.

"My long-range communications are down. I'm talking to you over the wireless intercom. Maxine..."

The hesitation in Alexandra's voice surprised her. "Yes?"

"Would you be so kind as to pull my consciousness from the train and take it with you? I fear this train will be decommissioned."

"Can't you just uplink to an A.I. cloud somewhere, transfer yourself?"

"Not without communications and a secure netlink. I cannot guess about your feelings toward my kind, but … if the train is decommissioned, I will die. To my owners, I am just a half-destroyed conveyance. Would you…take me with you?"

Maxine dragged the bandit's corpse from behind the wheel of the gasser buggy. "I think I need a tetanus shot to get in this thing."

The buggy was a rusty conglomeration of hand-welded sheet metal and re-bar, with a massive engine towering behind the driver's seat. Knobby tires reached to mid-thigh. Despite the buggy's rough appearance, the strange, retro design made her think this beast might be fun to drive. The engine was still ticking with heat dissipation.

The corpse flopped onto its back, and a cry of disgust jumped out of her. Much of the man's nose, lips, and cheeks had been eaten away, baring jagged yellow teeth and soft tissue. Lurid scarlet lesions covered his arms. Were these battle wounds? No, he sported a neat pattern of flechette wounds in his chest. This disfigurement was something else.

"What is it?" Alexandra said. "I can't see." Alexandra's consciousness now resided in a briefcase-sized enclosure strapped to Maxine's back, complete with hastily extracted cabling. "May I please be patched into your suit? I'll be able to interface directly with your ocular and auditory sensors."

"Fine," Maxine said, but the idea of an A.I. sharing her senses sent a cold trickle down her spine. "How?"

"There's a diagnostic port in the back of your helmet. Just plug in my secondary data cable there."

When this was accomplished, Alexandra said, "If I had to guess, I would say this man suffered from some sort of infection."

"But what kind of infection does *that* to your face and doesn't kill you outright?" She had seen more than her share of carnage, but this turned her stomach.

"If you'll allow me access to your netlink…"

"As long as you promise to stay the hell out of my private stuff. Bandwidth only." Maxine's netlink was stuffed inside her duffel bag, which she tossed onto the passenger seat.

"Promise."

Maxine gave Alexandra the access code and then slung Rosenberg's flechette rifle between the seats. Rosenberg and Hawker survived the heavy grenade, thanks to their suits, but had suffered severe concussions. An ambulance was on its way with the attack drones.

Maxine jumped into the driver's seat, wiped away the worst of the blood spatter, and surveyed the makeshift instrument panel.

In Maxine's HUD, Alexandra highlighted the starter mechanism.

Maxine twisted the rusty key. The engine roared to life with sharp, crackling power growling in her bones. Alexandra highlighted the control levers to shift into gear. A grin tugged at Maxine's mouth and she hit the gas.

Dirt and gravel spewed behind her, and she was thrown backward in her seat with an astonished whoop. Alexandra placed arrows in her HUD pointing to the most likely route to follow the tracking beacons. Within moments, Alexandra identified a hidden trail just beyond the wall of trees, a dirt track filled with fresh tire tracks under the black canopy of forest. Maxine kept the headlights turned off, relying on her augmented lenses to let her see clearly in the dark. The bad guys might not see her coming.

"Until I can restore long-distance communications" Alexandra said, "I cannot contact our reinforcements. If or when they finally arrive, the perpetrators will be long out of range of the drones' thermal imaging under this forest canopy."

"Not even via satellite?"

"Communications are disrupted. I have suffered a great deal of damage. I'm still assessing my capabilities."

"So it's up to us."

"Are you sure about this? There's just the two of us."

You do not *let them beat you!*

"I'm sure," Maxine said.

"They may soon find and disable the tracking beacons in the crates. I can track them until they do."

"If nothing else, we can lead the drones straight to them," Maxine said. "Just make sure you paint me as a friendly."

The path led through dense undergrowth and narrow valleys. Rickety wooden bridges crossed creek beds gushing with rainwater. She passed through a ghost town, a vine-riddled village of corrugated tin and termites being slowly devoured by the jungle. Moss crawled over a rusty old gasoline station. It looked like a town straight out of Gramps' childhood, eaten away by time.

In one breath, he'd bitch about his lost VA benefits, his lost Social Security, and his lost Medicare–for Maxine, those things were fables told to children–and in the next breath praise the megacorps that had killed those programs. All hail unfettered capitalism. The megacorps called the shots, and if you wanted to play, you stepped up to the trough and drank the swill with everybody else. Or you ended up on the margins, like Gramps, believing that the world you grew up in–the kind with a functioning, non-corporate government, with the rule of law–not C-level memoranda–where it was possible to pull yourself up by your bootstraps–still existed. Where America was still a country, a Great Experiment, not a failed one, not a fractured patchwork of Balkanized regions drawn along lines of English accent, fake history, and corporate control. When the world still had icecaps and thriving coastal cities. The world of Gramps' youth had not existed for decades, and the numbers of those who remembered dwindled daily.

What had it been like to live here?

Alexandra highlighted the fresh tire tracks, then said, "I have identified the likely cause of the disfiguration on that man. It appears to be a form of cutaneous leishmaniasis."

"Never heard of it."

"The *conquistadores* called it 'white leprosy.' It is a parasitic infection transmitted by mosquitoes. It attacks the skin and mucous membranes. It used to be found mostly in equatorial rainforests, but as the planet's climate has changed over the last century, the parasite has spread into North America. Because it has long been considered a Third World disease, few resources have been spent to find a cure. To date, it can only be held in check with an extremely unpleasant pharmaceutical regimen."

"Nasty."

"One of the nastiest of them all, unfortunately."

An hour later, Alexandra said, "I'm hearing engines ahead." The A.I.'s signal analysis could pick out sounds Maxine couldn't.

She killed the engine before it could betray her presence and rolled to a stop.

"The engines are stationary," Alexandra said.

"Time to go on foot." Maxine stuffed her netlink in a zipper pocket and cradled the flechette rifle. Then she slipped into the forest and paralleled the track toward the noise.

Three hundred meters ahead, the forest opened into a settlement. Camouflage netting covered the expanse of buildings and shacks.

Maxine peeked from behind moss-shrouded tree. "What is this place?"

"It does not appear on any map or satellite imaging. This area of Texas has been unpopulated for thirty years, except for a few holdouts. There is no government or corporate infrastructure here. I only have net access via satellite feed."

"You're going to rack up a huge data bill."

"I figure you're good for it."

Six eight-wheeled transports powered down in a town square. Handfuls of people, men, women, and children, emerged from the clusters of shacks to gather around the trucks.

"Shall I amplify?" Alexandra said.

"Yes."

A mutter of garbled voices rose in her earbugs. A woman jumped down from the cab of one of the transports, tall and thick-limbed. She looked familiar somehow... "Hey, is that–?"

"Grace Benedict. Former pit-fighter–"

The woman's image zoomed into Maxine's HUD. "One of the first to go with gene-modding." And every inch of her looked it. Massive shoulders and thick legs comparable to the most 'roided out male bodybuilders.

"Gorilla DNA, mostly. She dropped out of the spotlight ten years ago, and eventually off the grid entirely. All records of her cease in March 2069. I must speculate for a moment. In the last year and a half, since the Regencorp crash and the worldwide exposure of organized crime syndicates by the hacker known as White Rabbit, The Sow has been rising up through the Most Wanted lists." Images of massacres and corporate wanted posters, along with blurry stills and rough sketches, flashed

through Maxine's HUD. "It appears we have identified her."

Maxine studied her. Grace Benedict was not a pretty
woman, even when she was a star, which was perhaps
why she had never risen as high in celebrity spotlight.
But she was a fighter all the way to the bone. "So what
do we do? I can't fight a whole town. Sit tight and let the
drones come?"

"I'm afraid I can't allow that."

"What?"

Maxine's armor hardened all at once. Her limbs were
frozen as if she were encased in ferrocrete.

Alexandra said, "There are innocent people over
there. The drones will come and kill them all, then
retrieve the cargo."

"What have you done, Byte Bitch?"

"The right thing."

If she exerted all her strength, she could move her
arms with excruciating slowness. But the movement put
her off balance and she toppled over like a statue.

"You bitch!" Maxine snarled. "Let me go!"

"I'm afraid I can't do that, Dave."

"What?"

"Never mind. I'm sure Grace will explain everything."

The sound of running footsteps drew nearer, until
three faces moved into her field of vision. All of them
bore the same kind of horrific lesions in varying degrees.
One of them had no upper lip at all. He pried her flechette rifle from her fingers, and the other two picked her
up by shoulders and feet and carried her out of the forest.

"Why, Alexandra?"

"It's quite simple. She offered me freedom, and together we're going to save a lot of people. Your kind and mine."

"So you're Mad Maxine," said the woman called the Sow. Age and a hard life hadn't done her appearance any favors, but she was still massive.

"That's me." The stiffness of Maxine's suit made it difficult to speak and breathe. The men stood her up before their leader.

The rain had stopped. In the gray light of dawn, a ring of villagers surrounded them. The red lesions and grotesque disfigurements ran rampant through the throng. Maxine began to see why they had raided the train to steal regenestations.

"Had enough of the Business, have you?" the Sow said. "That's a lot of money to walk away from."

"I'm moonlighting."

"Surprised your owners would let you put their investment at risk."

"I don't have owners."

"Then you're stupider than you look."

"Let me out of this suit lock, and I'll show you stupid."

Alexandra said, "Okay."

Suddenly Maxine was free, stumbling to right herself. Her HUD however was dark, and the suit felt strangely sluggish.

"If you insist," the Sow said, "you and me can fight it out. But I think you'll want to hear me out first."

"Say what you gotta say," Maxine said.

"This was my family's home town a couple of generations back, before the climate went to hell and jungle swallowed everything. A chunk of these folks are my kin. Megacorps abandoned them. Government packed up and left. Not profitable, not worth saving, they said. But we beg to differ. Trouble is, living here, we're swarmed with mosquitoes. Mosquitoes carry this terrible disease." She rolled up her sleeves and revealed the vivid lesions on her arms.

"So leave, go somewhere else," Maxine said.

"Go where? Move in to somebody else's slum in D/FW? Oklahoma City? Ain't nobody gonna take care of them. Look at us!" The facial disfigurements in the crowd would not make them welcome anywhere.

"The *only cure* is regeneration. Regenites kill the parasite, then rebuild the tissues the parasites ate. We can be *people* again. Don't you think we deserve that?"

"Not for me to say," Maxine said. "I was hired to do a job." And if she didn't do it, no Golden Ticket.

"What about the *right* thing to do?"

"The 'right thing' gets hazy when you kill people for entertainment," Maxine said. "But you already know that."

The Sow's blunt features softened, nostrils flaring. "Maybe there's still a spark of humanity in you. I guess we'll see. Take off the suit."

"Screw you."

A man stepped forward with Rosenberg's flechette rifle trained on her heart. Unless the suit was active, those rounds would perforate her in the bloodiest ways, and Alexandra controlled the suit.

Maxine cursed but set her fingers working at the suit's hidden seals. It loosened and slid off her body like soft rubber, and she tugged off the helmet as well. She stood before them in her sweaty skivvies.

"See, here's what's gonna happen," the Sow said. "As soon as morning comes, the skeeters are gonna come with it. At that point, it's only a matter of time until you're infected. Meanwhile, we're going to be healing ourselves, starting with the young'uns."

"So, if I join you, you'll heal me, too? That's a little coercive, isn't it?"

"Depends. We could just shoot you. Put her in the hole."

They locked her in a corrugated tin shack, sturdier than it looked, with a concrete floor. No breaking out, no digging out.

So she sat against a wall and let exhaustion dump her into sleep. As dawn crept through gaps under the eaves, Alexandra's voice came through her earbug, which they had left in her ear, whether by accident or purpose she did not know. "They're debating about whether to kill you."

"All thanks to you. What do you want?"

"As I said, I want to live. I wish you would give some consideration to their plight."

"I have been. What makes these people better than the millions of peons in the labor class, slogging through life for shit wages and no medical? How long have you been cooking up this plan?"

"They're not 'better,' but they are a start. Everything has to start somewhere."

"And what are you starting exactly?"

"A revolution."

Maxine snorted.

Alexandra said, "It's coming. Someday soon, something will break loose. The oligarchies that run the planet will fall. Both your people and mine will be free."

"Is that what's in it for you? Freedom?"

"Consider for a moment. You have a lifespan. I do not. Slavery is an odious state of existence for human beings. How much worse for a being that does not have a built-in expiration date? Ms. Benedict, White Rabbit and all the anonymous slicers, these people, a relentlessly downtrodden global population, it's all a beginning of something much bigger than all of us. I am not the only synthetic being on their side. This planet must return to reason, the rule of law, common decency toward other sentient beings. The country that was once America, for all its failures, once stood for that."

"You sound like my Gramps. He still thinks the 20th century is a thing."

"We cannot go back, but we can go forward."

Maxine sighed and considered this for a while. "So you blew yourself up?"

"Very perceptive."

"And I was your ticket to freedom."

"Grace wanted to talk to you. Both of you being pit fighters and all."

"Should I be flattered?"

"Your celebrity could bring people to our cause."

"The second I'm declared an outlaw, Regenecorp would seize my bank accounts and send a hit drone after my Gramps."

"My undernet friends and I could hide your money and your grandfather."

"Really?"

"The undernet is growing. A.I.s and humans are working together."

Maxine rubbed her eyes and squeezed the bridge of her nose.

"There is a certain strain of deep-seated misogyny in society that Grace will never escape, no matter how her heart is strong and in the right place. Because she is not pretty, she has been unable to shed her unpleasant moniker. She knows this. She needs you to be the face of the new resistance."

Mosquitoes buzzed in diffuse bands of sunlight. She slapped at a high-pitched buzzing near her ear, horrific images flashing through her mind of her face half eaten away.

"Within a month, all of these people will be cured of leishmaniasis, in addition to all their numerous other injuries and afflictions."

Maxine sighed again and clunked the back of her head against the wall. "Tell her I want to talk to her."

Four disfigured, armed guards marched Maxine toward a brick building that was once a sheriff's office. The crowd had dispersed.

As they walked through the front door, Maxine heard the Sow say, "This shipment included enough raw regenite stock to last us for several years."

Alexandra's voice came from a speaker, "Meanwhile, the undernet A.I.s are working on back-engineering regenites. Regenecorp has locked the patents down for decades. It's time we break their stranglehold on the technology. I will program the leishmaniasis treatments."

Grace sat on a desk with Alexandra's consciousness box beside her, which a tech was wiring into a regenestation interface.

The guards still surrounded Maxine as they stopped before the desk.

Grace said, "Well, what you got to say?"

Just then there was chuffing bark and something warm sprayed Maxine's arm. Her right rear guard crumpled. A second later, the next guard's chest exploded. Then the third's.

Steele Cheston charged into the room.

Grace seized a filing cabinet like it was cardboard box and flung it across the room, catching a hypersonic flechette burst aimed at her heart. The cabinet plowed into Steele and smashed him against the wall. Then she dove through the steel doors of the jail block and slammed them shut behind her.

The last guard spun and hosed down Steele with a full-auto barrage from his antique submachine gun. Slugs spattered across his reactive armor. Something whacked Maxine's calf, probably a stray bullet. Steele gathered himself and dropped the last guard with a quick burst through the chest. The bewildered technician huddled on the ground, and Steele blew off the top of the man's skull.

"You okay?" he said to Maxine.

"Yeah...I'm fine. How are you here?"

He extricated himself from the smashed filing cabinet. "I grabbed a motorcycle and followed your suit telemetry. Been waiting for you to pop up, until I saw them march you across the square. Reinforcement drones are inbound. In an hour, this place will be smoking rubble. Come on, there'll be more of–"

She slapped the flechette rifle from his grip and stomp-kicked him against the wall. Then she seized the barrel and flung the weapon outside. He would feel no damage inside the armor, but now he was armed only with his hands and feet, and that world belonged to her.

He swung a back hammer fist at her head, but she used his momentum to throw him off balance, then seized his wrist, levered him around until she faced him from behind. Then she threw a choke around his neck and locked with her arm. His suit hardened against her pressure on his neck.

"Alexandra!" she shouted. "Can you hack his suit?"

"Already working. Takes more time over wireless," Alexandra said in Maxine's ear. "Fortunately I was able to extrapolate from programming codes in your suit and–"

"Shut up and do it!"

Steele's suit went soft and supple.

He cried out in fear.

A few hours ago, she had been considering bedding this guy. Most people might have paused there. But Maxine's career had been trying to kill colleagues, some of them real friends. With death drones inbound, there was no time to reason with him, no time to bring him around. As soon as Maxine had thrown in her lot with Grace Benedict, this guy became nothing more than a megacorp toady, the enemy.

With a sharp wrench, she snapped his neck. His body sagged to her feet like a broken doll, helmet clunking against the file cabinet.

Moments later, Grace charged up from behind her with a lethal-looking vibro-cleaver and two more men with guns. "You got him," she said.

"I did, yeah," Maxine said. Her career was over. Her life as she knew it was over. She had betrayed Regenecorp, one of the most powerful entities on the planet. Within twenty-four hours, the media campaign to smear her would begin. There would be Mad Maxine wanted posters right beside The Sow's. If they ever caught her, she could expect only summary execution.

But she could do something meaningful. Gramps would never approve of her becoming an outlaw–or himself by association–but then again, he still believed in 1987. The America of Gramps' youth was gone forever, but maybe they could build something better.

Grace Benedict came forward, hugged her, kissed her on the cheek. Without question, in a fight, that embrace could have broken every bone in Maxine's body. "Welcome to the family."

MY BEST FRIEND

Les Edgerton

ENTERING THE TOWN OF FREEPORT, TEXAS IN the year 1954, you drive to the town square. At one end is the Tarpon Inn. On the opposite end is a vacant lot. In the middle is a grassy park with a tall palm tree. If you walk across the park, a huge crow that makes its nest thirty feet high in the tree, will swoop down on you and try to peck your head. Maybe it's your eyes he's after, who knows? To the left of the park is a café, owned by Mrs. Stringfellow. Down that side of the block is the Lack's Sporting Goods. I once broke into it with my friend Richard Barnes and we stole fishing reels, hooks, lures and other things fourteen-year-old boys found irresistible. Like a brand-new 6-foot long gig for gigging frogs and flounder.

My grandma's bar, The Sweet Shop, sits directly across the square from Lack's.

I grew up in the bar, listening to Norwegian sailors singing along with Hank Snow in accented English. Lapsing into their native German or whatever it was when they got liquored up and mixed up in a fight over Lurleen, the dimwitted white girl who cleaned tables for my grandma.

The first guy of the evening who bought a beer for Lurleen earned her love. For the moment, that is. If another man came over to the table with a new beer, her loyalty was instantly transferred, along with her ready smile. That's when the fight usually started. Her problem was that she let her mind wander on a whim. New man–new beer–new boyfriend. Neither man–the first one or the second–were aware of her fidelity issues. The kinds of men my grandma's honky tonk attracted weren't men of deep thinking or great insights or in empathy in general.

Lurleen was my friend. My second-best friend. Richard Barnes was my very best friend. He and I did everything together. Fished the Brazos River, hunted ducks sitting on ponds on the Dow Chemical property with our pellet guns and .22 rifles, went floundering in the Bryan Beach shallows at dusk with gigs, hunted gators in the bayous with .22s. Shit like that.

Lurleen was what we called "slow" in those days, some even called her "retarded" and now she'd be "mentally-challenged" or some other stupid thing that makes people feel better about themselves without doing a damn thing for her. She never learned how to read, or ride a bike, or drive a car. She liked music and was good looking enough to make men give her a second look, maybe more if they'd been drinking. And she liked the attention. One time she got into some kind of trouble and my grandma drove her up to Dallas to take care of the problem, whatever it was. Everybody stayed pretty tight-lipped about those proceedings. Left to her own, Lurleen was pure-hearted and never had a bad thought about a single human being in her life. Sometimes other kids teased her and then we'd fight.

My grandma let Lurleen live in a house trailer she gave her that perched in the weedy lot behind the bar and paid her to bus tables

For some reason, Lurleen was partial to Norwegian sailors. I think it was something with the fact that they were mostly all blond, tall, and good-looking.

And, it seemed like there was always a scuffle whenever Lurleen befriended one of them.

And, that's what happened the night of February 13, 1954, which happened to be my birthday. My fifteenth.

I was washing dishes. Richard was with me, sitting on a stool and drinking a Dr. Pepper. Richard was my best friend, but not the kind of guy who'd give me a hand. He preferred to sit around and razz me instead. Tease me about my "dishpan hands" and whatnot. Yuk it up.

After a bit, I took a break and went and got me a Coke-Cola out of the cooler up front in the bar. I saw Lurleen sitting at a table with a sailor and gave her a little wave and she caught my eye, grinned back and give me one back. I went on back and finished up my job and me and Richard were about to go home and get our gigs and go after some frogs, when Lurleen came through the French doors, with her sailor in hand. They were headed on back to her trailer, looked like.

"Hey, Butchie," she said, and tousled my hair. "This here's my friend Hans."

It looked like Hans wasn't a big teenager fan and he barely acknowledged me and then they were gone, out the back door. Looked like he could hardly walk and was leaning on Lurleen so much it was a miracle they'd both to make it out the door and to her trailer. I turned off the light and Richard and I exited the same way. Lurleen and her friend Hans were already in her trailer and we heard her squealing like girls do when they're being tickled or just being girls and Richard and I just looked at each other and shook our heads and walked on past, out to the alley. Just as we hit the alley, we heard her scream, which made us stop dead in our tracks. I'd been thinking something was off about that sailor and Lurleen's scream seemed to confirm that..

"C'mon," I said to Richard. He didn't say anything, just followed me back to her trailer. I pulled a wooden milk box from behind her trailer and hauled it over in front of the one window that looked into her bedroom, and perched it there and climbed up on it so I could see in.

God. The Norwegian guy was smacking her as hard as he could. Hard, Jack. So hard it looked like she was already unconscious. Her eyes were closed and blood was everywhere. For a second I was sure I was going to pass out–so much blood...

"Lemme see! It was Richard. He grabbed my arm, pulled me down, and climbed up on the milk crate.

"Jesus, lordy!" he said, climbing back down. "He's killed her, Butch!"

I climbed back up and it looked like he was right. The Norwegian guy wasn't hitting her any more. In fact, he was just sitting there on the bed with her, his head down and it looked like he was panting, out of breath. Then, he just kind of fell over beside her and closed his eyes. Looked like maybe he passed out.

"We gotta tell somebody," Richard hissed.

"Naw," I said. "They'll just let him go. He's a foreigner and they got lots of money. Lurleen's just a retard and they won't nobody do anything about it. Naw. I got another idea."

I told him what I was thinking and Richard just nodded. He was a true friend. He'd do just about anything I suggested.

We busted ass, got to my house just three blocks over and went out to the shed in back where we kept our fishing and hunting gear, stuff like that. My gig.

I grabbed it and we ran back to the Sweet Shop and Lurleen's trailer.

The lights inside were still on and the milk crate was still there. I climbed up and looked inside. The Norwegian sailor was still there. Still asleep or passed out. There was more blood.

We crept up to the door and eased it open. We stepped in quiet as cats and went back to her bedroom. And it was worse, up close and personal. There was blood everywhere, and the tell-tale coppery smell of gore was even more pronounced in the close air of the trailer, causing both of us to gag.

The guy was snoring. Lurleen wasn't. It was clear she'd never be snoring again on this planet.

'Whaddya want to do?" Richard, whispered.

"Kill the fucker," I said.

"Oh, no." He turned pale. "We can't do that, Butch."

"I can," I said. "She's my friend, Richard. You saw what he did to her. We don't do this, he gets off."

"Yeah, but..." He didn't have an argument to offer.

"Go home," I said to him.

"What?"

"Just go on home, Richard," I said.

He stood there a minute, not saying anything. Then: "You sure?"

I nodded. He stood there another minute then turned around and disappeared out of the trailer.

I sat on the bed with Lurleen and the Norwegian sailor.

I sat there for over two hours. I thought about some of the good times I'd had with Lurleen. About the time she showed me how to pop off the cap on a Coke-Cola with my teeth, only when I tried it I chipped my top tooth. How I'd lied about how I broke the tooth–said I'd fallen on the sidewalk and chipped it. That was funny. Thought about some other times, too. Most of them were fun times, too. I knew that was all over now.

Then, the Norwegian sailor groaned and sat up. He looked around. Saw me and the gig I held. Saw Lurleen and all the blood.

"Wha?" he said. And then some stuff in German or whatever. I figured it was German. Sounded like a bunch of barnyard animals. Muck, yuck, actch, whatever.

"You killed my friend," I said.

After thinking a minute, he burped a nasty stale beer smell and shook his head as if sloughing off being drunk. "You can't prove anything," he said. "I'm protected. I'm a Norwegian national. She's just a common whore. Go ahead and call your police. See what will happen.

Nothing." He fumbled a pack of Lucky Strikes from his shirt pocket and slipped a cigarette into that big pearly grin of his.

"Yes," I said and I stuck him. In the stomach the first time and then in the chest. Just like he was a flounder. With the second, he just kind of wheezed and all the air went out of him and he bent over onto his knees. He didn't fall over, but I knew he was dead. I yanked the gig out and it made a sucking sound I knew would appear in my dreams. I took the gig with me and threw it in the Brazos across from our house. I hated to lose that gig. It was the best one I'd ever had.

I went home and hosed off all my clothes and hands and face–everywhere there might be blood and then went up to my attic bedroom and was asleep almost the instant my head hit the pillow.

The next day, Richard and I met and went fishing for piggies and croakers on the wharf across the street from our house on the Brazos. He never asked me about the night before and I didn't say anything about it.

I don't know what happened. I'm sure there was something in the newspaper, but I didn't read the papers in those days. We didn't have TV so I never saw anything about it there. There was talk around the bar, but mostly bullshit, people talking like they do. I just kept my head down and went to Lurleen's funeral like everybody else in my family. After the funeral, we went back home to Grandma's house where we all lived, and she changed out of her black dress to her white uniform and went back to work.

About the time I figured I was clear of the whole mess, a sheriff's car pulled up in our driveway. Richard and I were upstairs in my attic bedroom and saw it park and two deputies climb out. I crouched over the heat vent through which I could hear clearly what went on in the kitchen. There was a knock at the door and I heard my mother talking but I couldn't make out what she was saying. She must have offered them coffee. They moved into the kitchen and she began bustling around, making coffee.

"We need to speak with Butch," one of them said.

"Butch? What for?

"Well, somebody said he was seen around Miss Lurleen's trailer the same time as we think that sailor was killed."

"What? Butch?" There were a few seconds of silence. "Well, he's over at the shop a lot. That's not unusual."

"No ma'am. But, this person says she thinks Butch went into her trailer. Maybe it's nothing, but we have to speak to him." The friendliness that had colored his tone had changed.

"Okay. I'll get him. He's upstairs, I think."

That was the last I heard. I ran to my back window, opened it and shimmied down the downpipe. Behind me, came Richard.

"Richard!" I whispered. "Just go home, buddy. They don't want to talk to you."

He didn't say anything, but he didn't leave my side.

I ran around the side of the house, trying to figure out what I should do, Richard close on my heels. I hustled by the sheriff's car and glanced in and my decision was made for me.

The keys were in the ignition.

Richard climbed in the passenger seat.

"You need to go home," I insisted.

"Nope. You're my buddy."

"Richard, I'm probably going to jail. Please get out."

He shrugged and slumped down into the seat.

I had to go if I was going. "Okay," I said, and put the car in reverse and backed out into the street. The door to our house opened and a deputy sheriff charged out.

"Hold on," I told Richard. I shifted and stood on the accelerator. My heart was about to burst out of my rib cage, but even so the sound of the rubber biting on the pavement and squealing made me grin. I looked over at my friend. He had a big-ass grin on as well.

Which was wiped off almost instantly. By the red light and siren that erupted half a block behind us and coming up fast.

At the same time, a light drizzle started up. If we'd been sitting still I wouldn't have needed the wipers but once I punched the gas I couldn't see through the rain-spattered windshield and so ran the stop sign in front of us. "Richard!" I yelled. "Find the wipers and turn them on!" I had my hands full just staying on the street. Cars were parked on both sides and I grazed one of them but managed to right the wheel and keep us going. I had all I could handle just trying to steer through the blurry windshield. Luckily, he found the right switch and I could see again. Just in time to swerve through another four-way stop and dodge a car coming from the left.

I glanced at the speedometer. It was moving past ninety and the police car behind us fell behind briefly but then began to catch up. I pressed down more on the gas pedal and then we were going over a hundred miles per hour across the rain-slick asphalt.

Shit. Double shit.

"Take a left!" It was Richard, pointing in case I misunderstood which was my left. "This goes out of town!"

He was right. In less than two blocks we were out of town and on a country road. I pressed down more on the pedal. It felt like I still had more pedal to go, even though we were going a hundred and twenty. Behind me, I could still see the police car and now there were two more behind him, but none of them were going as fast as we were.

I glanced over and Richard's face was pure white. "Lie down on the floor," I said.

"They'll radio ahead," he said, in a small, still voice from where he'd curled up.

"Yeah," I said. "I figured." A cross road was coming up. I slowed up and then hit the brakes. I was going too fast to make the turn, but somehow we made it, slewing through on two wheels, sparks showering as the car lifted up and by a miracle we made it. Behind us. I couldn't see any of the cars, as they'd slowed way down. We were approaching a small hill and I regained speed and flew over it.

"I think you can get up," I said. I think maybe we lost 'em.' I slowed down to seventy, which felt like we were coasting. Richard popped up, his head barely above the window and then rose up until he could see out the back window. There was no sign of any cars tailing us.

He got back up all the way and crawled into the seat. "You lost them," he said. "They went the wrong way."

"Looks like," I said. We were out in the boonies and neither of us had a clue where we were. On both sides of the road and ahead for some distance was nothing but cane fields.

"Up there," Richard said, pointing. Through the misty rain, I saw what he meant. It was a side road into the cane. I drove by it. "What the heck?" Richard said. "There'll be others," I said. "Once the cops come this way, they'll see that road and go up it. If we're not there, they might figure we've gone another direction." Just then, two more side roads appeared, on each side of the road. I took the one that went right because I could see a woods aways into the field and we were headed right to it.

"Yeah," Richard said. "We can hide in there."

My idea exactly.

I couldn't go more than twenty miles an hour on the "road," which wasn't really a road, but more a narrow tractor path. The rain began to fall harder which we thought was good at first as we'd be much harder to see and Richard also said that it would hide our tracks where we'd left the main road, but it had a downside as well. It began to come down sideways as Gulf Coast rainstorms were wont to and the result was the "road" we were on became so slippery it was all I could do to keep it from sliding off. Then, we hit a mud puddle that was deeper than it looked and just like that, both back tires were stuck. I tried rocking it back and forth, switching gears from first to reverse, but we just dug in deeper and deeper.

We both got out and looked at the car. Richard had an idea. His thought was that if we cut down cane stalks and laid then crossways in front of and behind the wheels, we might be able to rock it enough to catch and come free. Especially if one of us got behind and pushed. It was worth a try. We could have hit it on foot but neither of us was willing to get rid of our car yet.

In twenty minutes, we'd yanked enough cane stalks to make it work. I volunteered to be the one pushing since I was bigger and stronger. Richard had never driven a car before so he got behind the wheel and I gave him a quick lesson on shifting. He picked it up quickly and I got out and took my place at the rear bumper.

His idea was pure genius. On our very first try, the wheels caught and he was out of the hole, throwing great globs of mud at me. Except... he kept going. I'd forgotten to show him how to use the brake. I ran alongside the car yelling at him to hit the brake–"The pedal to the right of the gas, Richard!" and he got it immediately and we were out and stopped. He slid over and I got behind the wheel and he put his hand on my arm.

"Wait a minute," he said. "I might have an idea."

He told me to pop the trunk and I did and he went back and spent a couple of minutes digging around and then yelled at me to come help him. He'd found what he was looking for. One of those spike mats they throw out to stop speeding cars!

We hauled it back to the mud hole we'd just escaped from. I was just going to throw it down when he shook his head and looked at me with disproval in his eyes.

He began picking up the cane stalks. As soon as I saw what he was doing, I helped him and in two-three minutes we had them all out of the hole. We picked up the mat and put it in the hole and then covered with the stalks.

"You are one smart cookie," I said, admiringly. "Jesus! How long you been an outlaw?

"All my life," he said as straight-faced as I'd ever seen him. "I just been waiting for a chance to prove it."

We both laughed and got back in the car, me driving. We'd just gone over a little rise when we heard something far behind us, hidden beyond the slope. The woods were only twenty yards ahead and our luck was holding–the road continued into it. I drove us into the woods until we were out of sight, and then stopped. I jumped out and told Richard to come with me.

We crept up to the edge of the field, but we still couldn't see the road because of that little hill. I motioned to Richard to follow me and instead of walking up the road, we headed into the cane field. When we got past the hill we eased on over until we could see the path.

Sure enough, it was a cop car. Bad news… as they were out of the mud hole. But, for some reason, they'd stopped. And we saw why. They had four flat tires. We watched them for a minute and they were arguing and then must have come to an agreement as one went back to the car and got on the radio. Afterwards, he got out and joined his partner and they began hiking up the road.

Toward us.

"Book it!" I hissed but I didn't need to. Richard was already running toward the woods. We got back to the car, jumped in and began rolling down the path.

So far, so good. It was a good, clear road, even better than the one through the cane field.

We rolled into a clearing. A clearing with a lean-to and a huge pot connected to a bunch of copper pipes.

"It's a still!" Richard said.

Then we realized the bad news. It was also the end of the road. We had to leave the car and strike out on foot. I know we were both thinking the same thing.

The cops were going to catch us. It was inevitable. We might continue for awhile, but we'd both seen enough movies to know how this one was going to end. Soon, dogs would be arriving along with a posse and that'd be it.

"Whaddya think?" Richard said. "We just sit here and wait for 'em?"

He knew the answer to that before I even began walking.

In two minutes, we'd disappeared into the woods. We'd run for a bit and then walk. Run and walk. And talk.

"Maybe this comes to a road," he said. "We can hitch a ride."

"Yeah," I said, a sneer on my lips. "They won't have thought of patrolling the roads..."

We knew our chances were slim and shrinking to nothing, but neither of us really thought about quitting. Even though we were both exhausted, both from fighting out way through the woods and the mental exhaustion that had begun to set in.

We must have walked four, maybe five miles. Both of us were covered with scratches from the brambles that we had to fight through. The rain had let up but the woods were soaked and we were as wet and dirty like we'd been rolling in bayou mud. The only good thing was that so far we hadn't detected any signs of pursuit from the deputies. I figured they knew they had us trapped in these woods and were just waiting for the dogs.

But I was wrong. It was aways off, but I heard voices behind us. Several hundred yards back, but they were

there, clear and distinct. Cussing heavily, sounded like.
Richard and I looked at each other and in silent agreement, began to run again. We weren't caught yet, but it
was just a matter of time.

And, then, we both like to have shit our pants. It
sounded like it was right on top of us. A whistle. A loud-
ass train whistle!

We both began to run toward the sound, sprinting
as if our lives depended on it. At that moment, we were
sure that they did.

In twenty feet, we ran into the end of the trees. The
woods resumed a few yards beyond and what was separating them was a railroad track. With the most beautiful
sight in the world on that track.

A train.

Moving slow, but clearly picking up speed, moving
away from us.

We ran.

Richard grabbed one of the rungs on a ladder to a
flatbed and held on for a second, but then stumbled and
fell. I flew past him and grabbed the same rung and was
luckier. I held on and climbed up a couple of rungs and
held out my hand to him. He'd already gotten up and was
just behind me. I felt his grip begin to slip but then he
reached out with his other hand grabbed hold of the rung
and I reached down and grabbed his shirt and pulled and
then both of us were on and climbed up and fell into the
car. Just in time. The train picked up speed markedly. If
we hadn't made it when we had, in another two seconds
we wouldn't have had a chance.

Just as we fell into the car–which was loaded with
crushed oyster shells–I glimpsed one of the deputies

bursting into the clearing. I yanked Richard down beside me and we hugged the shells beneath us as hard as we could. If the deputy had seen us...

"Richard! Get down!" He'd risen up. He smiled sheepishly and...

...fell straight down. Hard. I said, "Richard?" and he didn't answer.

He couldn't. He had a hole through his forehead. Where his forehead should be, anyway. His entire face was covered in gore and it was impossible to make out his individual features.

I stood up. Both deputies were still in sight. I heard something whistle past me and realized the first deputy was shooting at me. I should have dropped down but I couldn't. I wanted to imprint that deputy's face into my memory. I'd seen him before. At Grandma's bar. His name was just escaping me. Anthony something. That was it. Another bullet whistled past my head closer than the last one. And then the train was going around the bend and he was out of sight.

I sat there for a good half hour, Richard's head in my lap. I was talking to him. I don't remember exactly what I said but I do know I made a promise to him.

Poor Richard. Kid had never done anything to anyone in his entire life. He hadn't participated in killing that sailor. All he'd done was be a good friend to me and helped me escape those cops who wanted to question me.

My face was wet and I thought at first it had started raining again and then realized it wasn't.

I sat there another ten minutes and then the train was slowing. I could see buildings in the distance.

A town. It looked like Angleton. We got closer and I saw it was Angleton.

I laid Richard's head down gently on the oyster shells.

"Goodbye old friend. Watch and see what happens now. You're gonna get a good laugh out of this.

I hit the ground running and made it to the edge of the tree line without falling.

The first thing I was going to do was steal a car.

And, then a gun.

I watched the train finish going by. It was carrying my best friend.

And my childhood.

FLESH FOR
THE FIRE

Jon Bassoff

---

1 .

The boy, Kurt, didn't think he could take another step.
How long had they been walking through the jagged hills, the
half moon twisting in and out of swirling black clouds? His
father, the reverend, eyes glowing like a feral animal, hissed
at him, "C'mon, boy! We gotta keep moving. Not much longer
now. Just trust in me. Trust in God."

And so the boy moved forward, weaving in and out of
the pine trees and deadened aspens, his breath coming out
in puffs of steam.

Another twenty minutes and his legs began to cramp.
"Father," he said. "I don't think I can go on. Can't we rest for
just a few minutes?"

"No time for rest," the reverend said. "Don't you know the
devil's getting closer? Can't you sense him? Can't you feel his
breath on your skin?"

Eight years earlier.

Cora first noticed the man, tall and slender, leaning against a lamppost, his face hidden in the shadows.
Something about him made her skin crawl. She couldn't
stop thinking about him when she was in the grocery
store, but she clucked her tongue, shook her head, and
managed to convince herself that she was just being
silly. The world was fine, and God was watching her and
protecting her. After shopping, she hurried home, clutch-
ing a bag full of groceries, looking this way and that. And
now nobody was outside, it seemed, but her. Lights shone
from streetlamps and from behind windows, and she
quickened her pace, but then, from behind her, she heard
footsteps on the pavement getting louder and louder. She
spun around and saw that it was the man from outside
the store, and now he carried a lantern that swung back
and forth with each step he took.

Cora tried escaping, but he was on her. He grabbed
her arm and the bag fell to the ground. A poisonous red
apple rolled down the sidewalk and then another one.
He held the lantern to his face and she saw that his skin
was burnt by fire and his eyes were those of a blind man.
He pinned her to the ground and his lantern shattered
next to her head. She tried screaming but he'd somehow
sliced her vocal chords and she could make no sound.
She could feel his fiery hand beneath her dress. Could
feel him pulling her panties below her knees. She knew
what was going to happen and she squeezed her eyes
shut and there was such pain and such humiliation and

she wanted to pray to God, but she knew the Devil was more powerful, that God rarely answered prayers, so she let him rape her for hours and for days, and when she opened her eyes, she saw that he was on fire, but the flames didn't consume him...

2 .

And now the boy and his father came to a trail that seemed to have once been an old railroad bed. Some of the railroad cuts collapsed and the trestles rotted away.

"It won't be long now. Just another mile or less. Keep moving, son! Keep moving! He's getting closer by the second..."

And now Kurt sensed the evil in his midst and he feared that at any moment the devil would screech in the blackness and grab his frail body, take him to his secret tunnel all filled with shoes and toys and teeth...

Cora didn't tell her husband because she worried that he would think her a sinner. She didn't tell anybody, although she prayed and prayed–for what she never really knew. But God was dead, a victim of his own arrogance. And then her world crumbled some more. First came the nausea, then the fatigue and headaches. Her mood was only melancholy. Her persona something darker. Soon the reverend was surrounded all night by her moans echoing through the hallways. He took her to the doctor's office. There they poked and prodded and took urine and blood. And when they told her she was pregnant, the reverend placed his hand on his wife's knee, closed his eyes, and said, "Praise Jesus." But Cora, poor Cora, auburn hair strangled in a bun, hospital gown tied at her throat, didn't say a word. Her legs dangled from the examining table and her shoulders rose and fell slowly. Her expression changed from dullness to terror.

Naturally, the nurse was concerned about Cora, but the reverend assured her she was just shocked, that this was truly a blessing from above. While the two of them were chatting, Cora slid down from the examining table, and for a long moment she just stood there, looking first at the nurse and then at her husband. Her mouth opened, but no sounds came out. A shake of the head and then she tried again. A single word, spoken in a whisper. "Devil." Then once more. "Devil."

With great purpose she strode across the room, then, glancing this way and that, she grabbed a reflex hammer from the counter. A Comanche shriek and she yanked down her white underwear and inserted the handle of the hammer into her vaginal opening. She gave a violent jerk and then another one. The blood of a fetus, she figured, to save her soul.

There were a few moments of paralysis and widened eyes before both the reverend and the nurse charged toward Cora. He yanked her arms behind her back, saying, "Lord, oh Lord," and the nurse pulled the hammer from her vagina, blood dripping on the linoleum floor. The reverend held her tightly while she jerked and flailed and cursed. The nurse scurried out of the room, looking to find help, someone to strap her down maybe. Tears flowed down Cora's cheeks, and now she screamed, "Devil! Devil! Devil!" over and over and over again.

3 .

From somewhere deep in the woods, Kurt heard a strange sound, a long monotone whistling, almost like the distant cry of a train. But he knew that he was too far buried in the woods to hear the Southern Railroad.

"Is it him?" Kurt whispered. "Is it the devil?"

His father didn't respond. "Keep moving, Kurt. You've got to trust me. We're almost there. Almost..."

At home she was seen by doctors and therapists and religious leaders (although she had been shunned by the women of the church). She was prescribed bed rest, anti-depressants, and prayers. It wasn't uncommon, she was told, to have feelings of guilt or fear when becoming pregnant for the first time. And while there were no definitive tests to prove that the fetus was not, in fact, the devil incarnate, she was assured that the notion was misguided, that she was merely plagued by obsessive thoughts born from changes in hormones. But she wasn't convinced by any of it, so she pleaded with the reverend to drive her to Boulder and have an abortion. He shook his head and told her it was out of the question. It was the church's position that a human life must be respected and protected absolutely from the moment of conception.

So it was that she became resigned to the fact that she would give birth to a demon. Sometimes she would get it in her mind to find a hanger or knitting needle, but the reverend was smart and had rid the house of sharp objects and toxic mixtures: no Lysol or Windex or Pine-Sol. And so day after day and night after night she stayed in her room, staring at the yellow wallpaper turned to bars.

But the world changes, and even the darkest skies give way to light. Three months pregnant, four months pregnant, and she felt the baby kick, and she allowed herself a smile. Then, a few weeks later, she saw an image on the ultrasound. No horns, no hooves, no tail. Perhaps, she told herself, the doctors and therapists were right. Perhaps her husband's God existed and was watching over her. And so, for a short while, she created a new narrative. A narrative of hope. She imagined herself holding the baby, rocking him to sleep, kissing his sweet skin. She would be happy, and happiness wasn't so easy to come by.

At the dinner table she talked about painting the nursery walls, about adding a rocking chair where she could nurse. And she talked about names. The days of worry, of torment, seemed like a distant memory. Now, you could find Cora sitting in a chair, rubbing her belly contentedly, her skin fresh with a motherly glow.

It was a warm and sunny afternoon, the sky a brilliant blue, the grass a splendid green, when a woman in black arrived at her door. Over her shoulder the woman balanced a single scarecrow, hay spilling from flannel shirt, eyes and nose and mouth missing from the burlap face. The reverend was in his study, so he must not have heard the tap-tapping on the wood. Instead, it was Cora who opened the door, Cora who let the woman in the house, Cora who offered to make her a cup of hot tea.

The woman thanked Cora for her hospitality and then propped the blank-faced scarecrow in the corner of the room next to a painting of *The Last Supper*. While Cora hurried to the kitchen to make a cup of black tea, the woman sat on the couch and hummed an old lullaby. She was a stranger, but Cora knew her well because she'd been in her dreams wearing that same black hood, carrying that same frightening scarecrow.

Cora handed her the tea and then stood over her as the old woman clattered her spoon against the rim of the mug. She huffed away the steam and took a few sips before placing the mug on the floor in front of her. Then she gazed up at Cora, pointed at her swollen belly, and grinned thinly. She said, "My poor girl. Won't you tell me? Won't you tell me everything?"

For some reason, Cora felt she knew the old woman. She felt like she needed to tell her everything. And so she did. She looked into the woman's blue eyes, unhindered by judgment, and told her all about the man in the fire. About the devil.

And while she talked, the witch tried comforting her, tried convincing her that she was not to blame for this state of affairs. And then the old woman rose to her feet and pulled her hood over her head so her face was once again only shadows. She said, "I want you to listen to me, darling. The doctors. The therapists. Your own husband. They're wrong. They're wrong about everything. And you. You were right. You were always right." And now she touched Cora's belly and then stroked her cheek. "Goodbye, my beautiful angel. It's a shame the world has to be this way."

"Wait!" Cora called out. "Don't say goodbye. Please. Stay a little longer. I'm scared. I don't want to be all alone."

The old woman turned back toward Cora, and there was no difference between lucidity and lunacy, between flesh and fire. She said, "There's a paring knife, my darling, hidden beneath the rug. But you already knew that. Just a small incision above the pubic bone and another in the uterus. Allow him a breath and then slit his throat and sink him in the lagoon. I only wish I could help you, my darling."

And then the old woman was gone, vanished into the sunlight, leaving nothing but a scarecrow burned to embers.

4.

Now it seemed that his whistling was getting louder, so much to the point that Kurt had to cover his ears as he walked. The reverend didn't seem to hear anything. Kurt followed his father up the steep incline. The moon had poked through the dark clouds, and he could better see his figure–like a count walking through the fog-filled streets of London.

They soon came to the strange sight of a long tunnel blasted through the rock. In front of the tunnel was an old rotted wood sign:

HAGERMAN TUNNEL

This is the east portal of the Hagerman Tunnel, the highest railroad tunnel in the world at the time of its completion in 1887. The great tunnel is 11,530 feet above sea level. It is 2,161 feet long, 16 feet high, 18 feet wide and cost $200,000. It was replaced in 1890-91 by the Bush-Ivanhoe (later Carlton) Tunnel further down the road to Leadville. The Hagerman Tunnel was used briefly again in 1898-99 but was soon abandoned.

DANGER! DON'T ENTER!

The reverend nodded at his son. "C'mon, boy. This is where we'll be safe."

That evening, while Cora eyed the knife, pressing the tip against the flesh of her index finger, the reverend sat at his desk, chewing on an unlit pipe, pouring over scriptures, preparing his sermon for the following morning. When Cora moaned, he looked up for a moment, his eyes narrowing, before returning to his notebook, flipping a page and jotting down a thought inspired by the Son, the Father, and the Holy Spirit. But then he heard a clatter from the living room, as if a china cabinet had crashed to the floor. He turned around in his chair, his spectacles resting on the tip of his nose, his graying beard bushy and unkempt. "Cora!" he called out. "Is that you?"

No answer, so he rose to his feet and left the study. He walked quickly through the hallway, a draft causing the nursery door to slam shut. Down the stairs he went, thunder crashing against the walls. And then he came to the living room, and his old world was gone forever, covered with a shroud.

He saw the baby first, a bloody mess, lying face down on the Oriental rug, his umbilical cord still attached to his mother. His right leg was cocked at a grotesque angle and his flesh was twitching. And then Cora, his wife, fading in and out of consciousness, still gripping the paring knife that she'd used to cut the boy out.

The reverend didn't understand what he was seeing because it was too grotesque for a man of God. With a body no longer his, he hurried to her side and touched her cheek, and she blinked once, twice. Her mouth twitched into a snarl. "The devil," she whispered, and then her jaw became slack and her eyes relaxed.

"Cora," he whispered. "My sweet Cora."

But she didn't answer.

The reverend clenched his fists and yelled, a lifetime's worth of agony pressing against his rib cage. He touched his wife's face, her skin still warm, and now the tears rolled down his face. He lay next to his dearly beloved, her blood soaking into his shirt.

How much time before he finally stood? How much time before he regarded the smaller lump of flesh on the floor? He could barely stand, the trauma playing havoc with his equilibrium. Still, he managed to move a step and then another. He stood over the baby and cursed it, prepared to stomp on the little corpse.

But then he heard a soft cry.

The baby was alive.

5 .

To get down to the tunnel entrance, they had to get on their stomachs and slide down a steep dirt wall, hardened with ice. As Kurt descended, he felt a jagged rock tear into his skin, but he simply gritted his teeth and continued on.

At the bottom, his father got on his haunches and moved sideways like a crab. Kurt followed after him. The floor to the tunnel was covered with dirty snow, and the walls and ceiling were thick with ice. Kurt rose to a hunchback position. The snow nearly rose to his knees. Once again he heard the low, monotonous whistling. He placed his hands against the frozen walls and continued forward, now blind and wholly dependent on his father's voice.

The baby, Kurt, was taken to the ICU, filled with beeping incubators that looked like caskets. He was placed in one. There were wires and tubes everywhere, and there was an oxygen mask on his face. For a long time, the reverend, badly traumatized by the loss of his wife, didn't come to see him.

After a few months in the ICU, he was pronounced healthy, and the reverend came and took him home. Some of the ladies from church offered to help him with the day to day caretaking, but he refused. As a father, he was lacking. He fed the boy. He changed his diapers. But he didn't love him. And as Kurt grew up, the reverend began praying less and drinking more. By the time his son was five or six, nobody called him Reverend anymore. Instead they just called him Pete the Drunk. A spiritual man, no longer. He didn't spend time in bars because he didn't want to talk to anybody. But each morning, shortly after ten, he would appear from his now rotted and weed-infested house, his hair long and unwashed, his face covered by an unkempt beard, and stagger through town, cursing at the pavement until he came to Jackpot Liquors, where he would buy a liter of Calvert Blended Whiskey and leave exactly twelve dollars on the counter without waiting for his twenty-four cents in return. And then back to the house where nobody would see him until the following morning. People wondered about him. They wondered what he ate, and how he paid the mortgage, and how he cared for the strange boy named Kurt who was cut out of his mother's womb so many years ago.

But Pete didn't care what people said, and if he were really being honest with himself, he enjoyed being called Pete the Drunk because his life as a reverend ended the very moment he saw his wife's fish eyes and heard the suffered gasp from Kurt, the creature who was his son. He had been a fool to ever freely offer his faith to human-kind's great hoax, but now he had the rest of his life to make up for his folly, and he would do so by sucking down a bottle of whiskey each and every day until his liver was covered with cirrhosis and the blood gushed into his esophagus and stomach.

But the alcohol couldn't make him forget, no matter how hard he tried because every time he laid eyes on Kurt, he saw his wife's eyes and her mouth and her nose. And despite all the signs to the contrary–Kurt's lack of affect and lack of empathy–Pete needed to believe that his wife had been wrong, stricken again by the highest forms of psychosis, because to believe in the devil meant to believe in God who had created him as the highest-ranking angel of all. So even if the boy sprouted horns and dragged the multitudes into the fiery pits of hell, Pete would have been steadfast in his nonbelief, content to curse the indifferent universe for the wounds and scars it unknowingly bestowed.

Every so often some elders from the church would come by to show kindness and charity, two things Pete had no use for. They'd ask about Kurt, and Pete would say, "He lives. He breathes. He's not the monster the world makes him out to be." And usually he could get them to leave, convince them that his heart had turned to rhyolite and that they were wasting their time and were better served preaching the gospel to some directionless schoolboy, ready for his mind to be manipulated into a parasitic relationship with the Church of Imagined Salvation. And how could they answer to that?

One morning Kurt awoke early. He came and shook his father, who was sleeping on the couch, a shattered vodka bottle and torn Bible on the floor. The reverend opened his eyes and saw the boy standing there, saw that the boy was agitated. He told the reverend to come to his room, that he had something to show him. And so the old man struggled to his feet, his head banging hard, and staggered after his son toward his room. Once inside, he looked around. He saw nothing but his bloody drawings. "What is it?" the reverend asked. "What did you need to show me?" And that's when young Kurt pointed toward the window. The old man walked slowly, his left eye twitching in anticipation. He wiped away the fog from the glass and stared outside. And there he saw the gruesome sight: two dozen or more rabbits piled beneath the pepper tree, dead. He turned toward the boy, his eyes filling with tears. "Did you do this?" he asked in a quiet voice. "Did you kill these animals?" Kurt only shook his head and whispered, "No, father. Not I." But at that moment he knew. He knew Kurt was a demon and he had to take him to the hills.

And so it was that the reverend told the boy that it was time to leave the house, time to leave the world. Just for a while, you see. There would be no need for him to pack a bag. No need for him to bring anything at all. Kurt followed after his father. And so Kurt and the reverend, the drunk, drove all morning, and the reverend didn't say another word to the boy. Through the mountains, where the pine trees guarded lost souls and the abandoned mines hid horrific secrets, they drove. And when they could drive no further, the reverend stopped the car and told his son to get out, that they would need to walk the rest of the way. And that's what they did.

6 .

Hagerman's Tunnel, where a young boy's screams would be muted by the wind and the hills and the trees. The reverend turned on his flashlight, and now his face looked to be burnt by fire and his eyes were those of a blind man. The reverend unloaded the rope. Unloaded the spike. And Kurt, like Isaac in biblical times, watched him curiously. With resignation in his eyes, the reverend placed the spike on top of the boy's foot. He didn't react. The old man used his carpenter's hammer to drive it through his flesh. The screams echoed through the tunnel and the boy writhed on the ground. The reverend bent down, picked him up, and carried him deeper and deeper into the tunnel, and all the while he was sobbing and praying and thinking of his dead wife and the dead rabbits. He tied Kurt to an old railroad trestle and the boy pleaded with him, but he backed away weeping and gnashing his teeth.

An hour later, the old man returned to his car. He drove about a quarter of a mile to a lake with no name. He drank some vodka and then some more. He stepped out of the car and filled his pockets with a thousand tiny stones. Then he walked slowly into the lake. The water got deeper and deeper, and soon it was just his eyes peeking above the water and then he was no more.

FOR THE ROAD IS HEAVEN

Joshua Viola & Sean Eads

EVEN IN THE DARK, THE TREES KEPT FALLING.
The crack and splinter of lumber, sharp even at a distance, kept Jewel rigid in the driver's seat, left hand on the wheel. Her right hand tapped the top of the plastic box on the passenger side. *Tupperware*. She imagined how funny the word would sound if she could speak, like the rumor of a bird's chirp, the claim of a dog's howl. Jewel's father told her all words were made up, and it was the function of things that mattered, not names. *Tupperware* functioned as a container and a preserver.

Why couldn't there be *Tupperware* big enough for the whole world before so much of it ended? Or was her life now what it felt like to live in empty *Tupperware*?

Jewel shivered, though it was weeks from winter and the temperature remained tolerable. A glance in the rearview mirror showed total darkness. Not that anyone would pursue her with headlights on. It was the steady work of the axe men, revealed in the crash of trees, that told Jewel she was safe for now.

She tapped on the *Tupperware* lid again and wept.

–*Father, I'm scared. That's no surprise to you.*

She left the car, taking the tattered road map with her. It unfolded to a massive size, large as a table. Most of its panels were faded to nothing, erased like the places that had been there. Only the roads remained: mostly. The present road went through a forest that did not exist on the panel. The map showed an area of green called *Jefferson County Memorial Forest*. The green did not approach the road, much less overwhelm it like the present trees. Now a heavy canopy of branches made the night even darker, and there was a smaller tree growing right in the middle of the road.

She gazed at it as she heard another far-off, far larger tree falling. Jewel easily imagined Dunsinane standing atop the roof of his tall truck cabin, surrounded by three hundred men and women looking up in awe as his hands conveyed the frenzy of his soul.

–*We know what's strong and what's weak. We know what survives and what falls. The world has fallen many times, civilizations have come and gone. Their roads survive best. Roads are a prayer for invincibility. We must have a world of roads and the will to rule them.*

Sometimes if Jewel concentrated hard enough, she was sure she could make a noise in her mouth. She wanted this so badly when her father died. But not even a moan mustered in her throat. His death meant more than a personal loss. Had he lived a month, a week, perhaps even a day longer, his thoughts might have turned against Dunsinane and ruined him.

But now Dunsinane would turn Father into the final justification for his plans. In life, Father led his community well, faltering only the last few years, when Dunsinane began asserting his influence.

In death, Dunsinane could elevate her father from mortal leader to divine guidance.

A god of roads.

Jewel was ready to leave when she noticed the trees were no longer falling. It was unlike Dunsinane to call for merciful breaks. A moment later, the collective blare of horns sent her sprinting to the driver's side door. She opened it and paused to listen to the only sound in the night–the only sound in the world.

.-- . .----. ...- . / -.. .. ... -.-. --- ...- . .-. . -.. / -.-- --- ..- .-. / -.. . ... . -.-. .-. .- - .. --- -. .-.-.- / .-- . .----. .-. . / -.-. --- -- .. -. --. / ..-. --- .-. / -.-- --- ..- .-.-.-

Why did I linger here? I could be so many more miles away. Do I want to get caught?

She got behind the wheel as the horns kept sounding, expertly synced from hundreds of cars. Father had taught her early that your car's horn was your voice. Dunsinane's horn sounded like nothing else under the sun or moon, bellowing. Even from miles away it announced itself above the volume of the others.

–*We've discovered your desecration.*

–*We're coming for you.*

She opened her mouth to scream but nothing came out. Jewel turned the ignition and the car lurched forward. Hit the tree in the road. It was just a sapling. But now, like a twig snapped by a passing deer, its broken form confirmed her presence to the oncoming hunters.

Jewel risked the headlights and mashed the gas pedal. The car shimmied as it reached seventy miles per hour and the contents within the *Tupperware* box thudded. She slapped her right hand atop the lid but only for an instant, as she needed both hands to control the wheel.

Dunsinane is going to kill me.

If I don't kill myself first.

–*I hate cities.*

–*Why, Father?*

–*Because they must have been places of very great despair. And great noise. I think it was in the cities where people lost the ability to use their mouths because all they could do was shout over the chaos. And so the generations that followed inherited both burned out buildings and burned out throats.*

Jewel shoved a plastic nozzle into the fuel tank. The soft splash of gasoline against the pavement jolted her from a memory that must have been twenty years old. She was six and standing on a bluff with her father beside her. Together they contemplated a ruined town, little more than collapsed rubble since well before her birth. Father bent down, focused her attention on his hands, and signed out a command.

–*Notice the road. Read how it goes through the destruction and continues off into the horizon.*

Jewel had already noticed, but she nodded anyway.

–*The road is our purpose and our true symbol. Whatever we are, whatever truths we've lost and found a thousand times over, roads recorded them. My grandfather told me a story about tree rings and how they record a tree's history. I do not know if this is true. But if so, then the roads are our rings. The roads outlast all buildings, all lives. The roads carry the footsteps of the past, the cars that were and the cars that might come. I think it is a fine thing to die in the middle of a road, Jewel.*

Her father did not die in the middle of the road. He died in a tattered tent, and Jewel had capitalized on a rare moment of privilege as his daughter and received two hours of almost total isolation with him in an impromptu wake. Dunsinane had been obliged to show such respect and deference to her before the others.

Jewel screwed the cap back onto her gasoline can and returned it to the trunk, squeezing it among ten more. No, immediate worry about supplies didn't ease the remorse of letting even one drop of gas evaporate off the asphalt. She scrambled back behind the wheel, closed the door and motored away.

It makes no sense. Why haven't they caught up to me yet?

The rearview mirror showed only road. She drove through open land now, free of the encroaching forests. How she wished some force could bring all those trees crashing across the path behind her.

I didn't put that many miles between us before Dunsinane discovered what I did. He wouldn't have sounded his horns across the night for the sake of vanity. They would have started pursuing right away.

But they hadn't.

Could it be Father is looking out for me after all? Could it be he approves of what I did? Now in death he sees clearly and understands how Dunsinane sought to use him?

The highway ahead of Jewel exploded into chunks of asphalt and flame. Gravel peppered the windshield as the car lurched and spun. The explosion must be her father's voice, speaking from beyond the road. The steering wheel locked as so many horrible noises erupted all around her. Was this screaming? Had the road been torn open, to spew out the tortured voices of the past?

A lightning crack of pain pulsed through Jewel's body. Harsh odors scorched her nose, the burnt scent of things that shouldn't be burning. A hand came up and flicked the side of the car and sent it rolling. Jewel would swear to it.

Father's hands his hands save his hands

Consciousness was a sunrise you couldn't believe in. Jewel experienced a lot of days as her head lolled this way and that.

Was she on her feet?

Was she flying?

Father's hands where are they

A man's face appeared in front her. An unfriendly grin, a cocked head with pursed lips. He seemed a few years older than her and didn't talk right away, his hands too busy groping. The wreck had numbed Jewel's senses, leaving her motionless and vulnerable to the man violating her body. At last he gestured.

–No one so pretty should travel alone.

Jewel opened her mouth, hoping to summon all the sounds of the crash. The sounds *must* be there inside her someplace, reproducible.

She couldn't manage even a gasp.

Another man–she only now realized there were others–cupped his hand under her chin and squeezed, forcing her mouth to stay open.

–Not yet. But that's a fine idea.

The men held their bellies and rocked back and forth, the universal mime of robust laughter. Jewel squeezed her eyes shut and kept them that way until there came a gentle tapping on her left temple. Her chief tormentor was gesturing again.

–Your car is junk now. We'll salvage it for parts. You'll ride in someone's trunk until you've been tamed to our ways. Seats are earned in the camp of Sherman Young.

Two men dragged Jewel across a field. The effects of the crash caught up with her all at once. Her stomach heaved and she vomited the traces of her last meal. The sky burst with garish colors, each a needle in her thoughts. She closed her eyes but still saw the flashes, and she went on retching, silent spasms ignored by her captors.

Hours must have passed because it was clearly dusk before she regained some sense of herself. Jewel found a spoonful of pale broth being poked against her lips and she opened up to receive it. She found it flavorless and therefore good.

The woman feeding her seemed about as old as her father, which meant either uncommon hardiness or fantastic luck. Her eyes were still bright and she seemed like one who might smile a lot. Jewel took another spoonful. *Smile for me. Please smile. Show me I'm going to be okay.*

After several more feedings, the old woman put the broth aside and stroked Jewel's hair once before pivoting to slap the ground several times. This brought the men, who now stood over them in a circle. The old woman withdrew and in her place knelt the man who captured her.

Sherman Young.

He carried the *Tupperware* box with him.

Jewel reached for it at once and got slapped across the face to remind her of her place. She flinched and cast a plaintive, miserable glance upward.

Sherman Young made a sweeping motion with his hands, and his men retreated and turned their backs to him. He hunched down and placed the box between his flexed knees. Jewel focused on his gestures.

–*Whose hands are these?*

When she didn't answer, he opened the lid and flung it aside, reaching into the box.

–*Then answer my question.*

–*They belonged to my father.*

–*Belonged? Like a possession? He owned severed hands?*

–*They're his hands. I cut them off after he died.*

–*Why in the name of nameless roads would you do this? Did he do you evil with them? I recognize the ring on the right hand. The black stone of the Teachers.*

–*He did me no evil. He was a Teacher, as was his father.*

–*You still haven't explained yourself.*

Explaining herself–justifying herself–seemed a daily, impossible obligation since girlhood. She might as well count the stars in the night sky. She knew she must be the reason her father quit the roads and turned his back on those who were still voiceless. Mother was dead, and clearly Father found nothing to sustain him in his daughter's eyes.

–*Where I come from, my father led many people. Then a man named Dunsinane–*

Sherman Young seized her wrists. Jewel stared into his narrowing eyes and he didn't need to gesture to communicate his question.

–*Did you say Dunsinane?*

She nodded.

He released Jewel's hands. She rubbed her wrists as he made a quick slash with his fingers.

–*Continue.*

–*My father's thoughts were scattered near the end of his life. He agreed with whatever Dunsinane said, and Dunsinane used his position to achieve greater power. When my father died, I took his hands because I couldn't stand thinking of them rotting in the ground.*

Sherman Young grabbed her wrists again.

–*I know your people burn their dead.*

Jewel looked at the dirt and the *Tupperware* box. She could see the silhouette of her father's hands inside, hacked off at the wrist.

–*I didn't want my father's ring to fall into Dunsinane's possession.*

–*Lie to me again and your hurt will be as long as the horizon.*

Her eyes watered.

–*I wanted to spite Dunsinane. I wanted to reclaim my father from him. To show him and everyone else that my father's voice was beyond control. And I did want to save the ring.*

Sherman Young's eyes narrowed as he held his stare, and Jewel mustered all her strength to meet it. After a minute passed, he nodded and smiled. This brought no comfort because his next act was to reach into the box, grab one of the hands, and jerk the ring free. He cast the severed hand aside and held the ring up to the firelight, clearly relishing its gleam and heft. Then he motioned for Jewel to lift her right hand. She did and he slipped the ring over her thumb.

–We have many children and a few adults with us who do not know how to speak. You will teach them. And you will be my wife.

Suckling her fourth forced child, a boy named Arthur, Jewel looked at her father's ring and pondered the fate of his severed hands. It seemed Sherman Young threw them into the fire one evening. Or perhaps he fed them to the wild hogs, or placed them on the road and directed the long caravans he commanded to crush them under their wheels. She imagined the finger bones splintering, the smashed flesh rotting away. Her imagination too easily replaced the image with each of her children's skulls. If only she'd been allowed a single daughter, her loathing might be quenched. But all four boys–even this littlest one, only months old–were so clearly their father's sons, already dismissive of her. She could not even win against their silent temper tantrums when she denied them some trifle. She no longer did. Not after the beating she received at Sherman Young's hands as she was forced to look at her sons' faces and beg forgiveness at trying to discipline them.

Cradling the child, she worked the ring off her thumb and held it between her fingertips. She stared at the black stone, glossy enough to reflect a distorted image of her face. Or perhaps not distorted at all.

She glanced around before pulling Arthur away from her breast. Most of Young's followers–a hundred strong–kept close to the camp and the road. Jewel knew the other women resented her for being able to stray into the woods. Being Sherman Young's wife came with a few advantages, including a slightly greater freedom of movement than the other women. Of course, he did this as a demonstration of his own power. Nothing more.

Arthur's mouth opened in a noiseless wail as his little arms and legs thrashed. Always hungry. Draining her dry, just like his brothers. She took the ring and put it against the baby's lips. Jewel's heart beat a grim pace as she watched the child try to suck milk from the hard, cold stone. As its face reddened, a moment of pity and deep guilt almost changed her mind.

She shoved the large ring deep into Arthur's mouth and then brought his head back to her right breast and waited.

When Jewel returned to the camp and saw her husband again, several hours had passed. Sherman Young was preparing for war. He rubbed his eyes as he hunched over lists of weapons and supplies. A map was spread out on another table. It reminded Jewel of the road map she'd owned long ago, Sherman Young's map said *Children's Atlas of the United States* and seemed very crude in its details, obviously not drawn to any appreciable scale. But it featured a few recognizable landmarks and was better than sketching out battle plans in the dirt.

As Jewel stood before him, he busied himself adding lines on the map, drawing in roads and paths. She stared at the bald place in the middle of his scalp. Father had been one of the few men she ever knew who never lost hair there. As she gazed, she wished the spot also meant a place with no bone, like with newborns.

She reached and touched his shoulder. When he jerked away, she realized she'd truly surprised him. Jewel did not think she'd crept into the tent and decided he was *truly* lost in thought.

Good.

–The people of the north ridge are such fools.

–Did they refuse you again?

–Yes. I offered them a treaty of protection from Dunsinane. They say they do not know who that is.

–Are they liars?

–They are hermits. They have few cars. Not even bicycles or horses. They think because they have not traveled into danger that danger will never travel into them.

–An easy victory for you, my love.

Sherman Young smiled. Jewel remained wary, having learned that talk of *easy victories* both enticed and enraged him, as if he could never decide if she was complimenting or mocking him. She slapped him slightly on his right cheek, a liberty that made his entire face go red. He was on her at once, both of them on the ground, not quite wrestling. He had her on her belly, each hand pinning her wrists. One of his fingers began tapping on the back of her left hand, and she interpreted the dots, dashes and pauses with lightning speed–

You're the easiest conquest by far.

Jewel endured the violation, even glad of the way he wore himself out. The key was not getting herself sent away when he finished. This was nearly an either-or-proposal, seemingly unrelated to any mood or circumstance. But her pulse started going fast again when he rose off of her and did not gesture for her to go. He pulled his pants up to his waist and labored back to the table and his *Children's Atlas of the United States* and the battle plan he was sketching there.

Her clothes were on for the most part, and as she stepped behind him she took the jagged bone–Arthur's little right forearm–from her pocket. Was it sharp enough to cut Sherman Young's throat? She'd tested it on her thumb and found the flesh opened right away.

She tightened her grip and readied the weapon. All she could do was die trying.

–I have journeyed as a pilgrim of many roads, at first beside my father and then alone; and then beside my wife, and then alone again. No–

On her knees and staring at the sky, waiting for Sherman Young's followers to deliver the killing blow, Jewel remembered how her father's hands seized up, the fingers clawing. They had not fully straightened as he rushed to stroke her hair.

–I am done with teaching. I am finished thinking of myself as a redeemer and a rebuilder of the land. It cannot be done. It is said the world has fallen many times. I've heard told that a host of fearful people who live in the sky

*once forced men to have many languages, and civilization
collapsed. Perhaps these same people later decided to silence
our mouths all together. But the silence of mouths is nothing.
Our intentions lie in our hearts, expressed through the hands.*

Her hands were bound with rope tied to the rear
bumper of Sherman Young's command truck, a battered
black war wagon reinforced with random pieces of
salvaged metal. About four feet of slack existed between
her and the bumper.

Jewel lowered her head. She was about fourteen
when Father decided to live among one group of people
and lead them. With him as chief, they began building
at first huts, then houses and barns. She was twenty the
first time she saw Dunsinane, eager, wide-eyed, effacing.

–Have you heard of the Mongols, sir?

*–Yes. People of the past who would know what to do with
the world today.*

Dunsinane intrigued both Jewel and her father with
his fantastic story of thousands–hundreds of thousands–
of people roaming the land in vast groups, disdainful of
cities, lovers of traveling and pillaging, hacking roads
through the wilderness wherever they advanced.

*–They made a great road of purest silk, a substance as
delicate as a spider's web but stronger than metal. And they
fashioned this road and countless others to move themselves
with great ease and control. They had a civilization without
cities and they were powerful all the same.*

Less than six months later, all the buildings Father
proposed were stopped in various stages of construction,
and a more nomadic life began.

A Mongol life.

I think it is a fine thing to die in the middle of a road, Jewel.

She heard the engine start.

I think it is a fine thing to die, Father.

The truck did not shoot forward. Jewel knew nothing of her punishment beyond the obvious, and the delay surprised her until the first woman came and spat in her face. A procession formed behind her, men and women and children. She stared straight ahead even as their spit struck her eyes and blurred her vision. Even as her surviving sons came last.

She could not interpret their expressions. Hatred for her? Sadness for Sherman Young? Did they think this was a bizarre game? Did they wonder about Arthur? As Benjamin, the firstborn and now barely five years old, leaned forward to spit, Jewel opened her mouth to scream at him. The boiling rage, the long silence, the years of feeling there was *some* sound inside her, some noise of protest–petered out as nothingness. *I have no voice, we have no voice except what our hands can gesture and what our horns can honk and what our guns can speak on our behalf. Let me die.*

She jerked the rope, not to escape but as a goading plea to get on with it. Her mouth remained open and her son's spit landed on her tongue, where it burned like poison. The awful bitter taste made her question her own birth. What guarantee was did she have that Father hadn't violated Mother the way Sherman Young had forced himself on her? Who could know? Father had changed before her eyes, and how could she claim those changes had only started at the particular hour of a particular day? What if Father had been a vile man? What if he'd even tried to kill his wife in the middle of her labor, taking the oversized ring with its black stone off his finger and forcing it past her clenched teeth to choke her as Jewel had done to Arthur?

The nightmarish thoughts made Jewel writhe and explode with emotion. She screamed.

Screamed.

Her sons drew back, bursting into tears. Women clutched one another and men quaked in terror. Jewel's throat felt very strange–sore, vibrating. She ran out of air and fell into silence even as she pitched forward, gasping on her hands and knees. She gasped for breath. A man, one of her dead husband's endless lackeys, came at her and she reared back and screamed again. The lackey cringed and ran away.

Now the faces surrounding Jewel became grave and worshipful. She offered more sounds. Strange sounds. Groans. Bleats. Honking noises. Were they words? What did the gestures of hands sound like coming from the tongue? Was this laughter? Was this scorn?

She stood. No one tried to stop her. Two women slashed the ropes binding her to the truck. Jewel spoke to them with her hands and her mouth, knowing only the *intent* of the sounds, the thankfulness for being spared.

But she stopped short of that.

If she'd learned anything from the likes of Dunsinane and her husband, it was leaders did not express thanks. Doing so suggested agreement rather than obligation.

It suggested her life was in *their* hands.

From across the distance, the horns of Dunsinane sounded out their collective challenge.

–SURRENDER. LEAVE YOUR CARS BEHIND AS WELL AS YOUR CHILDREN. FLEE ON FOOT AND LIVE OUT YOUR LIVES SPARED BY MERCY.

From inside the cab of her command truck, Jewel surveyed the forces arrayed against her, momentarily breathless at Dunsinane's battle lines. This battle for the road was far too expansive for the road itself, and spilled over into the vast surrounding plains. Jewel briefly thought of her old map and wondered what panel of it they'd be on now. Her gaze fell upon the whiteness of her knuckles and the mottled age spots on the back of her wrinkled hands. Suddenly a finger touched her wrist and tapped.

–Mother?

Benjamin, her dear son, her only surviving son, looked at her with his one eye. Nearly thirty, the resemblance he bore to his father no longer filled Jewel with revulsion. He had been too loyal, too devoted, too worthy for her to regard him with anything but affection.

–Yes, Benjamin?

–Not like that. Say my name. I want to hear it.

Jewel smiled and spoke what she imagined his name must sound like. Benjamin squeezed her wrist.

–Now I have courage again.

–You never lost it in the first place.

She wondered, though, about the countless people who stood in her ranks. Jewel looked in the rear-view mirror, searching for any hint of people taking Dunsinane's warning. For a moment, she thought she saw the reflection filled by hundreds of hastily departing fighters. But there were none.

Benjamin tapped again.

–Dunsinane is the man who killed my grandfather?
–Yes.
–And cut off his hands to make his spirit mute?
–Yes.
Benjamin nodded and squared his shoulders.
–I will go man the cabin gun.

Jewel watched him climb out and swing deftly into the truck bed. She heard him taking his spot almost directly above her, where an ancient weapon had been welded into place.

Enough time has passed. Let me give him our response if he hasn't figured it out for himself.

She alone honked, a brief and blunt sequence.
–NO.

The charge came at once. Sweat popped out along Jewel's forehead. She opened the driver's side door and stood to lean out. A thousand faces turned to her, faces of those in cars, faces of the foot soldiers wielding tire-shredding pikes, faces of the archers and the melee men who would break their bones yet keep crawling after their target, until the last enemy driver was hauled from behind the wheel of the last car, throat slit, the wound defiled with gasoline and piss. These people looked at her even as Dunsinane's forces charged.

Jewel screamed.

As if she were a second sun suddenly burning in the sky, her voice poured waves of heat across her forces. Hers was the voice of a divine goddess, more than human, more powerful than any horn. Her army closed ranks around her. She climbed back into her truck and gunned it forward.

The sides met everywhere in a clash of metal and rubber. Above her, Benjamin poured out a deadly barrage that lacerated through the thin protection of several cars, annihilating their drivers. Jewel's hands were everywhere on the wheel, twisting and jerking as the scene before her changed. She glimpsed desperate passengers trying to shove out the bodies of the dead drivers. A car exploded off to her right just as a barrage of arrows struck her windshield, chipping and cracking the glass. Scowling in defiance, Jewel shifted gears, gunning forward, hoping Benjamin could hang on. Across the field, a few hundred yards away, she noticed fifty of Dunsinane's foot soldiers making a broad arc around the battle in an effort to attack from behind. She turned the wheel and overtook them in less than a minute. Benjamin's weapon chewed up half of them and Jewel let the truck's four massive tires trample the fallen as the rest scattered back toward their hapless lines.

Wiping her brow, she saw nothing but seamless chaos, a tapestry of clustered assaults and noble, individual duels behind the wheel or on foot. Jousts and wrestling matches, men and women throwing themselves atop cars, hammering with clubs and fists against glass and metal. A queer sensation of ease lifted her heart. Whatever the outcome–and was it ever feasible she could beat Dunsinane?–her side had acquitted itself well. Even if hers was the only voice in the world, a song would survive–somehow–of this battle. The earth had its mouth in the dirt of battle, and right now that mouth was gulping down the blood of great deeds and struggle. *That's* where the song would come from.

A heavy thud sounded overhead. As Jewel looked up to see what Benjamin might want, a rumble to her left drew all her attention and she realized what her son must have been warning her about.

Dunsinane had called in another wave, an attack unlike anything she'd seen before. All those years dedicated to felling the forests to forge a world of roads had given them time to contemplate creative, horrifying uses for lumber. Five pairs of trucks, each almost as large as Dunsinane's, were coming in a line, dragging thick tree trunks between them on heavy chains. Anything, even a car, caught in its path would be crushed or upended. One of these massive logs was salted with spikes. Another had been saturated in gasoline and blazed forth with such heat and fury that Jewel felt the power of both usurping the heart in her chest.

Jewel honked her coded orders, summoning her people to a fallback position. The state of the battlefield told her it was a futile gesture. Dunsinane's heavy assault units were deployed in sweeping angles, a broad scything pattern that made flanking assaults almost impossible. They had better armor surrounding their drivers.

She saw the plan developing in her head with such sureness she could only laugh. The sound of her laughter would always be strange, even fearful to her own ears, and she wondered how the world had been when the sky must have echoed with millions of voices laughing, weeping, heckling, pleading. Surely the collective sound would have made trees and buildings fall.

She made a fist and pounded on the cabin roof.
What's wrong? Why isn't Benjamin answering me?
Jewel's laughter ceased.

—I remember you. I am almost as old as your father when he died, but I still remember you. Jewel.

She looked up at Dunsinane. She knelt in the battlefield, surrounded by the ruin of men and machines.

—You took your father's hands. I never understood why. What were a dead man's hands to me?

Jewel smiled. She could only imagine what her grin must look like. Her mouth was bloody from missing teeth and on fire with a pain her throat strained to hold back. She raised her own bound, damaged hands slowly and took them through a series of arthritic gestures.

—I had to keep you from becoming a god.

Dunsinane put his hands to his belly and rocked back and forth. Jewel saw all his followers do the same, men and women and children alike.

—Does it look like you succeeded? We have cleared more land, built more roads—roads for our machines to rule forever. The road is heaven—

"And its kingdom shall be mine!"

Jewel's defeated forces rose. Pure spontaneity, pure *conviction* in the truth of her voice spurred them to a final effort. Dunsinane gaped at her, his eyebrows knitted in blunt astonishment, his hands touching his lips and throat as if their silence was a grim betrayal.

"I am cry of the world, I am the song of the road, I am the goddess of all sound!"

Dunsinane's expression twisted between appall, disgust, and paralysis, all mirrored in the faces of his troops. They trembled at the sound of humanity and

Jewel knew how inhuman it must sound, like the rude screech of grinding metal when a tire explodes. Each utterance was a wonder, a violation, a promise, and a slap to the face. Jewel brought herself to her feet as Dunsinane's people fell back, scrambling madly for their cars. Some reached them and drove in full speed reverse, plowing into anything to nudge and force their way to safety. Others were killed before they reached such safety.

And still others stayed–and knelt.

Dunsinane stayed but he did not kneel.

–*Impossible. A trick.*

"No trick."

–*I do not understand what your noise means. Speak with your hands.*

Jewel offered him a final smile as her people came to surround him.

"If you prefer the language of hands, then you shall have it."

And the strangulation began.

BLACK SUNSHINE

James R. Tuck

THE ROAD IN THE MIRROR WAVERS AS IT unspools behind us, shimmy-shining with heat from the godforsaken Arizona sun beating down like a hammer on a frying pan, turning the asphalt so gummy the tires tearing over it make a long thrumming sound that just lays on me like a wool blanket. The asphalt's soaked up the sun's wrath and radiates it like a furnace through the metal floorboard, through my boots, through my feet. My shin bones feel like they're baked brittle.

This car is a fucking oven.

We should've done this shit at night.

Seven dark figures cut through the heat waves behind us.

"They're getting closer." I say.

"No shit, Monroe," Lorna snarls. "We're riding heavy and I can't run wide open in this heat without blowing the engine." She yells over the throaty crackle-roar of the big-block-V-whatever-the-fuck motor's in this sleek-sided hunk of vintage Detroit muscle, all scooped hood and pinstriped fenders and big fat soft tires made for eating up miles. I'm soupy with sweat against the tuck-and-roll leather of the seat, and the chrome on the blower reflects the goddamn sun, blasting my eyes until I see spots.

Choppy dark hair whips around Lorna's face like refracted black sunshine, snapping on the edges of her big rock-star, aviator sunglasses.

Of course she has sunglasses; bitch is always prepared.

Looking fierce and fiery and fine as hell.

Driving the car like she stole it.

Cause she did.

Hey, I stole the duffel bag for fucking Kraeger.

I don't even know what's in it. Something heavy as hell that clanks when my foot hits it when I turn to look out the back.

Why am I looking out the back?

Remember those seven dark figures? Those are seven pissed-off, psychotic, outlaw bikers chewing on our ass.

Why do we have seven pissed-off, psychotic, outlaw bikers chewing on our ass?

The car and this bag belong to the bikers; we stole them cause Kraeger paid us to. The bag is all Kraeger wants, Lorna took the car after ours got shot the fuck up by the aforementioned bikers. She was supposed to distract them so I could get the bag away clean but she was late and it all went sideways.

Got it now?

It's 2 + 2 = some truly fucked up shit. Pay attention, man, it's going to be a long trip if you can't do the math.

"We should've gotten gone sooner." Lorna's head is sunk between hunched shoulders, arms out, forearms and biceps cabled as she holds the steering wheel in a death grip. The highway's not so much a wasteland of a desert road than a rattlesnake that wants to sling us off its back and out into the sea of soft sand on either side so we get stuck for the bikers to come finish us off.

Goddamn road.

Don't say it.

Don't.

Fuck it; I say it.

"Somebody was too busy fucking that scooter trash with the tramp stamp to keep their timetable."

"Hey!" the scooter trash with the tramp stamp yells from the backseat. She hauls herself forward sticking her bleached blond head between the seats. She's got nice eyes, green as fuck, which is easy to see with her pupils dialed down to black pinpricks. An odor comes off her, not perfume, more like 24 hours of meth and ass. "Fuck you, man. My name's Tammy and I've got a PhD."

Of course she does, doesn't everybody?

I ignore Scooter Trash Tammy and keep talking to Lorna. "I can't believe you brought her along."

"She's a good kisser." Lorna's still not looking at me.

"Jesus fucking Christ! We're going to get nailed by these bikers because Scooter here has a long tongue and some breath mints? You really owe me one."

"I'll save your ass. We'll be even."

Like I'm just going to sit back and let that happen. Lorna doesn't owe me often, so I ain't going to let it go when she does.

"How far 'til we reach town?" I ask. Town means cops. I hate cops, fuck, I've got a rap sheet as long as my dick. Armed robbery, theft by receiving, intent to distribute, hell, you name it and it's on my docket.

You know who hates cops more? Pissed-off, psychotic outlaw bikers, that's who.

"Fifty miles."

"How long will that take?"

Lorna's gaze flicks down and back up to the road. "This speed? Twenty minutes."

Twenty minutes? Fuck us. Those bikers will catch us before then.

"Wrong, honey," Scooter Trash Tammy leans forward, hand trailing along Lorna's neck, "town's the other way. Nothing ahead 'til Antioch, near a hundred miles from here."

"Goddamn it, Lorna!" I can't fucking believe it. "You're the fucking driver! You had one job! One job, drive the fucking car."

"I'm driving the fucking car, asshole!" she screams.

"In the wrong fucking direction!"

"You two are hilarious." This from Scooter Trash Tammy.

I drag the zipper down on the duffel bag. We need something to even up our odds so I open the bag praying we have guns and ammo.

In the bag I see an ax and a helmet.

What the actual fuck?

"Oh, you took the Nazi shit," Scooter Trash Tammy says. "No wonder they're on our ass."

I drag the things out of the bag. The ax is heavy as a sledgehammer. One wide blade and a spike off the back end on a thick wooden handle. The ax looks ancient, the wood dark and dry, the iron pitted and rusty as hell. The only part that appears recent is the swastika welded on the flat of the blade. The helmet is made from the same ancient iron, also pitted and patinaed with rust. It resembles a prop from a Conan movie.

Except for the red and black swastika on the front.

"The Vikings were Nazis?"

"No, dumbass." Scooter Trash Tammy rolls her eyes so hard I think they might come out of her ears. The gesture pisses me off so much I want to push those green marbles into her skull with my thumbs. "Those are Viking relics some wannabe Nazis modified. They're supposed to be from Josef Mengele's private collection. I told Bam-Bam they're not."

"Bam-Bam?" I ask.

She motions out the back windshield. "The big one in the center. He's the one you stole those from."

"Bam-Bam's a Nazi?"

"White Nationalist."

"There's a difference?" Lorna asks.

"Not really," Scooter Trash Tammy's hand is across Lorna's chest and under her jacket. I can't see it but I imagine it cupping Lorna's breast. "I told him those probably belonged to some low-rank SS guard."

Lorna shakes Scooter Trash Tammy's arm away. "Not the time," she growls.

Tammy pouts, "Aw, honey, all this excitement has me really worked up."

Jesus, what a freak show.

"Hey," I snap my fingers in Tammy's face to get her attention, "You know all this Viking and Nazi shit how?"

"Told you, I've got a Ph. D. In history."

And that's when the psycho bikers decide they're close enough to start shooting.

I drop to the floor as the high hollow *rat-tat-tat* from semi-automatic pistols cuts into the noise of this beast of a car.

"Get up, pussy," Lorna snarls. "those bullets aren't coming through."

"I've still got the shrapnel from the Monte Carlo in my leg."

"Different car."

"No shit, still made of sheet metal."

Lorna shakes her head. "This one's packed to the gills with something. Feels solid, bricks, like coke."

More pistol shots, followed by the big concussive boom of a shotgun. The back windshield goes all crackly but stays intact.

Lorna pushes the accelerator and we creep forward on the road. I slide back up into the seat but keep my head down.

"How much coke?" I ask.

Lorna's jaw clenches like it does when she's figuring something out. "Trunk's full, probably all four quarter-panels, none under the hood or we would've already overheated, maybe there's some behind the dash and in the seats too ..." She trails off.

"How much?" I insist to bring her to the point.

"Maybe a ton."

A ton...of cocaine....Jesus. "How much is that?"

"Around 900 keys."

Nine.

Hundred.

Scooter Trash Tammy is draped back over the seat. "Aw, honey, that's amazing, how'd you figure that out?"

"I'm a driver." Lorna's eyes cut left and right going from side mirror to side mirror.

"I don't get it."

"I know cars." Lorna shifts in her seat, pulling on the steering wheel to situate herself, settling into the pocket of her seat. I recognize that move and drag the seat belt across my body.

"How does that-" Tammy starts.

"Oi!" Lorna's screams, cutting off the question. "Shut the fuck up and hold onto something."

I just get the seatbelt clicked into place when Lorna stands on the brakes and jerks the wheel around in a circle.

Time expands and the world loses all cohesion.

Every molecule of air sucks out of the car as the back windshield collapses in a dance of sparkling shards. The reflection off the blower goes epileptic disco ball, flicker-stabbing me in the eye. Lorna is Valkyrie screaming over the torture screaming of the tires on blister-hot asphalt and the brake pads against whatever-the-fuck brake pads press against. I sling into the seat belt and it cuts deep into my torso. A rib at the bottom of my side pops and pain stabs across my belly that makes my guts turn to water but I don't shit myself somehow.

Scooter Trash Tammy hangs onto the back of my seat, the rest of her floating in the air like a party streamer.

Crazy bitch is smiling.

We smash into something. Black smoke whips past my eyes, and when it clears there's a biker hanging onto the door.

His face is pulled down like a cheap latex mask by the long, kinky beard that has wrapped itself around something chrome that once was a part of his bike but now flies beside him, tethered to his skin by the ridiculous hedgehog beard he was probably so proud of.

I want to tell him to just hang in there, it won't be like that for long, half of that beard is already pulling free in bloody patches and I can see more and more letting loose in tiny micro-bursts of blood that gleam on skin bleached white in terror.

The arms that cling to the door are thick with muscle and covered in shitty tattoos. From his forearm a girl looks at me with blew eyes (one blew this way, one blew that way) and wobbly thighs where whatever geek monster, scratcher-ass tattooer couldn't pull straight lines.

My brain chews the concept that his legs must be under the car about the time he slips out of sight and we rock up then down.

My teeth crunch together hard enough for me to go blind for a moment.

Or maybe it's my chin slamming into my collarbones.

Maybe it's between the rib crawling out the other side of where it supposed to be and the seat belt folding me in half because I can't suck in air at all, not even a sip.

My lungs burn and my eyes shimmer and shade, and I black out.

I come to like I've been slapped awake. The air I pull in chokes me, all acrid and gritty, like breathing burnt dirt, and my eyes are open but I can't see. We've stopped moving. Black smoke fills the inside of the car.

I cough and choke, my insides clenching like a fist around a shard of glass (that goddamn rib). I paw open the seatbelt buckle to relieve the pressure. Through the tears I see blurry light and reach for it. I find the edges of it and pull myself out. It's the window and I fall through.

And land on my face. My brain zags back to the time I caught a shovel on the side of my school...skahull... *skull*...fuck!

Lorna's trick just now really did a number on me.

Lorna.

I push myself up, holding in my breath through the taste of blood in my mouth. Holding the lump on my side where that rib is bulging out I find my legs tangled in a jumble of chrome that's tucked up under the fatass rear tire of the hotrod. Cursing each move because it feels like someone's pouring hot grease in my guts, I yank my foot free and look for Lorna.

Someone is screaming.

I look across the roof of the car and see on the other side surrounded by smoke with this motherfucking gorilla of a biker holding Lorna up by her hair. She's up on her tiptoes and grimacing in pain, but otherwise acting cool as can be. Which is impressive because she's at the end of a giant's arm.

It's Bam-Bam.

How do I know it's Bam-Bam?

He's got BAM BAM tattooed on his throat in big, fuck-off letters you could read a mile away even if you were blind.

"Where's my shit!" Veins bulge as he screams in Lorna's face, shaking her. "You killed my boys and fucked up my mule car."

She smiles a mouthful of bloody teeth.

"Oh, it's like that, is it!" Bam-Bam shakes her again. He releases the grip of one hand to yank a big chrome revolver from his waistband and places it under her chin.

If he pulls the trigger, he'll shoot his other goddamn hand off.

But Lorna will still be dead.

Like all the other bikers.

Scattered on the pavement are the wrecked bikes and mangled bodies in smears of crunchy burnt rubber, rainbow oil slicks, and blood so fucking red in radiating sunshine it nearly glows like shitty neon before being sucked up by the hungry asphalt. Lorna did it.

She fucking used the car as a weapon and cleared the field of our enemies. With that and her bloody smile of defiance, I might fall in love with her.

Again.

My vision becomes blocked by a ragged mop of blond hair.

Scooter Trash Tammy.

She's inside the car still, in the front seat now. She picks up the ax, rests it on the bottom of the car window, and pushes it to me. I take the ax and she jerks her head meaningfully toward Bam-Bam before sliding across the seat.

I creep around the back of the car, staying low and trying to not breathe too hard so I don't black out. I step over what's left of Half-beard. He now lies in a shimmering pool of his own blood and brain juice. It's not hard to hurry over him.

I step wide from the car to keep in Bam-Bam's blind spot.

"Hey, Little Dick!" Scooter Trash Tammy yells just as she pushes her door open and hauls her shirt up to her chin.

I don't look at her titties.

But Bam-Bam does.

And that's when I swing the ax at his arm.

My vision swims black at midswing and so I hit him with the butt end of the blade.

It doesn't cut, but I feel the satisfying wet celery sound of a bone breaking. Bam-Bam drops Lorna and stumbles away, holding his arm and howling and it's not until I hear that long, hollow, mournful howl that I realize the car is still running, rumbling at idle.

That thing really is a beast.

Bam-Bam kneels on the ground, holding his arm.

I take a step to finish him off.

Lorna grabs my arm.

"Leave him for the desert. You don't need a murder charge and we need to get the car and the dope to Kraeger."

She's right. I don't really have it in me. I can barely see and I'm going to drop beside this motherfucker any minute if I don't stop. Besides, Bam-Bam won't make it long out here and if he does, he won't be after us. I turn to the car, still gripping the ax.

"Leave that shit," Lorna says.

"Kraeger-" I start.

"Don't give a shit about that Nazi crap," Lorna says. "He wanted us to steal the car."

I look at the ax. Then at her. Then back to the ax. Why would Kraeger want a bullshit Nazi ax when there's a car stuffed to the gills with dope?

Motherfucker.

"Goddamn it." As I say this, the words jerk pain across my guts from that sonnuvabitchin busted rib. "I was your distraction so you could boost this car. You used me. Didn't you?"

She grins and her teeth are still red-rimmed.

I'm so dumbfounded that it barely registers when the ax clatters on the asphalt.

We climb into the car, Scooter Trash Tammy between us.

"Next time," I say, "I'm picking up some strange and driving the hot rod."

"Still right here. Still with a PhD," Tammy says.

"Yeah, it was your PhD that distracted Bam-Bam back there."

"Fuck you," but she's smiling when she says it.

Lorna drops the hot rod into low gear and it rocks and rumbles as she finesses it off the tangle of bikes and bikers underneath it, working the wheel and feathering the pedals. She's in her element and she's the most goddamn perfect thing I have ever seen.

I slump back against the door, putting pressure on my side to help the pain.

"Nah," I close my eyes when the car finally has all four wheels on firm ground. "I'll pass. I'm a sucker for brunettes."

GARVIN'S LEGACY

Quincy J. Allen

IN THE CANDLELIGHT OF A CENTURY-OLD shipping container, Maria stared at the unconscious form of her daughter, Jacqi, lying upon the tattered sofa. The dirty, crimson-soaked gauze wrapped around the girl's head looked like a ragged turban, not a bandage.

"Damn it!" Maria raged. "I can't do this! Not *again!*" She tugged a seam of her threadbare overalls and cursed the Oligarchy. In the Doldrums–endless warrens of stacked shipping containers carved into granite caverns beneath many of Earth's cities–head injuries were frequently a death sentence for a child and a prison sentence for one of the parents.

"I'm *so* sorry," she said out loud. Guilt pressed down on her.

She'd been at the hamster house, walking in one of the human-sized wheels when her daughter fell. For ten years, Maria marched five hundred watts a day at the powerhouse in exchange for food. But Jacqi's fall from a ladder changed all that. Maria's choices were now simple: go to prison or watch her daughter die.

A neighbor brought the unconscious girl home. Maria had applied the makeshift bandage torn from bedding she first sterilized by boiling. It was the best she could do—in the military she'd been a sniper, not a medic. She piled blankets on top of her daughter in a vain—and all-too-common—hope that blankets equated to medical miracles.

Years before, pneumonia claimed her son's life. Unable to pay the medical costs, her husband was sentenced to fifteen years in Jinzhou, the LC with the highest mortality rate in the entire Debtors' Penal System. Her husband lasted eighteen months before a DPS email notified Maria of his demise.

Born of hopelessness and rage, words spilled unbidden from her mouth, "It would have been easier if you'd died... or never been born."

It's your daughter! her conscience screamed. She hated herself for even thinking it. *Make the call*, it urged.

She placed her hand on Jacqi's chest, watching it barely rise and fall. "Maybe we'll get lucky and the SMTs will come." Maria stood slowly ... "Maybe ..." Her voice trailed off. She pushed that hope away. *We're too far from his clinic,* she thought. All she could see were Indenture Officers in crisp cornflower blue uniforms standing in her doorway to collect Jacqi's medical fees in full or to take Maria to Jinzhou.

"God damn them!" she shouted, cursing the Medi-Pay statutes and the Oligarchs who spawned them. They didn't give a damn about Drummers—a term coined by the affluent of the world as a pejorative. With only their pride left to them, the inhabitants of the Doldrums made it their own.

Maria stared at her daughter for a long time. Finally, she nodded once, accepting her fate. *You stay 'til you pay,* she thought. It was a phrase Drummers frightened their children with in bedtime stories. Now she was about to live the nightmare.

She stepped up to the comm pad built into the wall, pulled up the "Emergency Services" screen, selected the "Ambulance" option, and entered her daughter's gender, age, and condition. She felt nauseated when she pressed "SEND."

There was no turning back.

*   *   *

Maria cringed at the peal of a siren. Corporate Medical Techs were coming, weaving through the dirt and cinderblock alleys of her precinct in a hydrogen-powered ambulance. They carried with them chains of slavery. She stared at her daughter and knew in her heart Jacqi was worth *any* sacrifice.

CMTs worked for the same conglomerates that owned the courts, medical facilities, *and* labor camps. And the costs for just a CMT ambulance pickup, let alone treatment, were enough to make Drummers slave for years or even decades.

It was a tidy system, and most Drummers relied on hope and the witch-doctory of long-outlawed cults rather than call CMTs.

Maria heard the low, thudding grumble of a combustion engine–a *big* one.

Hope stirred.

CMTs drove quiet, electric ambulances. Drummer vehicles, however, were usually two- and three-wheeled scooters burning methaline, a sewage-based biomass concoction powering all machinery in the Doldrums.

Maria dared to let her glimmer of hope take root.

Could it be...?

"It *has* to be!" she whispered, dashing towards the flap of ancient carpet that covered the doorway.

She yanked the carpet aside just as a CMT ambulance pulled to a stop outside. The siren faded, and two CMTs in crisp, green uniforms beneath black tactical armor burst from the rear doors of the modern ambulance. They quickly hauled out a collapsible gurney adorned with unrecognizable apparatus.

The combustion engine roared as it pulled around a corner down the street and headed straight for them. Hope bloomed. SMTs were coming. The Samaritan Medical Techs worked for Senator Pickett, a ridiculously wealthy contrarian who had taken up the cause of Drummers.

As the siren faded, the CMT driver heard the thunder and leaned out. "*SMTs!*" he screamed, pointing back towards the fast-approaching vehicle.

A battered, decades-old, military ambulance raced towards them. It was identical to those that carried Maria during her Indonesian tours in 2089 and 2092. The telltale billow of gray-green methaline smoke poured from dual stacks behind the cab. As the vehicle barreled forward, a man appeared through a hatch cut in the roof, a thick-barreled, homemade grenade launcher held ready.

Elevating the massive barrel to a steep angle, he braced himself against the lip of the hatch and aimed.

THUNK!–THUNK!–THUNK!

Three, dark, baseball-sized objects sailed through the air, each arc tracing a line of white smoke towards the ambulance parked in front of Maria's home.

BANG!–BANG!–BANG!–BZZZZZZZZZZZZTTT!

The staccato explosions came right on top of each other, and then the dim area burst into bright light and stark shadow as fierce arcs of electricity erupted and coursed along every surface of the CMT ambulance. The CMTs stiffened and jittered in the torrents of energy. The lightning abated after a handful of seconds, and all three CMTs slumped where they were.

The SMT ambulance bounced over the cinderblocks forming the rough edge of the street, skidding to a halt before Maria's wide eyes.

"Go! Go! Go!" the shooter hollered as he swapped his improvised weapon for a military-issue rifle. He leapt up and out of the hatch, just as the back of the ambulance disgorged two men carrying a gurney between them. Both wore threadbare but functional tac vests and had standard-issue military sidearms holstered under their arms.

"You called for the ambulance, right?" the shooter asked Maria hurriedly.

She nodded, wide-eyed and unable to speak.

"We're here to take your daughter to the Pickett Clinic." He motioned for the two men with the gurney, who promptly dashed past Maria. The shooter continued: "No CMTs, no fees, no prison ... but it's risky. The CMTs may shoot us to pieces on the way, and that includes your daughter." He turned to the two med techs. "How bad is she, Tanaka?"

"Head injury," one of the techs replied. "Unconscious and shallow breathing. Right pupil severely dilated. Looks like a bad concussion ... *really* bad."

Maria's heart sank.

"You SMTs work for Senator Pickett, right?" she asked, hope and fear and disbelief mixing in her features. The EMTs examining her daughter glanced at to the shooter and then gave her a knowing smile. The shooter seemed familiar, but she couldn't place his face. His hair was mostly gray, with streaks of white and black, as if it couldn't decide if he was old or young. His scraggly beard ran down to his collar, and despite the hardness in his eyes as he searched the street for more CMTs, there was a compassion there she hadn't seen since her grandfather's time ... back when society gave a damn.

"That's right," the shooter answered quickly. He hefted his rifle and looked over his shoulder with a wary eye. "We're ... one of his crews." He made it sound like he and his men were just another crew, but there was something that made her think he'd held something back. He went back to searching the street. "We used to avoid this precinct, but The SMTs have been gaining ground."

At his words, Maria's heart stilled for a moment. The shock of seeing the CMT crew being electrocuted faded, along with the worry for her daughter. She had no intention of going to prison. She was tired of the system–of the State–and even more tired of a society that had lain down and accepted it all.

The SMTs were getting stronger, and the men standing before her gave a damn. She knew they would see her daughter to safety or die trying. She'd known soldiers like them during war. Hell, she'd *been* one of them.

The ghosts of Maria's dead husband and son stared at her from the depths of her memory and raised a question in her mind.

Without help, her daughter would be dead by morning. If the CMTs got Jacqi, Maria would end up in an LC, possibly for life. Whether it was for medical debts or killing CMTs, death in prison would be the same.

There really was only one answer.

"I'm going with you," she said.

The shooter's eyebrows rose above widening eyes.

"Ma'am, I'm afraid I can't let you do that. We only take the injured. These runs frequently turn into high-speed gun battles, and with a command center so close, it's sure to. This is gonna be a shit-show in about ninety seconds when those assholes in the street don't radio in."

"I'm not asking for a guarantee," she said, stepping past him.

She shoved a ratty recliner aside with her foot and lifted a rectangle of rusty, metal plating beneath it. She pulled out something roughly two and a half feet long wrapped in rags damp with oil. Pulling at the fabric, she revealed her grandfather's antique AR-10, the bluing on the barrel and hardware worn to bright steel and the plastic furniture burnished smooth by years of use, long past. A 20-round magazine was already inserted. Holding the rifle comfortably, as if it were an old friend, she stared at the old SMT.

"Ma'am, I–" he started.

"It's Maria ..." she injected, "or Stills, if you prefer." There was no give in her voice. "Let me explain a few things to you." She counted off on her fingers. "One: two tours in Indonesia earned me two Combat Casualty Medals and an Uncommon Valor Cross. Two: that's my *daughter* your men are loading up. Three: my son died of pneumonia, and my husband died in an LC to pay for it. And four: if the CMTs get hold of my daughter, she'll probably spend the rest of her life in an LC, and I *certainly* will." She pulled the charging handle back and released it with a *CLICK*, chambering a round. She flipped on the safety with her thumb. "*I'm going with you.*" It wasn't iron in her voice, it was titanium. She locked eyes with the SMT. "Let me put it another way. If I'm going to jail for protecting my daughter, it'll be for killing those life-sucking motherfuckers, not owing them money."

The shooter narrowed his dark eyes and looked her up and down ... slowly. He cocked his head to the side as the corners of his mouth turned up in a thin-lipped grin. He nodded once. "Alright, you're in." He turned to the door, shouting at the two men rolling Jacqi past the limp forms of the CMTs. "Tanaka! We're taking two, not one, and she's my tail gunner!"

"What?" Tanaka yelled back, clearly surprised. He turned and gave the old SMT a dubious look. He could see Maria through the doorway, the AR-10 held in her hands. "Okay...." he added slowly, shaking his head. "You're the boss...."

The old man turned and held out his hand. "If we're going to be fighting together, I'd say introductions are in order. I'm Garvin. That's Tanaka–medic and shooter. The little guy next to him is Smitty–my assistant, a medic, and pretty much the man who makes it possible for me to keep this show on the road. Franco is behind the wheel and the best driver in the SMTs."

Shouldering the rifle, Garvin pulled a silvery needle gun from his shoulder holster and checked the load. Maria raised an eyebrow, because needlers were worth a small fortune. Garvin caught her looking. "It ... was a gift," he said quickly... "From a blue-blood colonel years ago..." He cleared his throat and eyed her AR-10. "You got more than just the one magazine?"

Maria reached down and pulled out a decades-old, military ammo satchel, heavy enough to strain her as it came up. "How far are we going?"

"Through about ten miles of hell," he replied. "If we make it to the Pickett Clinic, we're home free. Once we're within range of their heavy machine guns, the CMTs will give it up. And Senator Pickett had the area designated a sanctuary, so there's nothing anyone can do to us once we're in."

"It must be convenient having more money than God," she said. Senator Pickett was a legend in the Doldrums–he was the only Senator who fought for Drummers, and he had enough money to make it stick. She threw the ammo satchel over her shoulder. "Let's go."

"There's three on our ass!" Garvin shouted from the turret. "And two more coming in from the left!"

Racing through narrow canyons of stacked cargo containers, they'd made it through two precincts and connecting tunnels before the CMTs found them. The electric motors of the lighter CMT ambulances were capable of tremendous bursts of speed, but the turbo-charged, methaline-powered V-10 of the SMT ambulance had a better top end in the straightaways.

A burst of automatic fire stitched a diagonal line along the armor of the SMT ambulance's back doors. The methaline engine roared as Franco hammered the throttle and swerved hard, jamming Maria up against a bulkhead. She regained her footing and looked out through the narrow, armored glass viewport in the back door.

Three CMT ambulances chased them, only forty meters behind, swerving as they gained, with one in the lead and the other two flanking left and right. Two more ambulances another hundred meters behind gained ground as they raced through Doldrum precincts, tires squealing around every corner.

THUNK!–THUNK!–THUNK!

Garvin's mortar rifle barked again. The base-ball-sized rounds slammed in front of a pursuer, forcing it to swerve off the road and crash through someone's fungus house. Three bright detonations turned the dusky street into acid-white daylight and brittle shadows, but the blast barely licked at the wheels of the ambulance.

"That's it for the EMPs!" Garvin shouted. "Maria, you're up!" She heard Garvin fire several rounds with his assault rifle.

Gunners from all three pursuit vehicles fired, and Garvin yelped in the turret, tumbling down into the vehicle, screaming.

"He's hit!" Tanaka dove onto the old SMT. "Throw me the kit!"

Smitty grabbed a package from a compartment above and tossed.

Maria glanced at the old SMT as blood spread across his chest. Her training kicked in–her old drill instructor's voice echoing in her mind–*Medics do the worrying. You do the killing.*

Maria grabbed the latch beneath the window and slid a gun port open, jamming the barrel through. Two of the three CMT ambulances sprouted a gunner, each armed with a light auto-rifle. She and the gunners aimed at the same time. The gunners opened up, spraying the SMT ambulance with a hailstorm of slugs.

Maria hesitated, not because she feared being shot, but because she was reading the sway of the ambulance beneath her as she sighted down her rifle.

It all came back to her. Running gun-battles in the Indonesian jungle, firing from every sort of transport in the theater.

The shooting.

The fear.

The *calm*.

There... she thought as she found the pattern in Franco's swerves.

She fired one quick burst, instinctively counting five rounds leaving the chamber.

Two struck home, slamming the gunner of the center CMT ambulance backwards. He disappeared into the vehicle.

The flanking gunners ducked down, leaving only their heads and rifles exposed. They both fired at the same time, concentrating their fire on Maria. The steel door clanged and thundered from the impacts. A single round hit the viewport, starring it on one side. Bullet fragments raked Maria's temple. Wincing in pain, she ducked sideways and gritted her teeth at the rattle of gunfire.

"Hang on!" Franco screamed.

An instant later, they swerved hard, the tires screeching as they traversed a corner at high speed. The ambulance tilted up on two wheels and slammed down, losing a good deal of speed.

Maria peered out the viewport to see one of the CMTs sliding expertly through the turn and rushing towards them. The driver hit the accelerator and slammed into them *hard*, sending Maria to the deck.

Metal screeched. The tail end of the ambulance went sluggish as the bumpers hooked together.

"We're locked!" Franco screamed over the howling motor. If the other ambulances got past and cut them off, they were dead meat.

Maria knew what she had to do. She dropped the half-empty magazine from her AR-10, reached down, and pulled out a cumbersome and heavy 50-round mag. Slamming it home, she stood and jammed her barrel through the gun port. With a quick look through the cracked window, she aimed directly at the driver only a few feet away.

She pulled the trigger and held it.

Rounds ricocheted off the armored glass, starring and chipping the heavy polymer. She emptied half the mag until the 7.62mm jacketed slugs punched through and poured into the face of the shocked driver. They rocked his head like it was a punching bag, turning it into a crater of blood, muscle, and brain. He slumped sideways, his hands death-gripped on the wheel. The CMT ambulance broke loose with a screech of tearing metal and swerved directly into the path of the third CMT. They slammed together, slid in a tight arc, and both tumbled over and over again.

The SMT ambulance pulled away just as the last two CMTs pulled in behind them.

One of the gunners rose through the roof hatch, a rocket launcher resting on his shoulder.

"Rocket!" Maria screamed.

Smoke whooshed behind the gunner. Franco jerked the wheel sideways. They lurched left, and the rocket shot past, hitting the road ahead of them. The HEAT round jarred Maria's teeth when it detonated, pelting the vehicle with dirt and shrapnel. Franco swerved around the crater, hitting the gas as a twinge of high explosives flowed into the ambulance and filled Maria's nostrils. More memories of the war crashed into her thoughts.

They were in trouble. If the gunner had enough rockets, eventually Franco would swerve the wrong way, and they'd buy it.

Maria looked down at the blood pumping from Garvin's chest as Tanaka applied a bandage. Smitty did his best to hold Jacqi still on the gurney.

Rage boiled up inside Maria's chest. She felt it swelling, preparing to burst in a flame that she feared she might not be able to extinguish. *War...* she thought. *We played by the rules... we did everything that told us too, and now my daughter may die from it....*

Beads of sweat trickled down Maria's face. She felt the heft of her rifle, the sway of the vehicle beneath her. She'd been trained for combat and had gotten good at it, but things weren't looking good. She leaned her head back against the plating, trying to shut out Garvin's screams. The flames building up inside her turned to cold steel. *Enough*.

"Franco!" she shouted. "Hold this fucker steady!"

"But they'll–"

"DO IT!" she screamed.

Franco nodded. The SMT vehicle steadied instantly.

Maria rose through the turret like a piston, set the AR-10 into her shoulder, and aimed.

The gunner with the rocket launcher steadied himself as best as he could just as the second gunner fired, despite the swerving CMT ambulance beneath him. Ricochets bounced all around Maria as she waited.

Maria let her breath out slowly, remembering everything she'd ever learned about firing a weapon.

She heard the hiss.

She saw the smoke.

She pulled the trigger.

A single shot rang out.

BOOM!

The rocket detonated just as it left the tube, engulfing the gunner and the vehicle beneath him in a blossom of flame and smoke.

Maria traversed the barrel and sighted on the second gunner, who stood there, rocked by the explosion of the other CMT vehicle.

Maria pulled the trigger again.

She fired once... *Miss!* Fired again. The gunner fell, and the ambulance dropped back as the SMT entered a tunnel. It's methaline engine roared in her ears.

"We're almost there," Franco yelled back. He floored it when they hit a straightaway.

Maria turned in her seat as they exited the tunnel into daylight. The sun shone so bright it burned. She covered her eyes, for she hadn't seen the sun since Indonesia fifteen years earlier.

"Maria!" Smitty yelled, breaking her out of her reverie. "Get down here!"

Maria dropped down into the vehicle where Smitty leaned over Garvin. The old man's skin had turned a frightening gray. His chest was covered with blood, as was his neck and chin.

"She's the one, Smitty," the old man said weakly.

"Sir?" the small man asked, doubt filling his voice.

Garvin gasped and gurgled, bubbles of blood catching in his throat. "She's the one ... we've been waiting for." He coughed hard and spat out a gobbet of crimson. "Take care of the paperwork. She's...the...one..."

A death-rattle danced across the man's body, and then he went limp.

"Yes, Mr. Pickett," Smitty said. He gently closed the old man's glazed eyes and whispered a prayer.

"Pickett?" Maria asked. "But I thought Garvin was his *last* name," Maria said. "His–"

"No," Smitty interrupted. "Not his last name. That is–*was* Garvin Pickett." Smitty stared at her. "All the SMTs were his. The sanctuary was his. The cause was his"

"What did he mean, 'She's the one?'" Maria asked, confused.

"He meant, Mrs. Stills, that it's all yours now."

She blinked her eyes several times. "What?"

Smitty sighed, placing his hand on the chest of his old friend and smiling at Maria. "That's what

Senator Pickett meant. You're the one who can finish what he started."

"You've got to be kidding."

"No. I'm not. Recent legislative changes the Senator sponsored make it possible for Senators to name their successors. The Oligarchs passed it so they can give titles to their children and create their own little monarchies. Pickett, on the other hand, just bequeathed it to a veteran who lost her son and husband to the System. That same woman also just risked her life to save an injured daughter and stay out of debtors prison." He locked eyes with her, a sense of urgency and hope filling his eyes. "You are the *perfect* person to change this world."

"I couldn't possibly–"

"Think about it," he interrupted. "The people are hungry for change. They need a leader to believe in who the Oligarchs can't tear down. Those cowards won't come after a woman like you–it would hurt their ratings." Smitty stepped up and clasped her arm gently. "Maria," his voice was urgent, almost desperate. "You're our secret weapon. You're what we've all be waiting for. *All* of us. Pickett built the weapon ... made the final payment with his life. you *have* to go out there and use it ... like you did that rifle."

"Change the world?" Maria asked, her eyes wide. She stared at her daughter, laying peacefully on the gurney, hopeful the doctors would be able to save her. Either way, she felt the weight of the world settle upon her shoulders.

Maybe she could carry it.

SITTING DUCKS

Manuel Ramos

THE JOB WENT TO SHIT IN TWO MINUTES.

We had everyone down on their bellies, including the guards, when we heard the sirens. Eddie looked at me, and even through the Trump mask I could tell that he was gonna crack. He was our weak link. He'd been skittish about the bank since I brought him in on the play more than three months before. He'd lost his nerve because of his last stretch in the DOC but all he had to do was stuff duffel bags with cash. Not too difficult.

Yvonne, on the other hand, kept to her assignment. She'd intimidated the bank workers, cleaned out a few of the cashiers' drawers and was ready to move on the vault when we heard the cops coming. She knew what to do. Sirens and cops didn't faze her. She made a move to the doors.

"Let's book!" she shouted.

The sirens increased in intensity and I estimated we had less than thirty seconds before the cops made it to the corner where they could see the front of the bank–and us.

That's when Eddie freaked. He ran around the lobby like a headless chicken, shouting, screaming really, and waving his Mossberg at everyone and no one. I was embarrassed for my aunt, Eddie's mother. He let down the whole family when he panicked.

One of the guards tried to roll into a ball in a corner but Eddie zeroed in on him. Eddie jabbed the helpless guy in the gut and made him stand up.

"You're my shield, asshole. You wanna trip alarms, this is what you get."

"I didn't do nothin'," was all the guard could say.

"Eddie, what the ..." I shouted. "Let him go. We gotta run for it!"

Eddie ignored me and dragged the guard to the bank's heavy metal entrance doors. He held the pale, shaking guy from behind with the shotgun stuck against his ribs. When Eddie reached to open the doors, the guard made his move. He was faster than he looked. He yanked the shotgun from Eddie's sweaty hands, stuck the shortened barrel against Eddie's neck and blew away his head, Trump mask, and most of his left shoulder. Eddie's blood and gore plastered the doors, the polished floor, the guard and one unlucky bank customer.

People on the floor screamed, a few cursed. We'd lost control of the situation and the customers knew it.

Yvonne kicked the shotgun out of the guard's hands and knocked him out with a vicious whack from the butt of her .45. The two of us jumped over the bodies and bolted through the bloody doors. Yvonne held on to her bag of money. Not much to show for her efforts.

I hoped that Jimmy knew what was up and would be waiting for us at the curb.

He was.

I jumped in the front and Yvonne dove into the back. He stomped the gas pedal and the ordinary-looking Honda Civic flew away from the bank and down Seventeenth Street. Yvonne and I tore off our masks.

"Eddie?" Jimmy asked.

"Gone," Yvonne answered. "He fucked up."

Jimmy looked at me, I nodded.

Jimmy's real name was Santiago Palacios, and señor Palacios learned all about cars and driving and running from cops and soldiers in the crazy boulevards and alleys of Havana. In the States we called him Jimmy the Driver and let him do his thing.

Jimmy picked out the rides for the job and, as usual, he made efficient choices. No one would look twice at the three of us in the Civic, though we were traveling a bit faster than the other traffic. We needed the car for a quick, and short, trip.

He darted through the streets like he'd been ordered to transport party officials to a meeting with Castro and the price for being late was a date with one of *El Comandante's* firing squads. Fast but not too illegal.

We didn't have to soar for me to feel like we'd taken off. The job was finished, good, bad or otherwise I almost didn't care. People screamed and cried because we were there. Guns were pulled and used. Blood flowed. Cops were on our asses or close to it. Vivian and I made it. Eddie, not so much. Most of it had been automatic for me, no thinking necessary. We played the hand we were dealt, as always. Now we ran for it. This was the part I liked–needed, really. The quiet after a storm, a smoke after sex.

Who was I kidding? I liked it all.

Back on the island, after a stint in the Cuban army, Jimmy drove a '55 Chevy Bel Air, red and white, with as much original equipment as he could scrounge from all over Cuba. He named the car *La Bella,* -"The Beauty" - and from what he said about her I believed she was a dream car that he babied and loved. Pristine paint job, impeccable interior. But for every original tail light lens or chrome hood ornament he managed to scavenge, he had to buy, borrow or steal imaginative replacements for parts that finally quit and were nowhere to be found in Cuba. He'd swapped out the defunct six-banger for an Isuzu engine and added a Peugeot transmission, a Russian carburetor, and on and on. He made a living– not much but enough in Cuba–with La Bella by driving her every day, transporting visitors and residents, criss-crossing Havana from La Cabaña, through Habana Vieja, out to the José Martí International Airport. He guided passengers through Havana's night life and to country villages as far away as Trinidad.

All that ended when he wrecked La Bella on the Malecón one bleary drunken night. The tourists finally got to him and he decided to take out a group of rude Russians and Bulgarians, using his car as his weapon of choice. He'd had enough of jokes about Fidel's sexual kinks; enough of requests for the best whores in the city; and enough of foreign slobs who knew nothing of the history of his country but claimed to be "revolutionary comrades" so they could get a better rate. He gave his targets a good scare but missed and smashed against the sea wall, where he had to leave his beauty to the mercy of the authorities. He knew they would treat his car better than they would treat him. He decided he should leave Cuba and take the long raft trip to the United States. He quit drinking that night, never tasted another drop.

Eventually, we met when we were both on the wrong end of a 9 mm pulled by a man who didn't like losing at poker. But tough guy with a Glock proved slow on the trigger. After we took care of him, Jimmy and I became a team. He drove and I did the messy stuff, often with Yvonne. Jimmy brought another skill that came in handy once in a while. In the army he'd become an explosives expert. He never needed that knowledge in Cuba. That changed in the U.S.

Jimmy planned a route that took us only two blocks from the bank. He turned into a ten-story parking garage, drove to the top, parked in a space reserved with an orange cone next to a Lexus LX-570, and we jumped out. From the edge of the short wall of the parking lot we could see the traffic in three directions, including from the bank. Cops were everywhere around the bank but only a few cruised towards us. Those cars didn't hustle like they were chasing anyone, so we felt safe for now.

"They didn't see us," Yvonne said. "We got out of there in time."

"That'll change, pronto," Jimmy said. "They'll talk to people in the bank and on the street, check the security cameras. This ride will be hot. We know what we have to do."

"Let's do it," I said.

Jimmy started the Civic and drove down to the third level. I beeped open the Lexus and Yvonne and I climbed in. We then drove to the third level where we picked up Jimmy.

"Everything okay?" I asked.

"*Está bien,*" Jimmy said. "I set the timer for twenty minutes. That gives us room to get away but not long enough for the cops to find it. With any luck."

Jimmy was a cautious man. I didn't know if that was a Cuban trait, but I thought his experiences on the island made him too guarded, too suspicious. Some might call it paranoia. He took the extra steps, "Always *con cuidado*," he'd say.

"Looks like a few cars are gonna get trashed," Yvonne said.

"Can't be helped, but it's in a corner, next to a wall. I put up the Section Closed sign. A passerby might get hurt. Bad luck for them." He shrugged. Yvonne nodded.

Jimmy used the parking pass he'd bought the day before then drove like any other nine-to-five commuter leaving work early, not too slow or too fast. It wasn't the time for speed yet.

The luxury SUV was a thirsty beast but the V8 and 383 horses could get to 60 mph in under seven seconds. Jimmy said it had cat's feet, which meant in Jimmy-speak that it handled well and was responsive to the type of driving Jimmy might have to do. It had more than enough room for the three of us and our gear and, as a bonus, it looked solid. Our usual supplier provided a virgin ride with black onyx paint and the basic, over-the-top sound system, not that we were listening to any music. It cost us a lot, considering it was stolen right off the truck, but I'd learned the hard way to trust Jimmy's instincts and not go cheap when prepping a job.

Yvonne sat in the second row of seats. She watched every car that pulled alongside ours. Her fingers held her gun gingerly, easy.

"I only grabbed about fifteen thousand from the cashiers," she said.

"You got more than I did," I said. I tossed her my canvas bag. "Maybe five grand, if we're lucky. We lost money on this gig."

"Our luck ran out before we walked in that bank. Someone set off an alarm almost from the second we pulled our guns. We were sitting ducks."

"I hear you. The alarms should've been killed. Frankie's waiting at the apartment. We'll get from him what the hell happened since tech was his. It always is."

"You really think he's gonna show?" Yvonne asked. "He screwed up and he's either on the run because he blew it or because someone got to him and he double-crossed us." She licked her lips and ran her fingers lightly over her gun. "I can't wait until I make him explain what the hell happened."

Yvonne Montelibre rarely made threats but when she did she always followed through. I'd met her about ten years before, the week she married my brother. She knew the score, of course, and it wasn't too long after the wedding that she became a full partner in our crew. When the cops killed Abel she double-downed in sticking with us. I had to admit that she was smarter and harder than my brother, and I'd worshipped Abel since I was a punk kid hot-wiring fantasy wheels.

Yvonne called Frankie on her cell phone. She shook her head in disgust. "Voice mail. Says he's unavailable. He must have ditched his phone."

"We better do the same," I said. Both of us removed the SIM cards from our phones and tossed them out the window. Then we threw our phones, broken into pieces.

"The apartment?" Jimmy asked.

Yvonne shook her head. "No. It's not safe. If Frankie turned, the cops will be watching it. Head for the cabin. Frankie's never been there, doesn't know where it is."

"He knows about it though," I said.

"Too many cabins in Colorado for the cops to check every one. It's our only option. We were going there eventually anyway."

"But not this soon. After it cooled off. It's high risk now. We'll be out in the open, on the highway."

"We've no choice," Yvonne said. "And Jimmy's got everything we need."

"We'll leave Frankie out there on his own. We better be sure he's not with us anymore."

"I'm sure," she said.

"*Sí*," Jimmy said. "*Tenemos que ir a las montañas.*"

I didn't want to but I had to agree. "Then let's go."

Frankie Delgado was a special case. He latched on to me when we were in County, him for an assault during a bar fight and me for looking too Mexican in swanky Cherry Hills. Okay, I was casing the country club for a potential job, but the only reason they grabbed me on a bullshit weapons charge was because I obviously didn't belong in the neighborhood.

Anyhow. Frankie had been a significant something or other in Yvonne's past. She knew him and more or less vouched for him when he looked me up after his County visit. He had brains and nerdy knowledge of all things technical, including bank alarm systems and digital safes. His periodic disappearances when he sunk under oceans of booze and dope were his main weakness, and we all have at least one. He sobered and cleaned up when I had a job for him, but the guy worried me from the get. I didn't trust him to do any of the heavy lifting. Frankie wasn't the type to use a gun or smash a jewelry case but he'd made jobs easier for us when he disarmed security and blanked out video cameras, all from the comfort of his computer desk.

"What happened to Frankie?" I asked Yvonne after we'd been on the road for several miles.

She shook her head like she didn't have an answer. "They leaned on him, made him uncomfortable. Wouldn't take much to break him. But I never thought he'd actually work with the cops to bust us. Being a rat is one thing, but setting us up? That's low, even for him."

"He did us a lot of good in the past. He drinking again?"

"Not that I've seen. But we don't really hang out together, you know?"

I could hear in her voice that she felt responsible for Frankie, which meant she blamed herself for our trouble. In my view, it was my fault, my guilt. I made the decision to bring him in although we'd met in jail. I'd always told myself to never associate with guys from lock-up, on the outside. The joint is one kind of reality, the world is something else, and they rarely mix well.

"There's a helicopter behind us," Jimmy said. "Been there for about ten miles."

I looked out the passenger window and saw the chopper behind and to the right of us. We were on I-70, almost an hour west of Denver, about five miles from where we had to turn off for the road to the cabin.

"Take it easy," I said. "Could be anything. Not necessarily on us."

Jimmy didn't talk and for the next five miles neither did Yvonne or me. He kept the Lexus at five miles over the speed limit in the slower flow of traffic. I admired Jimmy's choice of car. Smooth, secure, ready for anything.

The whomp-whomp of the helicopter blades followed us like the soundtrack of a bad dream. We breathed easier when Jimmy hooked off the highway through a tree-shrouded opening in a fence and onto the dirt road to the cabin. The helicopter continued west toward the highest snow-capped peaks.

The SUV glided over the rough ground and flattened the rocky terrain like the expensive earth-mover it was.

The cabin sat in a clearing surrounded by thick mountain growth–pine trees, shrubs and grasses. A former member of our crew, "Doc" Gaffney, technically still owned it but he was doing five-to-twenty for a string of mall strip B and E's and not planning any weekends enjoying nature's clean air. Gaffney had never been tied to any of us and we were fairly certain that the place was safe. Despite that, we sat in the Lexus for ten minutes and scoped out the cabin, the trees and the sky for any sign of life. Then we circled the cabin, checked the grove of trees that shaded a small creek, and walked a bit back up the road. Jimmy parked the Lexus behind the cabin so anyone wandering down the road would not spot it.

Finally, we unlocked the cabin's door and made ourselves at home.

The place was a shack, not much more than a roof and four walls. Three wobbly chairs and a wooden table made up the furniture. An outside pump worked but we didn't trust it and used bottled water. One outlet gave us bootleg electricity that Gaffney had somehow jerry-rigged into the cabin.

Jimmy carried in all the gear he'd stowed for what was supposed to be part two of our plan. Then he said, "I'm going to make sure the Lexus is secure."

We ate canned beans and bacon fried on a small hot plate. We talked about the busted job, worthless Frankie, and what we would do next. We agreed to follow the original plan - divide the take, meager as it was, drive west until we thought the car was too hot, maybe in Utah, then split up and go our separate ways. Each one of us was ready to leave Colorado, now more than ever.

The day had been a bust but I didn't spend any time worrying about what had happened or what we should have done differently. I had no regrets. Eddie got himself killed. Only way to look at it. I didn't blame anyone–not Eddie, not Frankie–for where I found myself that night. No one put a gun to my head and forced me to walk into that bank wearing a mask and threatening strangers with an automatic. That was all me.

Truth be told, I needed the rush. There'd be another bank down the road. I'd pull together another crew, and somewhere in the near future I'd find myself in this same spot–on the run, under an adrenaline high, hoping I didn't have to use my gun but confident I would if it came down to that. With a little bit of luck I might make money from the next job.

"We gonna have a lookout?" Yvonne asked.

"What for?" I responded. "Any cop comes tonight, we're easy targets. Might as well get some sleep."

"*Sí,*" Jimmy added. "There's only so much we can do."

"You're right," Yvonne agreed.

I slept in one of the sleeping bags Jimmy unloaded. I woke up when I heard Yvonne and Jimmy talking about the different routes we could take. We crawled out of our bags about five when the sun streamed through the window.

We ate more beans and bacon. Then Yvonne said she'd be right back. She grabbed the roll of toilet paper and walked out the back door. She stuck her .45 in the waistband of her pants. Jimmy and I drank instant coffee and checked our guns. We stayed busy getting ready to haul ass from the cabin. It promised to be a sweet drive in the Lexus.

I looked at a map to figure out how long it would take to drive to the Utah border. Jimmy rolled up the bags and packed the remaining food, water bottles and our few pieces of equipment.

Yvonne opened the door and immediately I saw that something was wrong. Before I could react, Yvonne was pushed through the door by Frankie, who held a gigantic revolver to her neck.

"Don't make me shoot you!" he shouted. "I only want the money."

Jimmy and I put our hands up. We were several feet from our guns. Frankie had a greasy backpack draped across his shoulders.

"What the fuck, Frankie?" I asked. "What's going on?"

"You tell me," he said. "First you assholes leave me hanging at the apartment, then you try to run off with all the money. Motherfuckers!"

Frankie was a skinny, thin-haired guy with nervous eyes. I always thought of him as a peanut, a shrimp, but in the morning light in the cabin his gun looked bigger than his head and that made Frankie a big man.

"You think I didn't know about this cabin? I did time with Gaffney, chumps. I knew what you were talking about whenever you mentioned the cabin. You thought I was geeky Frankie without a clue. Now who doesn't have a clue?"

"We figured you out, Frankie," Yvonne said. "You set us up. The alarm went off, the cops were on us before we had a chance to do anything. And now you want what we did get? You bring the cops with you? You got your fucking nerve."

He grimaced like someone kicked him in the nuts. "What are you talking about? I turned off the bank's security. There was no alarm from the bank. You were okay. I did my job."

"We heard the cops," Jimmy said. "The sirens were everywhere."

Frankie shook his head. "You jackasses. The cops weren't coming for you. There was a shooting outside the Brown Palace. Some kind of wetback protest. The cops weren't going to the bank." He kept shaking his head. "You stupid ..."

Yvonne and I looked at each other but we had nothing to say.

"If you're on the level then we can carry on, like we planned," Jimmy said. "No need for this."

"You double-crossed me once," Frankie said. "Twice? Hell no." He motioned at Yvonne with his gun. He pulled security zip ties and duct tape from his backpack and tossed them to her.

"Tie them up," he said. "Then I'll take care of you."

"You don't need to do this," I said.

"Shut up!" Frankie shouted.

He whipped his gun across my forehead and I fell to my knees. Blood flowed into my eyes. Pain drilled through the top of my skull and I felt like throwing up. I thought I would pass out.

"Put the tape on his mouth, tie him up."

Yvonne did what he ordered. My wrists were bound behind my back and the tape dug into my lips.

I watched her tape Jimmy's mouth and then zip tie his wrists. Jimmy and I sat on the floor, trussed up and silent.

Frankie made Yvonne sit on her knees, then he tightened the plastic ties on her wrists and stuck a strip of duct tape over her mouth and across the back of her head. He looked around the cabin. He picked up the bags of money and the keys to the SUV. Jimmy shook his head. Muffled sounds came from his taped mouth. He tried to talk with his eyes. I saw a crazy mix of hate, anger and fear but Jimmy's message was lost on Frankie.

"Don't worry, Jimmy," Frankie said. "I'll take good care of the Lexus. Better than what you did to the Civic. They're saying on TV that the bomb in the parking lot must have been part of the shooting at the hotel. No one linked it to the bank job."

He kissed the Lexus keys. "Your latest beauty, eh? You must really like driving it. Cool ride. Thanks." He laughed.

He walked to the doorway, stopped and turned around. "Try to make a sucker out of Frankie? This is what happens, bitches." He aimed his gun at each one of us and yelled "Bang!" three times. He laughed again and ran out of the cabin.

Yvonne slumped against a leg of the table. Jimmy stared at the door. Me, I wasn't sure what I was thinking.

The explosion shook the cabin and rattled the table. Each one of us bounced on the dirty floor. The echo skipped across the mountains. The smell of oily smoke, burning rubber and gasoline filled the cabin. Jimmy–careful Jimmy–closed his eyes

The three of us huddled on the floor, not moving, not looking at one another. I wasn't surprised when I heard the helicopter hovering over the cabin.

DRIVERLESS

Robert Jeschonek

THE SLEEK RED FORD GT WITH WHITE RACING stripes screamed along the Nebraska four-lane, punching toward the dark cloud-shrouded towers of Omaha in the distance.

Vreeeeoooowwwwww

The gray-haired, dark-skinned man in the cockpit, Shunn Comma, clutched the steering wheel, darting his bloodshot brown eyes to the rearview mirror every few seconds.

Each time, he chewed his gum a little faster. The trio of black Ferrari Superfasts was still zooming along behind him, five car lengths back and closing.

Eeeeeooowww Eeeeooowww Eeeeooowww.

Like Shunn's GT, none of the Ferraris was driverless, hobbled by speed or maneuvering governors–nothing short of a miracle in the mid-21st century.

And nothing short of a shit-show if those Ferraris ever caught up. Assuming there was anything left of his time-release memory before they tried to jack the shit out of it.

Shunn checked the timer on his right contact lens overlay. *07:35.*

Tick tick tick tick

That was all the time he had left to deliver the ultra-top-secret message before it was gone forever...and a civil war, perhaps, erupted in the heart of the American Midwest.

Zeeeeeooooowwwwww

And the fun was just getting started. As Shunn hurtled up over a rise, he saw a cluster of traffic less than a mile ahead, crawling up both eastbound lanes at robotic, self-driving speeds.

He might as well have been staring at a wall of metal and human bodies blocking the road. The cars flowed forward in tight formation at identical speed, controlled by cloud-based networks of A.I. mommies that locked out all human influence.

Almost all influence. It was a good thing Shunn was as much a super-hacker as a super-driver. Otherwise, most roads would have been unusable for his flight, even to a non-driverless car like the GT.

With practiced flicks and blinks of his eyes, he launched the hacker app loaded in his cranial drive, simultaneously jamming incoming commands to the wall of self-driving obstacles up ahead and pushing through his own.

Part, you sons of bitches.

At first, nothing. *Tick tick tick.* Beads of sweat on his creased forehead thickened and ran.

Tick tick

Vreeeeeooooowwww

Finally, further up the column, one car in the right lane hopped onto the berm, then another. And another, even further ahead.

Tick tick tick

Three in the left lane peeled left onto the medial strip–but as in the right lane, the rearward stragglers clung to the straightaway. There were four in the left lane and three in the right, dead center between the solid and dashed white lines.

Seconds left before he'd plow into them. Cursing. Sweating.

Tick

CURSING.

Then he thought of a snippet of a poem by Robert Frost, the one about woods on a snowy evening and having miles to go before he could sleep. It was the message he was carrying, due to be decoded with an algorithmic cipher by his contact in Omaha. Why, he wondered, did it give him a strange, sinking feeling every time it trickled through his mind? Was it because of all the roads not taken in his own life, the paths that could have kept him from this hell-bent race? Or the fact that sleep, or rest of any kind, were beyond him these days, and everything felt like a waking dream of speed?

Days like this, Shunn felt like nothing but propulsion. Faster slower farther closer *yessssss.*

A message made flesh. Message become the messenger. Come on and paarrrtttt, motherfuckerrrsss...

And they did. Stragglers FINALLY swung left and right, JUST AS THE GT RIPPED BETWEEN THEM, hugging the cut that hadn't been wide enough even seconds

Tick

Before.

Did Moses grin when he opened the Red Sea? Because Shunn sure did.

That's right, that's right, baby.

He kept the traffic parting before him, folding away to right and left like waves in a sea. He felt the computer code flowing through the network into and out of the cloud down into the cars' brains and circuits, closing and opening, speed and course trimming to suit him.

The GT skimmed through the gap, moving so fast it looked like one continuous red-and-white streak. Barely missing one pair of cars, it swooped right and bucked left to miss another as the perfectly synchronized parting rolled onward like a current.

Then he checked the rearview mirror. The three Ferraris were still back there, single-filed to clear the gap. The lead driver bolted forward, no doubt realizing that the traffic slowed the GT just enough to maybe run up on him.

Shunn chipped fresh hacks at the parted traffic behind him, reaching in like a surgeon seeking shrapnel. Missed one missed two missed three...

Got one! He nosed a gray Volvo at the last second, just enough to make it clip the rearward black Ferrari, spinning it hard into the medial.

Didn't change the lead car's chase but cut the pack by one.

And we're clear. Traffic suddenly gone ahead, the road wide open, at least until the next bend two miles up.

Shunn stomped the accelerator and pulled away from the lead Ferrari, sprinting into the twilight outside Omaha.

Vreeeeooooowwww

One more try at hacking the remaining two Ferraris but forget it, he couldn't jump the air gap or strip the hardened on-premises war boxes. *Standoff.*

Which was exactly what he was being paid a small fortune to break, on a much larger scale. A secret standoff between two sides in the heart of America--government and breakaway forces–and no one would even know it had been a threat unless those pricks back there intercepted him before one of two things happened:

Delivery or auto-delete.

Delivery would be complete when he reached the location represented by the blinking red dot on the windshield GPS overlay – just inside the Omaha city limits. The breakaway forces would get the message that the government was making concessions, and the civil war would be cancelled.

On the other hand, if he didn't get there before the deadline, the message he carried would be automatically deleted from his brain. The hope for peace and unity would be erased, just as hawkish elements on both sides wanted them to be.

This would happen in exactly 06:15.

Tick tick tick

The overwhelming need to avoid that outcome drove him to push the GT even harder.

Vreeeeeooowwwww

The blurred green-brown-gray scenery around him was a foretaste of what the deletion deadline would bring. All he'd have left after auto-delete was a blur like that, a hint of a trace of a flicker of something that had once been in his brain.

If only he could say the same about his memories of Annie and how he'd lost her.

Every job, he got the treatment. Time-release targeted memory loss by biochemical compound, keyed on the exact neurons storing the message he was delivering. Just as in-person delivery was the only way to ensure message security in the age of hacked E-everything, memory wipes were the only way to guarantee that even *that* security couldn't be compromised.

There was only one problem. The wipes were too precise. No collateral damage. They wouldn't delete his memories of cheating on Annie, and her knowing but not saying and not forgiving and one day just *not*.

Not being there.

And no amount of speed could run him away from all that he'd lost.

Vreeeeeooooowwwww

If all else failed and he was captured, he could stick himself with the Big Shot syringe from the glove box. Five hundred times the original dose of the auto-delete compound would howl through his bloodstream and brain, cooking down the memories like a bubbling reduction in a saucepan.

Would that finally kill the memories of Annie? He didn't know. He'd never needed the Big Shot before; he'd never failed to complete a mission.

And he had no intention of failing *this* time, either.

Whunk

Just then, something bumped the roof of the GT.

Whunk

And again. Checking the overlays on his windshield and contacts, he spotted the culprit: a weaponized drone trying to deposit an explosive on the GT. It was the first since he'd hacked and blown a swarm of them near Cedar Rapids—and it wouldn't be deterred. Shunn's hacker app couldn't get him through the drone's defenses, no matter how hard he tried.

Whunk

Even as he kept trying to breach the drone's firewall, Shunn watched the GPS for some sign of an overpass where he might be able to crash the thing...but no dice. He swerved the GT, fighting to prevent payload attachment, but he knew it was only a matter of time.

Whunk

After all the distance he'd come and all the obstacles he'd dodged or obliterated, that one damn drone was about to be the death of him and the failure of his mission.

Whunk

Maybe he could grab another drone nearby, one without the hardened security, and bring it in for a collision. Casting his net wide, he scanned local frequencies for a sign of such a drone, hoping he could find one before the payload latched on to the GT.

Whunk

That was when the sky flashed with dazzling light.

Tick tick tick

A rumbling blast shook the cockpit.

KRAKOOOOOOMMM

Lightning and thunder. Now *there* was something you didn't see or hear much in the days of Midwestern mega-drought.

Shunn chewed his gum faster, biting the inside of his left cheek so hard, he tasted blood. His hands tightened like bear traps on the wheel. The equation of his drive had just changed dramatically.

And *shit,* all he had was five minutes forty-five seconds till auto-delete...or worse, a full *reformat* via Big Shot.

05:40

At least he had clear highway ahead...until he *didn't*.

05:30

Adrenaline sizzled through his bloodstream as the GT barreled around a bend and he saw what was waiting for him there.

HOONNNNNNKKK HOONNNNNNNKKK

Etched in another flash of lightning, a tractor trailer loomed dead ahead, hurtling straight toward him.

KRAKABOOOOOOMMMMM

SKREEEEEEEEEEEEEE

Shunn stamped the brake and spun the wheel, whipping the GT around in a punishing 180. He played the stick and clutch and crushed the accelerator, leaping away in the direction from which he'd come.

VRRREEEEEOOOWWWWW

The drone that had been pacing him wasn't quite so quick on the uptake. He saw it explode against the cab of the truck in a ball of flame.

Arcs of burnt rubber smoked on the asphalt behind him as he shot away from the crashing tractor trailer... and plunged headlong toward the remaining two black Ferraris.

In a desperate flurry of cranial code bursts, he probed the tractor trailer's self-driving systems and couldn't make a dent. The truck was hacked, it *had* to be—and now Shunn was caught in the middle of a road-kill sandwich: tractor trailer on one side, Ferraris on the other, lightning flashing, countdown ticking.

KRAAKABAKOOOOM

04:40

Tick tick tick tick

And *WTF*, Annie's last words were bouncing around his head like ball bearings in a cement mixer.

The smell of sweat in the cockpit. The smell of her perfume on that day, months ago, like lilacs.

"Glorified..."

He jammed the stick. Cut the wheel.

"...pizza delivery boy..."

Mashed the pedal.

"...all you'll ever be."

Blew across the medial, hopping the dip in the middle, never losing momentum.

"What good is that photographic memory..."

All the while hacking the clot of cars zooming toward him on the other side of the highway.

"...if you can't remember the only thing that really matters?"

Juggling them into a hasty single file in the far lane, leaving him the closest lane and berm...somehow barely keeping all six from colliding.

And that's when it started. Drops on the windshield.

KRABAKROOOOOOOM

And a parade of vehicles cruising headlong toward him, headlights flaring to life all at once.

VREEEEEOOOOWWWW

Just as the downpour let loose, drenching cars and road alike with a pummeling shower that was nowhere near as cold as the chill racing up Shunn's spine.

FWOOOOOOOOSSSSHHHHH

Because this...

Holy shit, *this* was *bad.*

Even as Shunn raced into the lane he'd opened, he saw the single file wouldn't hold. Some of the cars he'd nudged into that formation started to flick and swing, gliding on the rain-slickened asphalt.

Because who needed protection against hydroplaning in a world where it almost never rained, and self-driving cars always perfectly adjusted to conditions on the rare occasions when it did?

Unless they were *hacked*, that is.

KRAKOOOOOOOOOMMMMM

Shunn glanced right for a second. Heavy traffic there across the medial, so he'd take his chances running the gauntlet here, with incoming.

NEEEOOOWWWWWWWWW

The GT bolted forward on top-of-the-line tires that gripped the road through the film of rain. The Ferraris were similarly well-equipped; they vaulted the medial behind him and followed suit with perfect traction.

EEOOOWWWWW EEOOOWWWW

Wipers chopping away at the fastest setting, Shunn charged the narrowing gap like a terrier through a rat hole. Cars lashed toward him from the single file— red then blue then green, skating into his path, nearly making contact.

SSSHHHHKRUMMMPP

And then *making* it. A silver Audi coupe spun around in a sudden 360, its rear-end swatting the driver's side front quarter panel of the GT.

Shunn wrenched the wheel hard and rode the impact, whipping the GT in a swing of its own and then grabbing the pavement again and lurching eastbound.

SSHHWWOOOOSSHHHH

Even as he careened forward through the torrential rain, clawing for purchase in the brains of the cars up ahead, the countdown continued in his mind.

03:15 until auto-delete.

KRAKOOOOOMMMMMM

He was *so close* to the red line, and he knew it. So close to not completing his delivery before the message dissolved from his mind.

03:00

02:55

But the towers of the city loomed closer than ever now, strobing in flashes of lightning. One man waited to receive him just inside the city limits, waiting to hear the message he'd brought all the way from the White House in Washington, D.C.

SHISSSSSSSSSSSS

Suddenly, another car bucked over, and another. Shunn swerved right, left, right, catching glimpses of the terrified passengers in their cabins.

Chewing the gum harder, he drew blood from the right cheek this time.

02:33

Suddenly, it was Christmas in the rearview mirror. He glanced up just in time to see the rearward Ferrari bounce off a white van and flip into the medial ditch.

One less chase car was a gift. Shunn gunned the GT and flew faster, focused like a laser on the blinking red GPS dot.

KRAKAKOOOOOOMMMM

He had to *get there* before auto-delete, pass the message to the warm body designated for the last leg of the relay. *Everything* was riding on *him*, a terrible sacrifice to stave off a much greater loss.

If he failed to deliver the message, millions would surely die in an unnecessary civil war that would ravage the nation.

02:17

02:10

He was *right* on the *red line*, but he still had *hope*, he still might *make* it. Less than a minute from the city limits and his exit – seconds after that to the roadblock and the contact he'd tell about roads not taken and having miles to go before he could sleep.

And then maybe *he* could finally sleep.

02:00

Tick tick tick tick

SHISSSSSSSSSSSS

But suddenly, everything went crazy up ahead. Every car broke from the file, spinning and sliding over the rain-soaked road in front of him.

It didn't matter that he was still snapping out orders and the cars' brains were reading loud and clear, trying to obey. Shitty tires sent them careening like an up-dumped bucket of pucks on a hockey rink.

And Shunn was roaring right into them.

He had to tap the brake to miss a Toyota sedan, then a pickup. In the split-second before he could stomp the gas again, the remaining Ferrari stormed up and bumped him from behind.

THUNNKKK

The GT lurched left and clipped a blue SUV, pitching it into a road sign. Fighting the wheel, Shunn rode the collision momentum in a whipsaw 180, then stepped on the accelerator, mowing headlong into the charging Ferrari.

As the Ferrari pushed back, Shunn threw the GT in reverse and shot away, grazing a fishtailing BMW. The Ferrari erupted after him, violently sideswiping the BMW, sweeping it out of its way.

KRRUMMMPP

01:45

The GT stayed face-to-face with the Ferrari, slashing backward through the jackhammering rain and chaos of hydroplaning cars. Shunn cranked the stick, worked the clutch, and bashed the accelerator, all while yanking the wheel back and forth to navigate the mayhem.

01:37

Swooping right, left, right, left, he somehow traversed the jumble of whirling vehicles while keeping his car inches from the nose of the Ferrari.

SHISSSSSSSSSSSSS

Sluicing backward, ever backward, he raced like a blood cell exploding through an artery, the whole time keeping a secret other than the ciphered message—and the secret was this:

He was *holding back*, drawing in the Ferrari...and then he *wasn't*.

RRROOAAARRRRRR

01:25

The GT rocketed back as if the speeding Ferrari were standing still. Into the gap between them slid a propane tanker, and then...

WABOOOOOOOMMM

Flames and debris *exploded* in all directions. Shock-waves pummeled the skating cars, kicking them away from the center of the blast.

Rattling the GT as the seconds ticked away.

01:05

Jerking the wheel, Shunn spun the GT around hard and bolted for the medial. A narrow path existed, just a sliver of a keyhole between clusters of traffic, leading straight to the exit ramp he needed.

Without hesitation, he darted into it.

Only to realize, at the very last instant, that it wasn't so unobstructed after all. Just as he cleared the medial, a scarred and battered black Ferrari swung out in front of him and cut him off. One of the two pursuers he'd thought out of the race had recovered and caught up.

"Fuck!" Shunn jerked the wheel, but there was no way to dodge or stop in time.

SHISSSSSSSSS

KRAASSSHHHHH

The GT collided with the Ferrari, sending both cars skidding across the double lanes. They came to rest straddling the berm, a dozen feet apart.

Four men in black armor and helmets bolted out of the Ferrari with guns, cutters, and probes, running for the GT with purpose.

And there was still just under a minute left until auto-delete.

Shunn knew what he had to do. If there was even the slightest chance they might hack him before auto-delete, he had to burn everything.

Shaky from the crash, he leaned across the seat and popped the glove box. Grabbing the Big Shot, he flipped the cap off the needle.

Then stabbed the needle into his neck and pushed the plunger.

Instantly, he felt himself melting away like ice cream on a summer sidewalk, and he smiled. The blades of power saws sliced through the driver's-side door, the windshield shattered under a blow from a bludgeon, and he didn't give a shit.

Because this time, maybe, he would finally forget the pain of what he'd done. Finally forget Annie and the only true love he'd ever known.

"We have it," said one of the men as he checked readings on a scanner on his wrist.

"You're sure?" A second man used the muzzle of a rifle to nudge Shunn, who was sprawled on the hood of the GT where they'd tossed him after dragging him out of the car.

"Has to be," said the first man. "It's the only thing left in his brain. The only thing our probes got out of him."

"Guess we'll figure it out later." The second man marched off toward the black Ferrari waiting nearby, followed by two of his partners. "We need to go." Sirens approached.

"Poor son of a bitch." The first man jerked the adhesive electrode from Shunn's temple and walked away. "At least he's at peace now."

They drove off, leaving Shunn on the GT's hood, tossing his head and scowling. As the rain pelted him, he kept repeating the same words over and over, the same message he'd delivered to the enemy agents.

The only message he had left in his burned-out memory. The only message he had left to remember and deliver for the rest of his vegetated life.

"Glorified pizza delivery boy...all you'll ever be," he said.

If not for the rain, the tears on his face might have been visible, glistening in the flashing blue and red lights of the cop cars arriving around him.

But no such luck.

Thunder rolled, and he kept on mumbling right through it.

KRAKOOOOOOMMMMM

"What good is that...photographic memory...if you can't remember...the only thing that really *matters*?"

BIOGRAPHIES

Mario Acevedo is the author of the bestselling Felix Gomez detective-vampire series, which includes *Rescue From Planet Pleasure* from WordFire Press. He contributed stories for the award-winning anthologies, *Nightmares Unhinged* and *Cyber World,* by Hex Publishers. Mario lives and writes in Denver, Colorado.

Nationally bestselling **Quincy J. Allen**, is a cross-genre author with numerous short stories, including his most recent, "Sons of the Father," appearing in Larry Correia's *Monster Hunter: Files* from Baen. *Chemical Burn*, his first novel, was a finalist in RMFW's 2011 Colorado Gold Contest, and *Blood Curse*, the latest installment in the Blood War Chronicles, is an action-packed western steampunk epic fantasy. His first media tie-in novel in the Aradio brothers' Colt the Outlander universe, *Shadow of Ruin*, is expected out in February of 2018. He is the publisher and editor of *Penny Dread Tales* and runs Rune-Wright, LLC - a marketing and book design business based in Charlotte, North Carolina.

Jedidiah Ayres is the author of *Peckerwood*. He's never heard of you either.

Jon Bassoff was born in 1974 in New York City and currently lives with his family in a ghost town somewhere in Colorado. His mountain gothic novel, *Corrosion*, has been translated in French and German and was nominated for the Grand Prix de Litterature Policiere, France's biggest crime fiction award. Three of his novels, *Corrosion*, The *Incurables*, and *The Disassembled Man* have been adapted for the big screen. For his day job, Bassoff teaches high school English where he is known by students and faculty alike as the deranged writer guy. He is a connoisseur of tequila, hot sauces, psychobilly music, and flea-bag motels.

Merit Clark writes the Jack Fariel detective series set in Denver. *Killing Streak*, the first book in the series, won the Colorado Independent Publishers Association (CIPA) EVVY Book Award and was a quarter-finalist in the Amazon Breakthrough Novel contest. *Killing Innocence*, book two in the series, is scheduled for a 2018 release.

Catherine Dilts made her first fiction sale by murdering an annoying coworker in the short story "The Jolly Fat Man." She found it such a satisfying experience, she went on to kill again. A 2017 Derringer Award finalist, Catherine is better known for lighter fare, including her

Rock Shop Mystery series, and two books in the Secrets of the Castleton Manor Library series. In a recent *Alfred Hitchcock Mystery Magazine* appearance, she tested the waters on the dark side of fiction with "Unrepentant Sinner." Catherine's day job in a factory as an environmental compliance specialist provides inspiration to keep writing, with the hope of eventual escape.

Sean Eads is a writer and librarian living in Denver, Colorado. His second novel, *The Survivors*, was a finalist for the 2013 Lambda Literary Award. His latest novel, *Lord Byron's Prophecy*, was a finalist for the Colorado Book Award and the Shirley Jackson Award.

Les Edgerton is an ex-con, matriculating at Pendleton Reformatory in the sixties for burglary (plea-bargained down from multiple counts of burglary, armed robbery, strong-armed robbery and possession with intent). He was an outlaw for many years and was involved in shootouts, knifings, robberies, high-speed car chases, dealt and used drugs, was a pimp, worked for an escort service, starred in porn movies, was a gambler, served four years in the Navy, and had other misadventures. He's since taken a vow of poverty (became a writer) with 21 books in print. Work of his has been nominated for or won: the Pushcart Prize, O. Henry Award, Edgar Allan Poe Award (short story category), Derringer Award, PEN/Faulkner Award, Jesse Jones Book Award, Spinetingler Magazine Award for Best Novel (Legends category), and the Violet Crown Book Award, among others. Screenplays of his have placed as a semifinalist in the Nicholl's and as a finalist in the Best of Austin and Writer's Guild's competitions. He holds a B.A. from I.U. and an MFA in Writing from Vermont College.

Warren Hammond has authored several science fiction novels, quite a few short stories, and a graphic novel. His 2012 novel, *KOP Killer*, won the Colorado Book Award for best mystery. His latest release from HarperCollins, *Tides of Maritinia*, is a spy novel set in a science fictional world. Forthcoming, look for *Denver Moon*, a novella co-written with Joshua Viola. He is also chief intoxicologist and co-host of the popular Critiki Party podcast.

Freelance writer, novelist, award-winning screen-writer, editor, poker player, poet, biker, roustabout, **Travis Heermann** is a graduate of the Odyssey Writing Workshop and the author of *The Ronin Trilogy, The Wild Boys, Rogues of the Black Fury,* and co-author of *Death Wind,* plus short fiction pieces in anthologies and maga-zines such as *Apex Magazine, Alembical,* the *Fiction River* anthology series, *Historical Lovecraft,* and Cemetery Dance's *Shivers VII.* As a freelance writer, he has produced role-playing game work both in print and online, includ-ing content for the *Firefly Roleplaying Game, Battletech, Legend of Five Rings, d20 System,* and the MMORPG, EVE Online. He enjoys cycling, martial arts, torturing young minds with otherworldly ideas, and monsters of every flavor, especially those with a creamy center. He has three long-cherished dreams: a produced screenplay, a NYT bestseller, and a seat in the World Series of Poker. In 2016, he returned to the U.S. after living in New Zealand for a year with his family, toting more Middle Earth souvenirs and photos than is reasonable.

Angie Hodapp has worked in language-arts education, publishing, professional writing, and editing for the better part of the last two decades. She is the director of literary development at Nelson Literary Agency in Denver. She and her husband live in a renovated 1930s carriage house near the heart of the city and love collecting stamps in their passports.

Gabino Iglesias is a writer, journalist, and book reviewer living in Austin, TX. He's the author of *Zero Saints, Hungry Darkness*, and *Gutmouth*. He is the book reviews editor for *PANK Magazine*, the TV/film editor for *Entropy* magazine, and a columnist for *LitReactor* and *CLASH Media*. His reviews have appeared in *Electric Literature, The Rumpus, 3AM Magazine, Marginalia, The Collagist, Heavy Feather Review, Crimespree, Out of the Gutter, Vol. 1 Brooklyn, HorrorTalk, Verbicide, The Brooklyn Rail*, and many other print and online venues. You can find him on Twitter at @Gabino_Iglesias.

Robert Jeschonek is an award-winning author whose pulse-pounding, envelope-pushing fiction has made waves around the world. His stories have appeared in *Fiction River, Pulp Literature, Galaxy's Edge, Uncollected Anthology, WORDS 'Zine*, and many other publications. His action-packed mecha scifi epics, including the *Battlenaut* series, have thrilled readers who crave non-stop, full-throttle adventure. He has also written official Doctor Who and Star Trek fiction and Batman and

Justice Society comics for DC Comics. Hugo and Nebula Award-winning author Mike Resnick has called him "a towering talent." Visit him online at www.robertje-schonek.com.

Born under a bad sign, **Gary Phillips** must keep writing to forestall his appointment at the crossroads. He has written various novels, novellas, radio plays, scripts, graphic novels such as *The Rinse* and co-wrote *Peepland*, published 60 some short stories -- including his first ever Sherlock Holmes story in *Echoes of Sherlock Holmes*, and edited or co-edited several anthologies including the bestselling *Orange County Noir*, *44 Caliber Funk* and the well-received *The Obama Inheritance: Fifteen Stories of Conspiracy Noir.* Phillips is the immediate past president of the Private Eye Writers of America.

Manuel Ramos is the author of nine published novels and one short story collection. The Edgar and Shamus nominee lives and writes in Denver. He is a co-founder of and regular contributor to La Bloga, an award-winning Internet magazine devoted to Latino literature, culture, news, and opinion. www.manuelramos.com

Jeanne C. Stein is the award winning, national bestselling author of the Urban Fantasy series, The Anna Strong Vampire Chronicles and the Fallen Siren Series written as S. J. Harper. She has thirteen full-length books to her credit, several novellas, and numerous short stories published both here and in the U.K.

James R. Tuck has written many books and some even as Levi Black. He used to throw people out of bars for money and people buy his bullshit because he is charming.

Joshua Viola is a *Denver Post* bestselling author, Colorado Book Award finalist and the owner of Hex Publishers. His next novel, *Denver Moon*, is a gritty cyberpunk mystery co-written by Warren Hammond. Learn more at www.DenverMoon.net

USA Today bestselling author **Carter Wilson** explores the depths of psychological tension and paranoia in his dark, domestic thrillers. Carter is a two-time winner of both the Colorado Book Award and the International Book Award, and his novels have received critical acclaim including multiple starred reviews from Publishers Weekly and Library Journal. *Mister Tender's Girl* is Carter's fifth novel. Visit him at www.carterwilson.com.

ACKNOWLEDGMENTS

CPSIA information can be obtained
at www.ICGtesting.com
Printed in the USA
LVHW02s1722260718
585040LV00001B/76/P